Parents Behaving Badly

A Novel

Scott Gummer

A TOUCHSTONE BOOK
Published by Simon & Schuster
New York   London   Toronto   Sydney

Touchstone
A Division of Simon & Schuster, Inc.
1230 Avenue of the Americas
New York, NY 10020

First Touchstone hardcover edition April 2011

TOUCHSTONE and colophon are registered trademarks of Simon & Schuster, Inc.

For information about special discounts for bulk purchases, please contact
Simon & Schuster Special Sales at 1-866-506-1949 or
business@simonandschuster.com.

The Simon & Schuster Speakers Bureau can bring authors to your live event. For more information or to book an event contact the Simon & Schuster Speakers Bureau at 1-866-248-3049 or visit our website at www.simonspeakers.com.

Designed by Renata Di Biase

Manufactured in the United States of America

10   9   8   7   6   5   4   3   2

Library of Congress Cataloging-in-Publication Data

Gummer, Scott.
   Parents behaving badly : a novel / by Scott Gummer.
      p. cm.
   "A Touchstone Book."
   Includes bibliographical references and index.
   1. Parents—California—Fiction. 2. Parent and child—California—Fiction. 3. Family
life—California—Fiction. 4. Suburbs—California—Fiction. 5. Domestic fiction. I. Title.
   PS3607.U5467P37 2011
   813'.6—dc22

                                                                      2010050140

ISBN 978-1-4516-0917-2
ISBN 978-1-4516-0919-6 (ebook)

For all the parents who live for—not through—their kids

Parents
Behaving
Badly

I.

Presumptuous is the parent who drops off a child at a birthday party, especially when the kid is too young to grasp that covered pools are not trampolines and some doggies don't like having their tails yanked. There's an unspoken expectation among parents that a child who is delivered to a birthday party will be returned in the same or similar condition having been fed aplenty and exercised sufficiently so as to guarantee a good night's sleep. These gatherings are among the last of society's handshake agreements, but by all rights Ben and Jili would have been wise to include fine print on the back of the invitations to Tommy's sixth birthday party.

DISCLAIMER: In consideration of your child's participation in this birthday party, you hereby release and covenant not-to-sue Benjamin Scott Holden & Jillian Highsmith Holden (hereafter "Ben & Jili") from any and all present and future claims for property damage, personal injury, or worse, arising as a result of activities related to this birthday party wherever, whenever, and however the same may occur. You acknowledge and accept that birthday parties are vigorous activities involving non-passive play and oftentimes roughhousing in a unique environment that may leave your child vulnerable and pose certain risks, including, but not limited to, death. Your voluntary delivery of your child to this birthday party constitutes your full and willing consent of your child's participation—active and/or passive—and hereby indemnifies and holds harmless Ben & Jili now and for eternity.

Ben's older brother, Fred, cracked open a beer and informed the hosts, "So I took the liberty of inviting my new girlfriend to the party."

"New girlfriend?" asked Coach. "I'm going to have to find a new hiding place for my Viagra!"

Coach and Fred doubled over laughing. Ben, not so much.

"Benny doesn't like to think about you and Mom doing the horizontal mambo," said Fred.

Who does, really, ever, at any age?

Ben thought about saying it, but in truth Ben was fine with his father's lame Viagra joke because the old man would never have said it were Fred not in the room, and Ben appreciated the buffer. Left to themselves, Ben and his father would have labored to fill the awkward gaps between recaps of safe subjects like how Ben's business was doing (just fine), how the old man was feeling (I'm on the right side of the grass), and what grades Ben's kids were in and how old they were now (Kate, ninth grade, age fourteen; Andrew, seventh grade, age twelve; Tommy, kindergarten, six today).

Without reason or warning, Fred jumped Ben and tried to get him in a headlock, but Ben saw it coming and ducked away, flicking his brother's ear with a loud *snap!* Fred had the height and weight advantage by three inches and thirty pounds, none of it muscle, but Ben had dexterity and speed on his side. He had never cracked six feet—a fact that delighted Fred more than it bothered Ben—but he was cut, relatively speaking. Not chiseled like David Beckham on the cover of the *Vanity Fair* magazine that Jili insisted remain on the back of their toilet, but the kind of sinewy build befitting a furniture maker.

"Knock it off," called Jili from the depths of the refrigerator, not needing to see them to know they were up to no good. Toting a bowl of her homemade guacamole, she spooned a dollop for Ben and asked him what it needed. Judging from her slight, athletic, yoga-toned build, she did not indulge in chips and dip or most of the rest of the birthday party smorgasbord. Fred, on the other hand, not only had the gut to prove he never met a snack he did not like but also the guts to scoop guacamole from the bowl with his fingers right in front of Jili.

"Watch it, Fredo."

The kitchen fell silent. Fred had been called a lot of names in his day, and deservedly so, but the one that set him off was Fredo, the bumbling Corleone brother from *The Godfather*. Ben remembered sharing this nugget with Jili one night while watching their favorite movie—then immediately regretting it. Fred shot Jili a cold stare. Jili set down the bowl of guacamole. *Uh-oh*, Ben thought, *here it comes.*

She placed her hands on her hips and stood slightly taller. She tilted her head just a hair to the right and pursed her lips. She narrowed her eyes and flared her nostrils and . . . wait for it . . . *Bam!*

The Gaze of Truth.

Inexplicable yet infallible, the Gaze of Truth was a mystical gift, a tractor beam to the soul that allowed Jili to see through the eyes, past the mind, and into the heart. Ben so named it after she used the Gaze to bust him for lying about Fred's paying for a hooker for Ben's bachelor party, though Jili was so pleased to learn that Ben lied to the guys about screwing the whore that she rewarded him with sex every day for a month. (That was fifteen years ago; Ben subsequently concocted a fib in an effort to earn the coveted reward again; however, when the Gaze sussed out his true intentions, he paid a dear price and went a full month without.)

The Gaze of Truth clouded the clearest of vision, calling certainty into doubt and twisting answers into questions into answers. *She does not know. Does she? How does she? She does know.* Confessions inevitably ensued. Over the years Ben had attempted to counter the Gaze by shutting his eyes, donning sunglasses, even childishly covering his face with his hands like the monkey who sees no evil. But there is no shield for the Gaze, no lead to its Kryptonite. Ben tried, on more than one occasion, to turn tail and run, but once the Gaze is fixed, it's over. The only feasible defense is to master the Gaze oneself, to use the force against the enforcer, and yet Ben, like young Luke Skywalker, proved too impatient to harness the Gaze.

Fred never knew what hit him.

"I'm sorry, Jili, that was not cool of me to scoop your guac with my fingers," Fred apologized. "Also, it was also not cool of me to brown down in your toilet and not flush it, but I thought it would be funny for Benny to find it later. I see how you might not find the humor in that, so I am going to go ahead and flush that. But rest assured I did wash my hands thoroughly after laying pipe in your bathroom and before finger-scooping your guac, which is phenomenal, as always."

Her work here was done. Jili disappeared like a superhero splitting the scene—though only into the next room to help Ben's mother, Patty, finish stuffing and sorting twenty-two goodie bags. It had been just four months since Ben and Jili had moved their family from New York City back to the central California hometown where they had both grown up. Tommy had not yet whittled down a core group of friends and he didn't want to leave anyone out, so every student in Mr. Austin's kindergarten class received an invitation. Jili figured a handful of kids wouldn't make it owing to basketball, family commitments, or parents who would find an excuse not to spend twenty bucks on a gift for a kid they didn't know, and yet, save for one kid named Dakota Callison, every single classmate RSVP'd.

Ben lugged a cooler out to the patio, where he caught wind of his older son Andrew before he actually saw him. Middle schoolers no longer showered after PE class, a development that Ben blamed for the advent of the oppressively pungent deodorant sprays with (oxy)-moronic names like Arctic Heat and Blazing Chill that had become required spritzing for teenage boys. The upside of not showering at school was it spared prepubescent boys like Andrew, who had less fuzz than a peeled peach, the same shame his hairless Chihuahua of a father had suffered in seventh grade having to strip naked next to the likes of Geoff "Sasquatch" Trusco.

"Go jump with Tommy," Ben said, nodding to the inflatable shark on the backyard lawn. Andrew grunted, his nose, as ever, buried in a book. He was a boy of few words, enabled by a family that had come to oblige him. "Where is your sister?"

Andrew pointed to the stately oak tree that Ben had climbed a thousand times as a boy back when their house belonged to the family of his friend Billy Mendes. Ben looked around but did not see Kate. Andrew pointed up, and there, sitting in the tree, was Kate striking a familiar pose: sulking and texting.

The doorbell rang. Ben checked his watch. It was 11:35 a.m. The party didn't start till noon, and it wasn't like his sister Nancy to be early. Ben started inside but got shoved aside by Tommy, who heard the *ding* and, before the *dong*, dived out of the jumpy, sprinted across the lawn, hurdled Bear, the family's bark-happy chocolate Lab, tripped on the patio door track, fell, popped up, dodged Jili, and answered the door.

"Hi, Tommy," said the boy.

"Hi, Dakota. Wanna go play on my shark jumpy out back?"

With that the boys were off, and so too, in the opposite direction, was the woman who had dropped Dakota off.

"Excuse me?" Jili called to the woman. "Is that your little boy who just came in the house?"

"Yes, I'm Ellen Callison, Dakota's mom."

"I'm Jili Holden," she said, offering her hand to shake but not moving out of the doorway. The woman seemed peeved about being made to traipse up the walk to shake Jili's hand. Ben started toward the entry to see who was at the door, but he stopped short when he heard the snip in his wife's voice.

"Please come in," Jili said.

"Thank you, but I've got to run."

"I'm so glad Dakota could make it. We hadn't heard whether or not he'd be coming."

"Really? I told Dakota to tell Timmy to tell you."

"It's Tommy, and I can't imagine that we didn't get that message." Ben tiptoed silently backward, but Jili hauled him into the doorway. "This is my husband, Ben. Are you sure you won't come in? The party doesn't start for twenty minutes."

Ellen peered over Jili's shoulder and through the house to the boys bouncing in the jumpy. "If it is a bother for me to leave him . . ."

"No bother at all," said Jili backing off, her point made. "We'll see you back here before 3:30."

In the time since the Holdens had moved from Manhattan to Palace Valley, Kate, Andrew, and Tommy had attended birthday parties at the ice rink, the roller rink, mini-hoops, indoor soccer, the swimming pool at the rec center, the batting cages, the gymnastics studio, the movie theater, and Bounce Bros. Fun Factory. Jili would have been more than happy to have Tommy's party at any of those places—save for Bounce Bros. Occupying a cavernous warehouse on the outskirts of town, Bounce Bros. had multiple mammoth inflatable jumpies, Habitrail tubes for humans, rock climbing walls, and pools of plastic balls. Tommy couldn't get enough of the place until the day he dove into the balls and came up with a pair of soiled skivvies on his head. Some kid had crapped his pants and ditched his undies at the bottom of the ball pit. Ever diligent with the camcorder, Ben caught the episode on tape. Not only did it lead to Bounce Bros. agreeing to clean each and every ball pit each and every night—when they emptied the pits after the incident they discovered, among other things, car keys, sunglasses, a dime bag of weed, $16.49 in change, a used condom, and a training bra—but Ben and Jili figured the video would draw big laughs someday at Tommy's rehearsal dinner.

Having the party at the house was Ben's idea. Jili lobbied to have it at Pistol Pete's Pizza, though she flatly refused to call it by its new name, Pirate Pete's. A few years back a group of sanctimonious parents organized a boycott of the pizza place over the gun-toting namesake. Pete Peterson, who opened the Main Street institution back in the 1950s, succumbed and changed cartoon Pete from a prospector to a pirate. Placated by the removal of the six-shooters, the offended parents signed off on the revised logo, evidently not bothered by new Pete's wielding a menacing sword and clenching a dagger in his teeth. Nor did they catch the phallic last laugh Peterson got by setting Pirate Pete astride a long cannon flanked by two round kegs of gunpowder.

Having the party at the house would save money, Ben reasoned, though his true motive was to avoid having to entertain Coach, who was guaranteed to sequester himself in the den in front of whichever game was on TV. Jili was not sold on the idea of hosting the party at home, not even when Ben promised to be in charge of the drinks, jumpy, piñata, game organizing, cleanup, and thank-yous. Only when he threw in a gift card to Palace Valley Spa & Massage did she concede.

The doorbell rang and Ben welcomed his sister, Nancy, her

husband, Paul, and their children, Parker, Portia, and Payton, ages five, four, and three, respectively. They looked like a page torn from a Nordstrom catalog. No kid willingly dons madras for a birthday party, thought Ben, nor was there any way that dull-as-dishwater Paul wittingly selected pinstripe slacks and a fuchsia sweater. For her part, Nancy wriggled into jeans that, according to fashion plate Kate, cost more than the entire birthday party.

Scampering up the entryway behind them came a young Asian woman wearing stiletto heels, a spaghetti-strap camisole, and a skirt that Ben quietly suggested to Nancy might actually be a tube top. The woman's heaving bosom did not bounce as she bopped, and she sported more makeup than Jili had cumulatively worn in her entire life.

"Hurry the hell up!" she barked toward the sidewalk. As she turned, Ben and Jili got an eyeful of the elaborate tattoo of a bird whose wings spanned shoulder to shoulder across the woman's back. Shuffling up the walk came two dour kids, a nine-year-old African-Asian boy and a seven-year-old Hispanic-Asian girl.

"Hello, I'm Jili Holden, Tommy's mom, and this is my husband, Ben."

"I'm Krystal," she replied with a slight lisp. "Krystal with a *K*." Her speech impediment might have been natural, but Ben suspected it was a result of the barbell piercing in her tongue. "This is Justin and Britney—yes, as in Timberlake and Spears, but who ever thought they would break up, right?"

Your tattoo looks like the hood of a Trans Am.

Ben thought it but bit his lip.

"Your tattoo looks like the screaming chicken on the hood of a Trans Am," Jili said.

"Good eye, girl!"

Jili asked Krystal with a *K* if Britney had Mr. Austin, as Jili did not recall seeing the girl's name on the class list. Krystal stared blankly back, then suddenly her eyes lit up and she ran into the house and into Fred's arms, wrapping her legs around his waist.

"How did I not see that coming?" Ben whispered to Jili.

• • •

"Hey, Dad?" asked Kate as Ben set up the piñata. "Do you know which kid is Jesse Barnes?"

"I don't, honey. Why?"

Kate presented her cell phone to her father. "Because he just posted this on Twitter."

This party blows, but Tommy's mommy's a hottie!

Lunch provided a brief respite, what with the kids all corralled and their mouths full. As Ben collected paper plates littered with half-eaten pieces of pizza and juice boxes that had barely been sipped, he thought it odd when he heard one little girl gripe that she did not get a pretty balloon from the piñata. He had filled the papier-mâché shark with candy, not balloons. Seeing Fred sniggering as their little neighbor Wendy struggled to blow up a multicolored latex tube confirmed Ben's suspicion that his infantile older brother had tossed a rainbow condom in with the loot.

"Who wants cake!" Jili's timing was impeccable, as Wendy ditched the rainbow balloon and joined the other kids in a mad dash for more sugar. Patty handed Ben a corner piece of cake thick with frosting.

"No thanks, Mom. I've been snacking on junk all day."

"Take it to your father. If he thinks I don't know, it will taste all the better."

Ben spied Kate sitting in a corner, texting. He presented her with the piece of cake.

"Gross."

"Please take this to your grandfather in the den."

"Why can't you?"

"Excuse me?" Ben shot her a look suggesting that were they near an ocean, her cell phone would be sinking to the bottom.

"Fine!" she snapped, the exclamation sounding like a cat coughing up a hairball.

Ben followed Kate into the den, where Coach sat on the couch cursing the TV and pounding on the remote control. "How do you turn up the damn volume!" he squawked. Ben snatched the remote, and Kate gave Coach the cake.

"Did your grandmother see you bring me this?"

Kate looked to Ben. He shook his head. Kate shook her head, and Coach smiled.

There was no way of knowing how long Coach had been pressing buttons on the remote, but he had managed to reset the TV to Luxembourg time, order seven pay-per-view movies, delete channels 236 through 347, change the menu language to Mandarin, set the DVR to record every episode of *All My Children* through 2022, and erase *Braveheart, Gladiator, Stripes, The Great Escape, True Grit,* and *The Godfather,* parts one and two but not three.

"Come here, princess." Coach pulled Kate onto his lap and presented her with a shiny nickel. "Here's a quarter for bringing me the cake."

"That's a nickel."

"Really?" Coach passed his hand over his palm, revealing a quarter.

"How do you do that?"

"Do what?" Coach closed his fist, knocked three times on Kate's head, then nodded for her to open his hand. She pulled back his calloused, sausage-thick fingers and found a crisp dollar bill. Coach gave Kate the dollar and a kiss, and she shuffled out of the room.

"Pick up your feet," Ben said to no response as football reappeared on the TV. He set the remote control next to Coach and pointed to the volume buttons. "Up for up, down for down, and don't touch anything else."

Andrew poked his head in the den. "Presents."

As Ben started toward the door, Coach took Ben's hand and patted it gently. "Thank you."

Ben looked down and considered his father for a long moment. The way he said thank you seemed curiously sincere for his having simply restored football to the television. Ben's eyes darted to the floor behind him, where he half expected to see Fred on all fours, in cahoots with the old man to push Ben over backward. But they were alone. Ben had become accustomed to looking past his father—at the kids, Jili, the clock—but as he looked at Coach now, Ben noticed freckles and spots between the follicles of his father's thinning hair. His skin looked pearlescent, more white than pink. Pockets of green tinted the corners of his mouth where birthday cake frosting had collected in the crannies around his lips. His eyes drooped, and his jowl sagged. He was an old man.

It wasn't the thank you that caught Ben off guard so much as Coach's taking and patting his hand. Ben's mind flashed to the last occasion on which Coach had expressed physical affection; it was not a stretch to remember because it was also the first time his father had expressed physical affection.

September 3, 1995. Ben and Jili's wedding day. As the newlyweds emerged from a shower of rice, Coach called Ben aside. "I probably should have said this to you a long time ago." He struggled with the words before declaring, "You just put the pencil in the sharpener and grind awhile."

"Good thing you told me, because Fred said—"

"Don't listen to anything Fred says. Ever."

"That right there may be the best fatherly advice you've ever given me."

"You know how Mother and I feel about you and about Jillian."

Ben nodded.

"Good, because if you screw this up, we are keeping her."

In a gesture that marked the height of his capacity for affection, Coach shook his son's hand with vigor.

Ben did not hold it against Coach. He was of a different generation. Had Ben been in the waiting room instead of in the delivery room when his children were born, he would've missed out on a life-changing experience. Plus Jili would've kicked his ass. Back in Coach's day, roles were more defined than shared. Ben had no clue whether his father had ever changed a diaper, but if he had, it would have been because Patty was on her deathbed, not traveling for business or enjoying a girls' night out. Ben believed that fathers and children alike are infinitely more enriched for the recent enlightenment, but the circumstances of the times did not make Coach any less of a loving father. Coach loved Ben, and Ben knew it. Even if he had never heard his father actually say it.

"It's a picture of a family I don't even know," groused Tommy. "Gee, thanks, whoever. Next!"

Jili *thwapped* Tommy upside his head and told him to mind his manners. Aunt Nancy tried to explain to Tommy that the picture was just a placeholder and the frame was engraved with his initials, but he was already on to the next best thing. Jili added the frame to a list that included a chocolate Lab stuffed animal she'd bought Tommy as a gift from her mother (Jili had thought about having Mitzi to the party, but her Alzheimer's-stricken mother was just as happy at the home watching the endless loop of *Murder, She Wrote* episodes Ben had set to run round the clock), a replica New York Yankees jersey with the number six and the name KING on the back from Coach and Patty, an Ultimate Cage Fighting DVD from Uncle Fred, five gift cards for Target, three for Barnes & Noble, two for iTunes, one each for Jamba Juice, Sports Emporium, and Pirate Pete's, and nothing from Dakota Callison.

Portia ran in from the den dragging her baby brother by the hand. Every last ounce of makeup Nancy had in her purse appeared to have been applied to the boy's face. He looked like Heath Ledger as the Joker—after being hit in the face with a shovel.

"I'm sure your mother will be very surprised," said Ben.

"You should see Grandpa Coach!" Portia giggled.

Wondering what exactly Portia meant, Ben ducked into the den and found Coach playing possum on the couch, his cheeks rosy with blush and his lips painted Lady Bug Red. He was a good sport with the grandkids, but this was above and beyond.

"The coast is clear," Ben said, expecting Coach to peek out of one eye. Upon closer inspection Coach looked to be asleep, but he was not snoring, which struck Ben as peculiar considering his father was notorious for thunderous snoring that could pull nails from the floorboards.

"Coach?"

2.

The parents who did dump-and-run from Tommy's birthday party were understandably freaked when they returned for their children only to find the Holdens' driveway blocked by an ambulance, fire engine no. 1, a battalion chief, and two PVPD cruisers. Had Ben and Jili been thinking clearly, they would have had the remaining kids wait out front with Krystal and Paul. Or maybe just Paul. Having the kids play out back in the jumpy kept them busy but added to the chaos as terrified mothers and fathers parked haphazardly in the cul-de-sac behind the emergency vehicles and raced into the house screaming after their children.

Milking the free babysitting for all it was worth, Ellen Callison showed up twenty minutes late to pick up Dakota, only then kicking into concerned parent mode, sobbing to her son, "When I saw the ambulance, I prayed some other kid had died and not you." Halfway out the door—without a thank you, *natch*—Dakota darted back inside and filched three goodie bags. Bear caught the little thief red-handed. The dog snarled menacingly, his saliva the color of fresh blood from the scarlet frosting he'd licked off the top of the unattended birthday cake. Bear barked, and Dakota turned tail, dropping the goodie bags and squealing after his mommy. Rooting through the bags, Bear helped himself to Jili's otherworldly chocolate chip cookies.

The paramedics worked on Coach with such nonchalance Fred wondered—aloud—if they got paid by the hour. In truth, their expedient precision only felt slow as time stood still for the family. Nancy held her mother's hands so tightly Patty's fingers bruised. Kate wept in Jili's arms. Andrew held his breath and tried to be strong standing next to Ben. Fred's son Vern videoed the scene with his cell phone, catching his father pointing to the red case with the lightning bolt and shouting, "Fire up the gizmo and hit him with the pads!"

One of the paramedics stood and faced Fred. "I'm sorry." He turned to Patty. "I am so sorry."

As the family shuffled out, the paramedic stopped Ben. "I don't know if you remember me, but I'm Travis Heston."

"Of course," Ben lied. "I didn't want to interrupt you while you were working." The Travis Heston Ben remembered was a scrawny, long-haired runt who wore heavy metal concert T-shirts, always reeked of pot, and was the kid brother of the girl Ben had spent his entire adolescence pining for, Liza Heston.

Since the moment they'd decided to move back home to Palace Valley, Ben wondered when he would bump into Liza Heston. It was inevitable, Ben told himself, if only to have one thing to look forward to. Surely he would recognize her, even if she might have packed on a few pounds, which he seriously doubted since Liza Heston was a runner. She was always the fastest girl in school, and she was a key reason Ben went out for track in high school—a fact that endeared her to Ben all the more because if not for Liza Heston, he would not have run track, which got him a college scholarship, which got him out of Palace Valley.

In the same way he used to go out of his way to pass through G Hall in high school just to happen past Liza Heston's locker, Ben now occasionally patronized the Starbucks in Olive Heights, the north side neighborhood where Liza Heston grew up—this despite the presence of no fewer than eight more convenient locations between Ben's home and his studio on the south side and the fact that he had no clue whether she still lived in town much less her old neighborhood. Preferring to see Liza Heston before she saw him, Ben kept his eyes peeled in public. He did not want a repeat of his encounter with his sophomore homecoming date, Kelly Jarvis, whom Ben bumped into at the vet's office one day when he was slathered in fetid dog barf. Were Ben not presentable at the moment his path crossed Liza Heston's, he would happily settle for a stealth whiff of her hair. The smell of her flowing blond ringlets—strawberry with a hint of honeysuckle—never left him.

What is your sister up to these days?

Ben started to say it but his senses caught up to his curiosity and he stopped short, knowing that this was neither the time nor the place.

"It looks to have been a massive heart attack," Travis said. Mistaking Ben's pause as a sign that he'd been overcome by emotion, Travis wrapped Ben in a hug. "It's OK, I understand. He was a great man. He got me to quit smoking dope and on the right path. I don't know where I would be today if not for him. I get it. I know. Let it go, bro. Let it go." Ben felt a damp spot on his shoulder where Travis's tears pooled.

The official cause of death was coronary atherosclerosis, not the piece of cake as Patty had feared or frustration-induced stress over the TV remote control as Ben had suspected. Two of Coach's arteries were 90 percent blocked, and if he had been feeling any discomfort in the days or weeks leading up to the birthday party, he never let on. Coach did not complain. He did not make or accept excuses. He did not acknowledge pain or take medication to ease it. To his mind, aspirin and heroin were one and the same. The only pill Ben found among Coach's toiletries as he was cleaning out his father's belongings was half a Viagra. Ben chose not to imagine what had become of the first half of the little blue diamond.

In the days following Coach's death Nancy took on the task of making calls to relatives and getting programs printed for the funeral. Paul saw to placing the death notice and the obituary. Fred dealt with the mortuary and the cemetery and arranged the venue for the service. Krystal offered to make coleslaw. Jili planned and cooked for the reception and, more importantly, kept Patty busy and out of the house while Ben sorted through Coach's things. Coach was a purger, not a hoarder. If he did not use it, he did not keep it. Fred got a set of cufflinks engraved *HHH*, their great-grandfather's pocket watch, and

Coach's nerdy sunglasses, which according to Kate were now back in style. Nancy got her father's vintage Leica camera and Royal typewriter. There was really nothing Ben wanted or could actually use, but feeling like he should have something of his father's, he got the old barber's neck massager that Coach inherited when his brother, Floyd the barber, died a few years earlier.

Life as Patty knew it ended the day Coach died. Her existence, her identity, everything she had been and become over the past forty-nine years was gone. Nancy asked to stay with her that first night after the birthday party, but Patty needed to be alone. She was a bad-news-first kind of person, preferring to confront her fear and be consumed by her grief because, as Coach used to say, time heals all wounds except those we keep running from. He would not have wanted her to wallow. She knew he wanted her to move on, and more than anything she did not want to disappoint him.

She hung her coat on the rack just below his favorite PVHS ball cap. He was rarely without it, except in the house. No hats in the house, that was her rule, no exceptions. She stood in the living room, truly alone for the first time in a space she had shared with him from the time she was a twenty-year-old bride until that morning. She stood in the kitchen and stared at his favorite coffee mug sitting in the sink, the one with I ♥ G-PA painted on it that Kate made and gave to him last Christmas. She stood in the family room and stared at the half-finished jigsaw puzzle they had been working on together of Monet's *Ice on the Seine at Bougival*, which they had seen at the Louvre last year, the one time in their lives that either had traveled outside the country.

Objects that, hours before, were inanimate now possessed a deep, personal meaning, and the deeper she walked into the house, the more personal the objects and their meanings became. The tattered slippers at the foot of his bed. The biography of his hero, Teddy Roosevelt, on his nightstand. The black Ace comb beside his sink. The flannel pajamas folded neatly on his side of the closet. Patty held his pajamas to her face and inhaled his essence into her being. Then she took off her clothes, pulled on his pajamas, crawled under the covers on his side of the bed and cried herself to sleep.

A Celebration of Life

Harvey Harold Holden
"Coach"
1939–2010

Holden Memorial Baseball Field
Palace Valley High School

Welcome
Fred Holden

"Desiderata"
by Max Ehrmann
Nancy Aycock-Holden

Salute
Homer King   Ben Holden
Tommy Holden

The Lord's Prayer
Trish Rhodes & Vern Holden   Katherine, Andrew & Tommy Holden
Parker, Portia & Payton Aycock-Holden

"Take Me Out to The Ball Game"
Palace Valley High School
Barbershop Quartet

It is not the critic who counts: not the man who points out how the strong man stumbles or where the doer of deeds could have done better. The credit belongs to the man who is actually in the arena, whose face is marred by dust and sweat and blood, who strives valiantly, who errs and comes up short again and again, because there is no effort without error or shortcoming, but who knows the great enthusiasms, the great devotions, who spends himself for a worthy cause; who, at the best, knows, in the end, the triumph of high achievement, and who, at the worst, if he fails, at least he fails while daring greatly, so that his place shall never be with those cold and timid souls who knew neither victory nor defeat. —THEODORE ROOSEVELT

• • •

"I did not know my father's real name until I was seven years old and he signed my first Little League registration form," Fred said into the microphone. "Coach, as he was known by all, was born Harvey Harold Holden on April 22, 1939, right here in Palace Valley."

It was a curious choice of a name, Ben thought, for there was nothing palatial about a town whose tallest structure was a silo, plus it was not really in a valley at all. The Sierras rose to the east, and to the west Higgins Butte offered a panoramic view of the city, but to Ben's mind you had to be bordered by more than a butte to call yourself a valley. The palace part was likely attributable to the wishful thinkers who settled the town during the gold rush days; their vision of gilded mansions most likely did not include the town's claim to fame (before Homer King) of being home to the largest lamb slaughterhouse west of the Mississippi. In a report on the history of his hometown in Mrs. Laskelle's second-grade class, young Ben suggested that any prospector who did strike it rich would have been stupid to come back to dumb old Palace Valley because he would be rich and could take all of his gold and move somewhere totally cool like Hawaii or Africa or New York City.

"Coach had the opportunity to leave Palace Valley in 1957 when the Philadelphia Phillies offered him a professional baseball contract out of high school," Fred continued. "The Phillies had high hopes for Coach, a slick-fielding shortstop whose first stop was to be the Olean Oilers of the New York–Pennsylvania League. He had his bag packed and a one-way bus ticket from Sacramento to Buffalo, New York," said Fred, pulling from his breast pocket one brittle, yellowed, never-punched Greyhound bus ticket. "He had every reason to go and one reason to stay: Patricia Miller."

Patty sat in the first of two rows of folding chairs on the grass between home plate and the pitcher's mound. Around her sat her family and before her stood Fred, speaking into a microphone placed at home plate beside a casket and a small table draped in PVHS green and gold. Atop the table sat a framed portrait of Coach. Every seat and square inch of standing room was filled at Palace Valley High School's newly dedicated Holden Memorial Baseball Field. Red, white, and blue bunting adorned the stands. Players from last year's varsity baseball team, dressed in their crisp home white uniforms, served as vendors, handing out programs, bags of peanuts, and boxes of Cracker Jack. A series of easels filling the length of each baseline displayed floral arrangements sent by mourners and admirers, none more beautiful or impressive than the one sent by the New York Yankees.

"Our father and mother were married on Sunday, February 6, 1960—the day before his first practice as varsity baseball coach at Palace Valley High. He was teaching English at the time and got the job because, he said, he wanted it more." A chorus of chuckles rose from the crowd but the joke was lost on Ben.

"Want it more. It was one of Coach's mantras. He may have wanted the job more, but he was also the one and only guy who applied for the job. *(Laughs.)* Last year Coach led his fiftieth and final squad to the state championship tournament. *(Applause.)* The Prospectors lost in the quarterfinals *(sighs)*, but not before knocking off Sacramento's top-ranked, highly touted, totally overrated, if-you-can-play-you-don't-have-to-pay private school St. Christopher Academy for Boys *(boos)*, or as we in PV like to call them, SCABs!" *(Cheers!)*

Ben spotted Geoff "Sasquatch" Trusco in the audience. He looked old, bald, and fat, but it was definitely him. When you've puked in a guy's face, you don't easily forget it. The incident was the singular event for which Ben would forever be remembered—not his star turn in *Tikki Tikki Tembo* in kindergarten or his administering the Heimlich to Lucy Erickson when she choked on a gluttonous bite of pig-in-a-blanket in the cafeteria in fifth grade or his winning back-to-back state cross-country titles as a junior and senior in high school. The fact that Ben's infamous spew occurred before the advent of camcorders was a double-edged sword, because while there was no physical record of the incident, the story had become embellished to the point where Ben was widely believed to have projectile-vomited directly into Geoff's open mouth. In truth, Ben had only caked the left side of Geoff's face. And in fairness, Geoff's parents shouldered the blame. Who throws a birthday party for a bunch of twelve-year-olds, serves sloppy joes, and then takes the kids out back for a few rounds of boxing? Things would have been so different had Ben drawn Jacob "the Shrimp" Berger, but fate frowned upon Ben when he got mismatched against Sasquatch in the main event. The mere thought of having to box in the first place made Ben nauseous, but it was an uppercut to the gut just two seconds into the bout that caused Ben to blow chunks. To this day, the mere smell of sloppy joes made Ben gag.

"There are so many more stories," Fred said, wrapping up. "But before I came up to speak, my mother reminded me that I am not too old to have my mouth washed out with soap!" Fred took a moment to take in the crowd. "Thank you all so much for coming and celebrating Coach today. He'd hate the attention but appreciate the sentiment."

"I was thirty-eight years old when I got married," began Nancy, turning and smiling at Paul. "I did not wait so long because I was afraid my father would not like the men I dated; I waited because I was afraid the men I dated were not like my father." Ben and Jili both leaned forward in their seats, looked past their fidgety children between them, and caught one another wearing equally puzzled expressions. This was news to them, as they had chalked up Nancy's matrimonial misfires to being so finicky she could have found a list of faults were she dating Jesus Christ.

- ✓ *needs a shave and a haircut*
- ✓ *limited upward mobility in carpentry*
- ✓ *wears a robe 24/7*
- ✓ *smells like fish*
- ✓ *acts kinda holier than thou*

Judged by her cover, Nancy was a catch: pretty, fit, stylish, straight teeth, nicely proportioned nose (postsurgery). She was bright, educated, well read, and well traveled, but she could also be obstinate, privileged, materialistic, quick to judge, persnickety, and predictable. The story of her love life read like a page out of Mad Libs.

Nancy and _____ had their first date at _____. Her first
     Name   expensive restaurant

impression was he looked like _____, but after _____ glasses
             ugly celebrity   3 or more

of wine he kinda looked like _____. Upon having _____,
            handsome celebrity   dessert or sex

Nancy proclaimed the couple exclusive, and for _____ _____
                     number   plural unit of time

everything was great. He was _____ and _____, and he
           compliment   praise

made her feel _____. Nancy thought _____ was finally
      flattery   Name

the one—until the day he _____. Suddenly she found
            seemingly inconsequential act

him to be _____ and _____. His _____ was too
     insult   criticism   body part

_____. He cared more about his _____ than Nancy,
  deficiency   team, possession, or mother

plus _____ always seemed to be staring at _____. He
    Name   any friend of Nancy's

kissed like a _____ and was an _____ in bed. He was too
      sea creature   invertebrate

_____ and not _____ enough. So Nancy arranged to meet
  this   that

him at _____ where she called him an _____ _____
    public place   expletive   slur

and dumped him.

Paul Aycock was different. Whereas Nancy's previous beaus were either too much like Coach or polar opposites, Paul fell somewhere in the middle. He was older, twelve years Nancy's senior. He was esteemed-looking if not exactly handsome. Like her father, Paul was a keen Civil War buff, which gave the two something to talk about for hours on end since they could not talk sports. The only child of a widowed beekeeper, Paul grew up neither a sports fan nor a participant. Playing in the backyard with Coach and the grandkids, Paul once asked which end of a football to hold. Coach laughed, certain he was joking until Paul threw him a two-handed chest pass.

Nancy enjoyed introducing him as a doctor—he held a PhD in microbiology—and noting that he chaired the department of viticulture and enology at the University of California at Davis, one of the country's foremost academic programs teaching the art and science of winemaking. Coming from her it sounded so worldly and grand, but Paul could kill the conversation in one fell swoop when he got talking about his interest in yeast biology and the genomics of lactic acid bacteria. The quality that endeared Paul to Nancy was his eagerness to please her. In guy parlance, he was spineless. But Paul did as she wished because (1) it made him happy to make her happy, (2) pretty, fit, stylish women with straight teeth and a nice nose had previously proved way out of Paul's league, and (3) he could not care less about things about which Nancy cared most: their McMansion in the tony, new, and also curiously named CascadeForest development of Sacramento, her Lexus hybrid and his Prius, their Pottery Barn furnishings, her Tory Burch shoes and matching handbags, his hair plugs, and the five-figure tuition at Parker's private kindergarten. Paul did not have a say in the alliteration-happy naming of Parker, Portia, and Payton, or in the mandate that the couple both take a hyphenated last name, although he did speak up and convince Nancy to transpose the order so that their children did not grow up as Holden-Aycock.

"The single most important thing I learned from growing up the one and only daughter of the one and only Coach is to love a person for who they are and not lament who you wish they were," Nancy said.

Unless you marry a human Gumby doll like Paul.

Ben would have whispered this mental parenthetical to Jili had they been sitting next to one another. He shook his head and expected her to be doing the same but was surprised to see Jili nodding along with the crowd. He looked to Fred, who was fixated on Krystal's breasts, which were pushed up so high and together so tight they practically served as a chin rest. The undertone behind Nancy's epiphany would have been lost on Fred anyway, but how did Jili miss it? Psychoanalyzing his sister had become something of a game, like Six Degrees of Kevin Bacon. The object was to connect Nancy's oft-perplexing deeds to the root cause of her deep-seated daddy issues. Just that morning Ben and Jili had had a go at Nancy's jaw-dropping outfit, which seemed better suited to the Oscars than an interment. Ben tied it to keeping up with Krystal, whose tube top skirt at Tommy's birthday party had diverted Coach's attention while Nancy bragged about Portia's spearheading a nursery school shoe drive for needy children in Haiti. Jili suggested Nancy went for glam knowing Krystal would go for gawk: indeed, Fred's girlfriend's little red number appeared to be backless and on backward. Jili linked Nancy's attention-getting getup to the countless events in her life Coach had missed due to baseball. "I didn't know Coach had a daughter" was the chorus of her childhood. She'd had to share her father with his 426 sons—the number of boys who had played for Coach—but there would be no missing Nancy on this day.

"My father kept this in his wallet." Nancy read a poem called "Desiderata," which offers earnest advice about things like the peace there is in silence and finding heroism in everyday life and aging gracefully. The poem concludes, "With all its sham, drudgery, and broken dreams, it is still a beautiful world. Be cheerful. Strive to be happy."

Nancy stepped back but did not immediately return to her seat. She lingered near the table and set her hand upon the casket. To the crowd, it appeared to be a touching moment. To Ben and Jili, it was an obvious stall tactic. Jili nodded toward the next speaker as he made his way to the microphone. Cued by the buzz that crackled through the crowd, Nancy timed her turn perfectly, away from the casket and into an embrace with Homer King. It was not every day that a stay-at-home mom from CascadeForest got to hug *People* magazine's Sexiest Man Alive.

3.

Of the 426 boys who played baseball for Coach at Palace Valley High, 47 had gone on to play in college or junior college, six were drafted by big league teams right out of high school, ten saw action in the minor leagues, three made it to the majors, and one became a bona fide big league superstar. At the opposite end of life's bell curve, one was serving fifteen years to life in San Quentin.

Clyde King, class of 1980, was a left-handed power-hitting third baseman who got drafted right out of PVHS but whose road to the big leagues did not stick to a storybook script. It would have made for a terrific movie: baseball star cradles his newborn son for the first time, looks in the baby's eyes, senses the promise, feels the greatness, sees the future, and then and there bestows on the boy the greatest name in the history of baseball: *Homer King.*

In truth, the name was mere coincidence. The boy's mother knew nothing of baseball; she just needed to fill in the blank on the birth certificate. Clyde's participation stopped after he'd stocked her pond with a hundred million tadpoles, one of which found its unintended target. By then, Clyde was out of baseball, his career having ended the week it started when, at his minor league team's welcome picnic, a drunk and belligerent Clyde hit on the daughter of his manager, then hit the manager in the mouth when he suggested Clyde learn some manners. Clyde did not make an appearance at the hospital on the morning his only child was born, instead marking the occasion at the

Dog House, the same seedy bar where the child was conceived atop the Pac-Man game. The irony was lost on Clyde as he toasted a life that might have been with his best and only friend, Jack Daniel's.

Clyde did not swing a baseball bat again until the night of June 26, 1997. Homer and his mother returned home from his Little League All-Star game to find their front door kicked in, half-burned legal papers demanding child support on the floor, and Clyde watching cartoons, waiting. A booze-fueled row ensued and ended with Clyde in jail, Homer in the hospital, and his mother in the morgue.

"I was a sophomore in high school when Coach and Patty opened up their home and their hearts to me," Homer told the crowd at the service. "I was angry. I was embarrassed. I was hurt. I was alone. I was everything that a sixteen-year-old kid should never be. But more than anything, I was scared."

He spoke softly and slowly, backing away from the microphone and taking a deep breath when he needed to swallow his swelling emotions. He did not care that his speech would wind up on YouTube within the hour or lead ESPN *SportsCenter* that evening; those were givens for the highest-paid player in baseball, the captain of the New York Yankees, and *People* magazine's Sexiest Man Alive. He did not care that he had incurred the wrath of sports talk radio loudmouths for taking bereavement leave during a critical series with the rival Red Sox. He did not care if more people saw him cry, not after he'd broken down in tears on national television when a heartless reporter chose the public forum of a postgame press conference to break the news that Coach had died. All Homer King cared about, ever, was making Coach proud.

"Coach and Patty gave me a place to live, clothes to wear, and food to eat. But more than material things, they gave me respect, confidence, purpose, hope, and love."

Homer King's story had remained largely a mystery before he spoke publicly for the first time about his past in a *60 Minutes* interview that aired shortly after he led the Yankees to victory in the most recent World Series. Homer now lived in Manhattan (proving Ben's point about the prospector who struck it rich moving somewhere totally cool like New York City instead of back to dumb old Palace Valley) but he returned home to give Steve Kroft a tour of his hometown, walking the halls of PV High, lunching at Pirate Pete's, which Homer twice referred to as Pistol Pete's, much to Jili's delight, and offering viewers a peek inside Ben's childhood bedroom, where Homer had bunked when the Holdens took him in.

"After what you had seen and been through, when you spent your first night in this room, what went through your mind?" Kroft asked King.

"I might have still been in shock, but I remember lying in this bed and staring at that wall and thinking, 'The poster of Fonzie has got to go.'"

Homer, Steve Kroft, and 15.8 million Americans had a good laugh at Ben's expense.

The majority of the *60 Minutes* interview took place at Homer King's gift to his hometown, the Palace Valley Big Time Ballpark & Sports Complex: four immaculate baseball fields, each an exact mini replica of a big league stadium—Fenway Park for Single-A, Dodger Stadium for Double-A, Wrigley Field for Triple-A, and Yankee Stadium for Majors, plus two softball fields patterned after the San Francisco Giants' and Baltimore Orioles' parks; a Wiffle Ball yard that hosts the annual World Wiffle Ball Championships; two practice diamonds with adjustable bases, mounds, and fences; batting cages and instructional areas; a snack shack; a sports grill with a root beer garden and closed-circuit TVs; little kids' playgrounds; four tennis courts; two basketball courts; an all-weather soccer field; a grass volleyball court; a sand volleyball court; a climbing wall; and a yoga studio.

"You tried to do this anonymously?" Kroft asked, sitting with Homer in the dugout of mini Yankee Stadium.

"My hope was that it would just appear like this field of dreams, but the plans got mixed up and I had to get involved to make certain Fenway was for the peewees and the big kids played in Yankee Stadium." Homer flashed the megawatt smile that made him the highest-paid endorser among professional athletes.

"Rumor has it that this cost close to ten million dollars."

"I didn't have much fun as a kid. Baseball was my escape. If this place gets boys and girls out from behind the computer or the TV, gets them to quit playing a video game or texting, keeps kids busy and active and out of trouble, then you can't put a price on that."

You can, however, put a price on a $750,000 video game endorsement, which Homer lost the morning after *60 Minutes* aired.

"If you played for Coach or had him as a teacher, you surely have a story of a life lesson that he taught you without you realizing it at the time," said Homer. It struck Ben that everyone seemed to nod except him. "During my junior year we made it all the way to the state championship game against a powerhouse team from Newport Beach, the Corona del Mar Sea Kings. On paper we had no chance, but we hung tough, took them to the last inning, and eventually lost by just one run. On the bus ride back we were having fun, joking around. We'd just come in second in the state of California! We were happy and feeling good when we stopped for dinner. Coach sat alone in the front of the bus. He stood, reached into the box with our trophies, took one, faced us, and held the trophy up in the air. We all clapped and cheered. Everyone was whoopin' and hollerin'. Everybody but Coach. He shook his head, put the trophy back, picked up the box, walked off the bus, and chucked our trophies in a dumpster behind the restaurant. Then he got back on the bus and muttered to the driver, loud enough so we could hear through our stunned silence, 'Keep driving. They're not hungry.'

"The only sound you heard the rest of that long ride home was stomachs rumbling. We were famished—but we were not hungry. Coach was not upset that we came in second; he was upset that we were happy we came in second. The following year we made it back to the state championship game against an even stronger Corona del Mar team. On paper we had even less of a chance than the year before, but this time we were hungry. We wanted it more. And we crushed them. That night we stopped for dinner at that same restaurant, only this time Coach bought each and every one of us the biggest, juiciest steak any of us had ever laid eyes on."

The sun glinted off the corners of Homer's eyes. "Of all the things Coach taught me, the one that sticks with me is to play dirty."

Homer stepped away from the podium and clapped twice. A couple hundred grown men leapt to their feet.

"Who are we?" shouted Homer.

"Prospectors!" answered a chorus of former players.

"How do we play?"

"DIRTY!"

"*D*?"

"Discipline!"

"*I*?"

"Integrity!"

"*R*?"

"Respect!"

"*T*?"

"Teamwork!"

"*Y*?"

Silence.

"Why?" Homer repeated.

"Because we are (*clap, clap*) PV! (*clap, clap*)."

In thunderous unison the crowd joined in.

We are (clap, clap) PV! (clap, clap)
We are (clap, clap) PV! (clap, clap)
We are (clap, clap) PV!

Homer King was the most successful player to play for Coach, but he was not the most talented. That distinction belonged to a five-tool phenom from the class of 1981 who could do it all: hit for power, hit for average, field, throw, and run. He was the first freshman ever to earn a spot on the varsity squad. By the third game he was starting. That year, he led the team in every significant category—offensive, defensive, and pitching. As a sophomore, he led the Sierra Foothills League in every significant category. By the end of his junior year he owned every significant school and league record. He once hit a grand slam by diving across home plate to swing at a pitch while being intentionally walked with the bases loaded. Fred never made an error, until the night he left a joint in his letterman's jacket.

Born in late November 1963, Fred was a handful from the get-go, all ten pounds, two ounces of him. Coach was never particularly fond of his own given name and flatly refused to dub the poor boy Harvey Holden IV, but he ceded to Patty's wish to keep it in the family as the baby's middle name. Patty had long wished to name a son after her father, who died of cancer when Patty was in middle school. Lee Harvey Holden was but one day old when that Oswald fellow sullied the name for all eternity.

Renamed Fred after Patty's brother, the boy was a naturally gifted athlete. The fact that, at any age in any sport, he could roll out of bed five minutes before any game and be the best player on the diamond/court/field did not help Fred in developing any semblance of a work ethic. God-given ability takes a person only so far—farther for some than others—but all eventually plateau. From there, where one goes is a witch's brew of intangibles, both controllable and unpredictable, a mix of will, opportunity, desire, timing, commitment, personalities, vision, and luck. Coach earned his opportunity with the Phillies by scrapping to overcome his lack of speed and inability to hit the curve ball. No one started earlier, practiced harder, worked longer, stayed later, or wanted it more, and had Coach boarded that bus to Buffalo, it surely would have been a brief pit stop on his way to the big leagues.

Fred excelled on pure talent, which he inherited largely from his mother. Patty was oddly adroit; she painted vivid landscapes without ever having taken a single art lesson, could juggle six apples, had perfect pitch, and scored a 206 her first time bowling. Had Fred inherited his father's grit, he might have enjoyed a career akin to Homer King's, if not greater, for as exceptional as Homer was in high school, even he could not eclipse in four years what Fred had achieved in three.

The stinging humiliation of kicking his star player, his own son, off his team for possession of marijuana was eased by its inevitability. Deep down Coach sensed it was a matter of time before Fred's auspicious talent got derailed by his inauspicious lack of common sense. If Coach had not found the joint in Fred's jacket, it would have been a cop finding an open container in Fred's car or a father finding his daughter petting Fred's trouser mouse or some other indiscretion. Frankly, Coach was surprised Fred made it all the way to spring quarter his senior year without a colossally idiotic slipup—or getting caught, anyway. Still, that did not stop Coach from blowing a gasket when he reached into Fred's pocket looking for car keys and pulled out a doobie.

Ben sat perched on the edge of the tub with a dollop of Keri lotion in one hand, his small, hairless penis in his other, and a *Playboy* centerfold splayed on the floor between his blue-jeans-draped ankles when Coach blew through the bathroom door that Ben had triple-checked was locked.

"Fred!"

Ben froze.

"Where is your brother?" barked Coach. He cocked his head to get a better angle on Miss March 1981, resplendent in nothing but a fur coat and knee-high leather boots.

Ben screamed.

Patty heard the scream and came running from the other side of the house. Coach left without shutting the door. Ben jumped to his feet but, shackled by his jeans, fell hard on the tile floor. She got a foot in the door, but Ben rolled up against it and breathed a deep sigh of relief at having blocked her from walking in. Then Ben looked up and locked eyes with his mother in the mirror.

Fred was in his bedroom searching furiously for something he was not finding when he heard the door creak open behind him.

"You shit bag," said Fred, thinking it was Ben. "Did you take my P—"

"Pot?" answered Coach. Fred was going to say *Playboy*. Coach presented the joint to Fred, who reached for it as if his father were there to return it. "You're through," was all Coach said. The vast disappointment in his eyes, his expression, his voice, and his posture said the rest. He waited to hear what Fred had to say, expecting something contrite and hoping for something humble. He'd have preferred feigned ignorance like "What's that?" or even a bold-faced lie like "It's not mine," anything but a challenge.

"You can't do that."

Coach pulverized the joint between his thumb and middle finger. Without a word he bent over and picked up the overflowing laundry basket Fred lived out of instead of emptying as his mother had incessantly asked. Coach emptied it for him, spraying clothes across the room like bullets from a Tommy gun, then he bulldozed Fred's trophy-filled shelves, scraping them clean and dumping every award and honor his son had ever earned into the laundry basket. On his way out of the room Coach grabbed Fred's baseball bag, and on his way out the back door he snagged Fred's letterman's jacket from a chair at the kitchen table.

Ben cleaned up and zipped up and followed Fred and Patty outside. Coach marched on a beeline across the gravel driveway toward the trash cans sitting under the carport. Then suddenly he stopped, his attention diverted by the hulking wood chipper parked beside the chicken coop. It made a menacing sound when he fired it up. It wasn't like that star-belly machine from the Dr. Seuss book *The Sneetches* that you could go back through again and again. This was one and done. Coach fed it a trophy, which it swallowed with a guttural snarl and spit out in a gajillion shards that sparkled in the light of a full moon. Coach shoveled in Fred's hardware like coal into the furnace of a train picking up speed. He unloaded the baseball bag and tossed in batting gloves, a jockstrap, a cap, a Snickers bar, a sweatshirt, two eight-track tapes, a wooden fungo bat, a pair of girl's underwear, and an unopened can of Dr Pepper to wash it all down. Coach paused momentarily to consider Fred's glove, an object into which the father and son had invested countless hours, breaking it in until it was perfectly soft and supple. The beast savored that juicy morsel, chewing it slowly and deliberately.

Coach lobbed in Fred's spikes, but the wood chipper rejected the metal, vomiting sparks and spewing shrapnel. One projectile cracked the windshield of Coach's car; another hit and killed Ben's pet chicken.

As Ben and Patty ministered to poor, innocent Clucksie, Coach shredded Fred's baseball bag, then served his letterman's jacket for dessert. In the process Coach unwittingly minced his car keys, which were in the pocket opposite the joint. If he had reached in the left pocket instead of the right . . .

And if my aunt had balls, she'd be my uncle, went another of Coach's favorite sayings.

Coach expected Fred to try to stop him—after the first trophy, before his glove, certainly to save his letterman's jacket—but Fred never said a word. The finality was an unexpected relief. Baseball had not been fun since Fred was twelve, Ben's age, playing on the big field in Little League. Before then it was all about having fun with your friends, playing your game, then watching theirs, spending entire Saturdays at the ballpark, grubbing snack shack food for breakfast, lunch, and dinner, then catching a ride home with Mr. Gotfredson, who locked up the park at the end of the day, then made the rounds through the neighborhood with a load of kids in the back of his pickup, back when kids still piled into the back of a pickup.

Since then, baseball had become a chore for Fred, the innocence sapped by expectations. Not only from Coach, but also from teammates and parents who assumed Fred would carry the load. Fred's potential would remain just that, and as he watched the last cuff of the sleeve of his letterman's jacket disappear into the wood chipper, that seemed to suit Fred just fine. He'd have quit baseball if he could, but that was never an option until Coach closed that door; in the process, he opened another to a relationship that was purely father and son.

Granted, it took a while for those ties to bind. Fred reacted to life without baseball like a repressed parochial school girl who goes hog wild at college after getting her first taste of freedom. He more than made up for all the partying he'd missed and capped his senior year by puking in the limo on the way to the prom and impregnating his girlfriend Annette on grad night. Fred married Annette, who missed her own senior year while carrying and then caring for a baby daughter they named Trish. Fred planned to become a fireman but failed the drug test. He had no Plan B. The situation was toxic, figuratively and literally, as Fred got a job managing a crematorium. The near-immaculate conception of a second child gave Annette renewed purpose, Trish an ally, and Fred a do-over at fatherhood. Eleven-year-old Trish wanted to name her baby brother Christopher Robin. Annette also liked the name Christopher. Fred suggested Vern, knowing Annette would hate it. He was kidding, but he was right—she hated the name. But desperate to avoid yet another knock-down, drag-out fight, she conceded, at which point Fred could not come clean with the reason he'd suggested the name in the first place. Annette took to calling her boy Buddy. Trish never called him anything but Christopher Robin.

Upon receiving her high school diploma, Trish kissed her mother, hugged her brother, gave her father the middle finger, and moved to Miami. Bangor, Maine, was the runner-up, and despite its being farther away from her father, Trish sacrificed the extra hundred-odd miles for the sunshine of South Florida. By then Fred and Annette had mercifully divorced. She paid a dear price in lost years and self-esteem, but Annette persevered, raising two children who loved her, earning her high school diploma, and working her way through nursing school. Fred was riding a one-way express train to Failureville when he struck it rich while taking a piss.

Drunk and teetering at a urinal at an Oakland Raiders football game, Fred spied an older gentleman sporting a Denver Broncos hat. Sensing Fred's glare, the man offered an awkward smile as he went about his business. Fred turned to the man and snatched the hat right off his head, soaking the gent's tasseled loafers in the process. Fred dropped the stranger's lid in the urinal and peed all over it. Later, while cooling his heels in the drunk tank and licking his wounds after getting his ass kicked by a septuagenarian, Fred had an epiphany: Potty Cakes. Urinal mints emblazoned with the logos of the visiting team. Within a year, every urinal in every stadium, arena, and ballpark in America sported Potty Cakes, and Fred was a millionaire.

• • •

"Live true." Homer King repeated Coach's mantra a second time, then a third. He bowed his head. He stood at the mic for a long moment, hands clutching the sides of the podium. He shook his head and walked away muttering. "Live true, live true . . ."

A smattering of uncomfortable applause preceded an extended awkward silence before Fred *thwapped* Ben upside the head. "You're up, butt breath."

Jili reached out and squeezed Ben's hand as he shuffled to the podium. She did not know what he was going to say—every time she asked, he shrugged—though she did know that addressing sizeable gatherings was beyond her husband's comfort zone. Ben had diarrhea for a week leading up to the kindergarten holiday play last Christmas after Tommy volunteered his father to act as the narrator. Ben appeared only slightly less uncomfortable as he stood at the microphone and cleared his throat, careful to pucker the sphincter guarding his nervous bowels. He considered the crowd and wondered how many people might show up at his own funeral if it were held today. It was an apples-to-oranges comparison, as a career coach and schoolteacher had a far greater pool from which to draw than a furniture maker who worked for and by himself. Plus, what percentage of attendees came just to get a glimpse of superstar Homer King and his Brazilian supermodel girlfriend, Natália Carvalho?

Ben hoped he might get a glimpse of Liza Heston. He scanned the stands and saw Kathy Moore, who went with Ben to the homecoming dance freshman year but made out with Mario Belmonte; Ernie Borgess, who smashed a Hostess fruit pie in Ben's face in sixth grade; Keith Campbell, Jili's high school boyfriend; Jenny Dennison, who wrote a best-selling memoir about her unrequited high school crush on Jili; Terry Taft, who apparently had not fallen into the grinder at the slaughterhouse and died; Tyler Skalr, who lost his virginity to Bill Warden's mother; and Bill Warden's mother, who'd had so many face lifts that if she wore a V-neck sweater, her pubic hair would look like a goatee. But no Liza Heston.

Beyond the bleachers, Ben spied an ice cream truck. In his mind's eye he saw a seven-year-old boy wearing a ball cap, T-shirt, and blue jeans pedal up, stop, lay his bicycle on the grass beside the curb, and contemplate the myriad options presented on the side of the truck. Drumstick? Fudgsicle? It's-It? Creamsicle? Rocket Pop? Push Up? Choco Taco? The boy ordered the Choco Taco, dug loose change from his pocket, and waited. Ben remembered waiting and thinking that it never took this long. He waited some more. Maybe they were out of Choco Tacos. He reviewed the options on the side of the truck and made a mental list in order of preference should he have to change his order. Ben called for the ice cream man, but he did not answer or appear in the window. Ben was too small to poke his head inside, so he got back on his bike and started toward the baseball field, but Coach was in the middle of practice and did not like to be interrupted, a lesson Ben had learned the hard way the weekend before when he had walked out to the mound and asked Coach for money for the ice cream truck and instead got to pick weeds behind the backstop. So Ben steered his bike to the back of the truck, stood on the pedals so he could reach the handle, opened the door, and saw the ice cream man bent over at the waist, his torso plunged deep in the ice box.

"If you can't find any Choco Tacos, I'll have an It's-It," Ben called.

Coach was throwing batting practice when he caught sight of Ben standing on first base. "What did I tell you?" he chided the boy.

"Not to interrupt you unless someone is shot, stabbed, bleeding, or dying."

"Is anyone shot, stabbed, bleeding, or dying?"

Ben shook his head.

Coach pointed to the weed patch behind the backstop.

"But what if he is already dead?"

Standing on the podium, Ben felt a tug at his sleeve. Jili eased him out of his daydream and into his seat. Tommy carried his chair to the podium, propped it up, hopped up, and read aloud a letter he had written:

Dear Coach I am sorry you are dead because I will miss the way you laugh and all the fun things we did together like going to the dump and fixing things in your workshop and washing your car and going to the pancake house and playing catch and shooting your gun which I promise to keep our secret until the day I die and see you in Heaven so make sure you introduce yourself to God so that when I say my prayers and tell God things to tell you he will know who you are even though he probably already knows because you were a great coach and an even better grandfather and my best friend.

4.

W hat's the deal with Ernie and Bert?"
        A lifetime spent listening to Fred speak with his mouth
        full helped Ben understand—as in decipher, not compre-
hend—his brother's question.

"They are Muppets," answered Ben.

"I know that, barf nugget."

An intimate gathering of family and friends joined Patty back at the house following the service. Patty made certain to spend a few moments with everyone, including Jili's mother, Mitzi, who sat on the couch sipping a Fresca and snacking on Bordeaux cookies, blissfully oblivious. Fred sucked a buffalo wing clean. "I mean are Ernie and Bert brothers or are they gay?"

"Writing your thesis, Fred?" Jili set a bowl of fresh guacamole on the dining room table.

"Ernie and Bert are brothers," stated Nancy. "They are not old enough to be in a consensual relationship. Adults don't collect paper clips and play with rubber duckies."

"So where are the parents? There seems to be a lot of unsupervised bathing." Fred lobbed the chicken wing through the doorway, across the kitchen, and into the sink using the window as a backboard. Ben wiped down the window and tossed the gnawed wing in the trash, saving his mother the trouble.

"They are not brothers, and they are not kids," countered Paul, careful not to sound like he was contradicting his wife. "Bert has an identical twin brother, Bart, whom Ernie had never met until the day Bart arrived, unaccompanied and 'by way of Buffalo,' to visit Bert."

"Notwithstanding the fact that your knowing that is creepy, maybe Ernie and Bert are stepbrothers and Bert lived with one parent while Bart lived with the other."

"Identical twins being separated so young?" questioned Jili's brother Fritz, who was five years younger than Jili and owned a brewpub in town.

"It happened in *The Parent Trap*," interjected Krystal, "before Lindsay Lohan went skank." Krystal downed her glass of chardonnay in one gulp.

"Ernie talks to a rubber duck, for chrissakes," Nancy said to Paul. "He is not an adult, unless you are suggesting he is mentally challenged and living as Bert's ward."

"Burt Ward played Dick Grayson, who was the ward of Bruce Wayne, better known as Batman and Robin the Boy Wonder," offered Fritz.

"Will you please go on *Jeopardy!* already," implored Jili.

"It's the headboards I can't get past," said Fred. "If Ernie and Bert are not kids and they are not brothers, then their matching headboards with their engraved initials are the giveaway that they are gay."

"Why the keen interest in Ernie and Bert?" asked Ben.

"Krystal's boy is totally into them right now." As Fred said this, Justin walked in from outside pinching the tail of a lizard. He politely said excuse me as he stepped past Mitzi to the fireplace, then giggled as he held the wriggling reptile over the burning Presto log. "Not Justin," noted Fred. "Krystal's little guy, whatshisname?"

"LaKevin," she slurred. "He's two. His father just got paroled. It was a bad situationship." Krystal lifted the wine from the ice bucket, polished off what was left, then set the bottle back in the guacamole bowl. "We hooked up . . ."

The story promised to make everyone feel the kind of dirty you can't wash off with an S.O.S. pad, so the timing could not have been more fortuitous when Homer King and Natália Carvalho ducked in from the kitchen, having slipped in through the back door. Krystal stumbled backward into a chair when Fred, who'd been propping her up, left his post unannounced to shake Homer's hand. Fred clamped down as hard as he could, and while Homer did not expect it in this setting, he got this all the time: a grown man's playground fixation with flexing his machismo. More often than not Homer simply smiled and slowly squeezed his iron fist until tears appeared in the other guy's eyes. Feeling charitable, he threw Fred the bone he so clearly desired.

"Easy, brother," said Homer, "I'm going to need that hand if I am going to hoist another World Series trophy."

Fred let Homer go and threw open his arms to Natália. She expected this, as she got this all the time: a grown man's transparent attempt to cop a feel. Natália's patented preemptive move saw her place both hands over her heart and tilt her head just so, an enchanting expression of her pleasure to have made the acquaintance. Be it sincere or feigned, most men melted and left it at that. Those who did not risked a quick lesson in Jiu-Jitsu from Natália, a sixth-degree black belt. Fred melted. So did Fritz, and so did Paul. Nancy milked another hug from the Sexiest Man Alive.

"Ben!" exclaimed Homer, shattering Nancy's fantasy that he too was contemplating where they could escalate this embrace in private. Homer broke loose from Nancy and, adding insult to injury, wrapped Ben in a more heartfelt hug.

"I was feeling you up there at the podium. Sometimes there are no words."

Natália cut in, taking Ben in her arms, pressing his cheek to her chest and stroking his face with her long, soft fingers. "When you say nothing," she offered in a thick, sultry Portuguese accent, "you say everything."

Her cleavage smelled of fresh pineapple with an undertone of vanilla almond and a hint of gardenia, Jili's favorite flower. Ben took one long, last whiff before coming up for air and introducing Jili to Homer and Natália. Homer took Ben aside.

"You know that buffalo nickel Coach used to always carry?" Ben did not. "One day my freshman year, Coach pulled me off the field in the middle of practice and sat me down in the dugout," Homer explained. "I'd busted my ass to make varsity and once I did, I let off the gas a little and started to coast. Coach pulled that buffalo nickel from his pocket and challenged me; he asked me if I was going to entrust my future to chance or to hard work. He asked me if I aimed to be good or lucky. He flipped the coin and told me to call it, heads or tails, and I picked heads. It was tails. Two out of three, he said, and I picked heads again. Tails again. Ten in a row I called heads, knowing that at some point it's got to come up heads. I lost all ten in a row, so I switched to tails. I called tails ten times in a row, and I'll be damned if I did not lose every one of them. Then he sat down next to me on the bench and looked me square in the eye and said, 'Son, you better get busy getting good, because you sure as hell ain't very lucky.'"

Just as he had done toward the end of his speech at the service, Homer turned introspective, as if he were talking more to himself than to Ben. "I'll bet we flipped that buffalo nickel a thousand times over the years, and never once did he let me win. I don't know how he did it; either it was a trick or he was right, and I just wasn't very lucky."

Ben gave Homer the once-over, spied Natália, then looked back at Homer. "It was a trick." Eyeing Natália, Ben asked, "What perfume is she wearing?"

"Natália."

"Yes, what is the name of her perfume?"

"Natália."

"Right, her perfume, what's it called?"

"Natália. It's called *Natália*. It's her own fragrance."

"I'd love to get it for Jili."

"Let me send you a bottle."

"You don't have to do that."

"It's fifteen hundred dollars an ounce."

Ben pulled out his wallet and handed Homer his business card. "Here's my address."

"How long was I up there?" Ben brushed his teeth as Jili toweled off after a shower. Kate, Andrew, and Tommy were in the den watching a reality show called *Brat Party*, wherein rich parents throw elaborate frat-style theme parties for their spoiled children. Ben argued that there is nothing real about an environment concocted by producers, surrounded by cameramen, and inhabited by attention seekers who know that the less real they act, the more airtime they get. He had asked Andrew to change the channel to something more appropriate for Tommy, but Andrew was lost in his book. Kate sat up, grabbed the remote, tuned in family-friendly fare, turned down the volume, and resumed lounging position all without missing a texting beat. Ben thanked her, then the moment he left the room Tommy snagged the remote and switched it back. Parents would hope that children who watched *Brat Party* would be aghast by the behavior of the spoiled kids and, in turn, treat their own parents with more respect and appreciation. That, and parents would see the folly in enabling misbehavior to curry favor. In reality, *Brat Party* made mini-celebrities of the little shits, most notably a wee-devil who plastered her daddy's shiny new Bentley with slices of bologna. Something in the processed luncheon meat eats away at paint—begging questions about what bologna does to the lining of one's stomach—and by morning the Bentley looked like a leopard. Rather than receiving a juvenile hall sentence, the girl got her own polka-dot clothing line for tweens.

"How long was I up there?"

"Two minutes?" Jili guessed.

"I didn't know what to say."

"It's not easy to put your feelings into words."

"That's the thing: I didn't have any feelings *to* put into words. All week long I tried to come up with something to say, something heartfelt, but I didn't feel quite right getting up and sharing, 'Maybe someday I'll find a reason to miss the ornery old coot.'"

Jili opened her towel and wrapped her arms around Ben. Hugging him from behind, her naked body felt warm and soft and smelled of sandalwood.

"I felt like I was at a funeral for a complete stranger," said Ben. "All those guys who played for him all talked about his sense of humor, but I don't remember Coach as funny. Crass, yes, but funny? I close my eyes and I cannot picture him smiling. I cannot remember one hug, not a single kiss. I got a handshake. Once." Ben recounted for Jili how, just moments before he died, Coach had taken and patted Ben's hand and said thank you. Then it seemed peculiar. Now it seemed prescient. "I am sorry if I embarrassed you," Ben said sincerely.

"You did not embarrass anyone."

Jili ducked under his arm and curled up between Ben and the vanity. She lifted his T-shirt and pressed her bare chest against his. Her breasts no longer pointed toward the sky like sunflowers to light as they had before she nursed three children, but Jili took good care of her body, and it showed. Ben's appreciation became readily self-evident.

She turned out the lights and slid her hand down the small of his back to the SpongeBob boxers the kids had given him for Christmas and gave him a hard, swift spank. Pressing her hips against his, she cooed and gave him a deep, deliciously minty-fresh kiss. She pulled off his shirt and, in a maneuver of impressive dexterity attributable to years of yoga, lifted her silky leg, pinched the waistband of his Sponge-Bobs between her pink-painted toes, and pulled Ben's boxers to his ankles. He began to caress her breast but she slapped his hand away, not to tease him but because she was hyper-ticklish, a lesson Ben first learned the hard way. Jili shivered, a combination of sexual anticipation and cold tile, as Ben lifted her onto the vanity, when the bedroom door burst open. Jili jumped down and draped herself in her robe. Ben darted for the toilet but, shackled by his boxers, tripped and fell. Paralyzed by flashbacks of Coach walking in on him and Miss March 1981, Ben lay frozen, facedown on the floor.

"What's the matter with Daddy?" asked Tommy.

"He's got a little tummy ache," was the best Jili could come up with.

"Looks to me like he's got a big butt ache," said Tommy, giggling and pointing to the red welt of Jili's handprint on Ben's left cheek.

Tommy stepped over Ben and set a flyer beside his face. "I want to sign up for Little League."

"Can this wait, little buddy?"

"Tomorrow is the last day to sign up."

"Can it wait till tomorrow?"

"Fine," Tommy said, slapping Ben's other butt cheek hard before tearing out of the room laughing.

Jili locked the door behind Tommy and let her robe fall from her shoulders to the floor. When the kids were awake Jili was normally either apprehensive about having sex or distracted when they did. Ben argued that a child walking in on his or her parents was like touching a hot stove: do it once and you learn never to do it again. But Jili was more modest about where and when, which made their sex life as predictable as their arguments about their sex life: he'd come to bed late and horny when she was spent and sleepy. Every not so often they'd have a go in the morning, but that meant either not kissing—they were a decade past the point where they would still make out with dragon breath—or getting up to gargle with mouthwash, but that risked rousting the dog, whose Pavlovian routine upon waking was to climb on the bed and flop down between his beloved alpha and the guy who fed him. Jili enjoyed a nooner, but it inevitably seemed that she was volunteering at one of the kids' schools or Ben was busy at his shop on the other side of town. He'd been after her to christen his shop since they'd moved back to Palace Valley, but to date they had yet to have a go on any piece of heavy machinery. The quickie while the kids were doing homework was better than nothing, but it ultimately exacerbated the issue, because after three kids, fifteen years of marriage, and twenty-one years together, Ben and Jili still genuinely enjoyed pleasuring one another and longed to recapture torrid moments like the time they got squirrelly on the Ferris wheel at the Rhode Island State Fair.

Ben dampened the mood when struck by a thought. "That is why Nancy was so insistent about reading the 'Desert Sonata.'"

"'Desiderata.'"

"She couldn't come up with anything nice to say either."

"I thought it was nice what she said about learning to love a person for who they are and not lamenting who you wish they were."

"I thought it reeked of resignation," Ben said. "If you can't beat 'em, join 'em."

Ben was not a joiner. He chose to run track in high school partly because it was a solitary pursuit, partly in pursuit of Liza Heston, and mostly because it conflicted with the spring baseball season. Ben had made up his mind that his last season in Little League was his last in baseball, for he knew that were he to so much as set foot on the PVHS diamond, there would be no way out. The night he kicked Fred off the team was difficult for Coach, but the day Ben told him he was finished playing baseball was devastating. The thread that kept them tethered had frayed, but Coach clung to the belief that once Ben got to high school and came out for baseball, the two of them would find common ground between the chalk lines. That thread snapped with a silent *twang* when Ben handed his freshman athletic participation form to his father to sign.

"You accidentally marked track instead of baseball," said Coach.

"That's right."

"That's right, you accidentally marked track? Or that's right, you are quitting baseball?"

"That's right, I am running track."

"Why?"

Because I do not want to play for you.

Ben thought about telling the whole truth.

Because I would rather not play baseball at all than play for you. All I ever see you do is yell. All I ever hear you tell kids is what they do wrong. I love playing baseball, but it's just a game, for chrissakes, and games are supposed to be fun, but playing for you doesn't look like any fun at all so I'm going to quit while I'm ahead.

Instead, Ben opted for the simple truth. "Because I am good at running."

"You're good at hitting and fielding too."

Indeed he was. Whereas Fred was a classic cleanup hitter, Ben was a prototypical leadoff hitter: he could hit to all parts of the field, was selective and patient enough to take a walk, and once he got on base, he was smart and lightning fast.

"I like running."

"You don't like baseball?"

In this moment young Ben learned a life lesson: adults have a curious habit of asking questions to which they really do not want to hear the answer.

Do I look fat in these jeans?

Why are you breaking up with me?

Which of our friends do you think is hot?

Still, they ask, and at that point the asker grants the answerer immunity to tell the whole truth. But Ben demurred. "I can ask Mom to sign it."

Coach scribbled his name and grumbled, "You could have asked her in the first place."

It wasn't just that Ben wanted to be closer to Liza Heston or farther from Coach. Running, and long distance in particular, suited his sensibilities. Whereas Fred always ran with a crowd and Nancy was never bereft of a boyfriend for more than one full rotation of the earth, Ben was suited to solitary pursuits. Seven years of mandatory Little League notwithstanding, Ben gravitated to swimming and tennis over team sports. He tried Cub Scouts but quit before Webelos. He preferred math class, where he could figure out problems on his own, to science, where he had to rely on a lab partner. His favorite elective was woodshop. His least favorite was chorus, despite a silky singing voice inherited from his mother that earned Ben the role of Prince Charming in the elementary school production of *Cinderella*.

It was fate that Liza Heston won the part of Cinderella—cruel fate that she came down with chicken pox on opening night. Her understudy was a little sassy pants with a face full of braces named Jillian Highsmith. Ben thought she was bossy. She thought he was a nerd. Neither was thrilled at the prospect of having to hug in public after the Prince places the glass slipper on Cinderella's foot. (In the movie it is the footman of the Grand Duke on behalf of the Prince who performs the actual fitting, but with so many fidgety kids on stage, the drama teacher economized the happy ending.)

At the moment of truth, Ben, on bended knee, slid the clear plastic pump on Jili's foot, only to learn that she was hyper-ticklish. She reflexively kicked, knocking Ben out cold and chipping his front teeth.

In addition to making a statement about the superficial nature of fairy-tale romances, the unexpected ending made for brilliant video for early adopter parents with toaster-sized camcorders.

Ben and Jili did not talk much after that, not until the night they graduated from high school. In yet another cruel twist of fate, the alphabet gods sat Jillian Highsmith in between Liza Heston and Ben Holden.

"Do you want to switch seats?" Jili elbowed Ben in the ribs.

"What is it with you and the need to inflict physical pain?"

"I asked if you want to switch seats. You are making me motion sick rocking back and forth trying to look past me to make googly eyes with Liza."

"What? I am not."

Jili shot him a glare, an unpolished precursor to the Gaze of Truth. "If you want to switch seats . . ."

"No, thank you," said Ben, turning toward classmates whose last names descended the alphabet.

"You'll outgrow her in a week. She's going nowhere."

"And where are you going?"

"Where do you think I am going?" Jili asked, intrigued.

"I think you and Keith Campbell are going to get engaged at Christmas and married next Valentine's Day."

"Really? Because I think you and Keith are going to get married and blaze the trail for gay marriage in America."

They shared a laugh, and despite what he might have thought about her, Ben could not deny Jili had a glow about her, or that she smelled delicious, like peaches and cream.

"So where are you going?" Jili asked as the class stood and the procession moved to shake Principal Middleton's sweaty hand and receive an empty diploma holder.

"Three thousand and thirty-eight miles from here."

"East or west?"

"East, to Rhode Island. Brown University."

"Very funny," she said, jostling him with her shoulder.

"How so?"

"I am going to Brown. I'm going there to swim."

"I am going there to run. I thought you were going to Stanford to swim."

"I thought you were going to Oregon to run. I totally called dibs on Brown!" As she climbed the stairs behind the stage, Jili pirouetted in her espadrilles and pointed a finger in Ben's face. "Where are you living?"

"One eighteen East Valley View—"

"Not here!" Jili barked. "At Brown."

"Jillian Marie Highsmith," announced Principal Middleton.

"Jameson House," said Ben.

"Jillian Marie Highsmith," repeated the principal.

"I am in Everett House," she said, "but I am pretty sure they are both right there on the Kearney Quadrangle."

"It's the Keeney Quadrangle," Ben corrected her.

"No it's not, it's Kearney."

"It's Keeney."

"You wanna bet?"

"Go!" yapped Janice Holliday from the stair behind Ben. Jili shot her an icy *Do not mess* look that rippled through the *J*s and *K*s clear back to Judy Leopold.

"I'll bet you a Guinness it's Kearney," proposed Jili.

"Jillian Marie Highsmith!"

"You're on," said Ben, as he twirled her around and pushed her out onstage.

Settling back into their seats as "Pomp and Circumstance" droned on, Jili offered a fantastically improbable prognostication. "Maybe we'll wind up one of those couples who meet in kindergarten and are meant to be together but don't get along as kids and don't get together until way later."

"And live happily ever after?"

Jili smiled and shrugged as if to say *you never know.*

"What about you and Keith?"

Again, Jili smiled and shrugged, only less smile and more shrug.

JiliandKeith, their names inextricably linked, had been boyfriend and girlfriend all through high school, but everyone knew she was destined for bigger and better things. He was a sweet, small-town boy whose ambition evaporated when his father walked out and whose lone source of self-esteem became the adulation he drew from being a three-sport star in high school. Jili was a go-getter who channeled her emotions over the death of her father in a car accident when she was six into motivation to achieve—grades, test scores, swimming, extracurricular activities, volunteer work—so that her options would know no limits.

"What about you and Liza?"

"I've had a crush on Liza Heston forever," he blurted. Ben caught himself and peered past Jili to see if Liza Heston had heard him, but she appeared to be faking laughter and interest in whatever it was Gary Haverford was saying. Ben looked back at Jili, her eyes radiating sincerity that Liza Heston's lacked.

"I've created this vision of her in my mind, and every time I get up the nerve to make my move, I can't help but wonder what happens if she doesn't fit the vision. What if she isn't perfect? What if—"

"Celia shits?"

Ben recoiled. "What did you say?"

"It's a poem, 'The Lady's Dressing Room' by Jonathan Swift."

"I know it's 'The Lady's Dressing Room' by Jonathan Swift. You know that poem?"

"I love that poem!" exclaimed Jili, reciting:

Thus finishing his grand survey
Disgusted Strephon stole away
Repeating in his amorous fits,
"Oh! Celia, Celia, Celia shits!"

"As for you and me living happily ever after, we tried that once," Jili reminded him.

"And thanks to Bert Mendes everyone in the country knows how that turned out." Indeed, Billy Mendes's father had submitted the clip to *America's Funniest Home Videos* and won $10,000.

"I am sorry about kicking you in the face, though I must say Dr. Dubach did good work fixing your teeth. You have a nice smile."

Principal Middleton announced Candice Zoeller, then directed the graduates to move their tassels from the right to the left, at which point all hell broke loose. Mortarboards flew, cameras flashed, music blared, someone lit a pack of firecrackers, parents wept, classmates hugged and kissed, and Ben mustered the courage to finally make his move with Liza Heston, only she was busy giving Gary Haverford a tonsil massage with her tongue.

Seeing Ben see Liza Heston kiss Gary Haverford, Jili stepped in and planted a kiss on Ben. Just lips, no tongue, but they both got a shock. Whether it was static electricity or animal magnetism, it left Jili light-headed and Ben with a ringing in his ears.

You Liza forget Keith dump I kiss think you love I.

Ben thought about saying something, but he could neither speak nor think straight. He could only watch as Jili ambled off dizzily and disappeared into a forest of green gowns.

They kissed again the following spring. Ben was at Brown hanging with friends in the Wickenden Pub, courtesy of Fred's California driver's license, a graduation gift from his big brother.

They'd spotted each other around campus and even had a class together first semester, Sociology of the Modern Dysfunctional Family, though the lecture hall was so cavernous that they did not cross paths until the day they took the final exam. Jili and Ben both found the course fascinating, as it not only made them feel better about their own families but it also explained a lot about the kids at Brown, where any sizeable gathering of undergrads was sure to have each of six basic roles represented: the Good Child, the Problem Child, the Lost Child, the Caretaker, the Mascot, and the Mastermind.

Pierce Barbour VI was a handsome, gentlemanly Connecticut blue blood who seemed like the Good Child when he asked Jili to dinner, but by the time appetizers arrived, he had flashed signs of split personalities covering all other five. Walking back to the dorms, he suggested they have dessert and recommended the bottle of Southern Comfort he had stashed in his room, but as they passed the Wickenden Pub, Jili spied Ben through the window and darted inside. Jili plucked two fresh pints of Guinness from a table of brainiacs or poseurs—it was often hard to tell—who were engrossed in a conversation about the false dichotomy of Rothbardian anarchism and Hayekian classical liberalism.

"You win," said Jili, handing Ben a Guinness. "It's Keeney Quadrangle, not Kearney."

"There you are, flower!" chirped Pierce, who only then noticed he was the only one in the pub wearing seersucker.

"Ben, this is Peter."

"It's Pierce."

"Pierre, this is my boyfriend, Ben."

Pierce appeared only slightly less surprised than Ben.

"Pshaw!" chortled Pierce.

Jili looked at Ben with puppy dog eyes that said, *Dude, my date just said "Pshaw," please, throw me a bone!*

Ben patted Jili on the head. She filled in the blanks and planted a kiss on Ben. First lips, then tongue, then Pierce dissolved and the pub melted away and time and space lost all definition as up became down and dark became light and by the time they stopped kissing they'd had sex five times and were spooning in her bed watching the sunrise.

Jili locked the door behind Tommy and let her robe fall from her shoulders to the floor. Ben eased his body against hers, patiently working past her ticklishness. She touched him in the place and in the way that normally made him shudder, only this night Ben felt a sharp, shooting pain. He'd never felt it before and shook his head like it was nothing, but when Jili reached down and touched him again, the pain made Ben's knees buckle.

5.

Over breakfast Ben made a last-ditch effort to talk Tommy out of playing Little League but it backfired exponentially.

"Andrew wants to sign up too," said Tommy.

"Really? You want to play baseball again?"

Andrew nodugged, Ben and Jili's term for his patented nod/shrug that meant more yes than maybe, as opposed to shrodding, the shrug/nod that meant more maybe than yes but was closer to no.

Andrew had played Little League back in Manhattan, and he enjoyed and excelled in the first two seasons of coach pitch. But the next two years of kid pitch, when he was nine and ten, bruised his body and his confidence.

"You really want to play baseball again?"

Andrew nodded.

When Santa Claus decided to bring Kate, Andrew, and Tommy new iPods last Christmas, Ben decided to get up early and hit Best Buy on Black Friday. By the time he arrived at 5:30 a.m., the line already stretched around the back of the building and all the way to Target—seven stores away. The line for Little League sign-ups was worse. As Ben made the trek past the multitude of dutiful parents waiting impatiently outside the Palace Valley Big Time Ballpark & Sports Complex, he noticed what appeared to be a short second line formed in front of the check-in table outside the gymnasium. Indeed, upon closer inspection, the second line stretched all of six people while the first easily numbered over a hundred. Ben walked back to the corner of the building where the disconnect appeared to occur and shared the good news of the second line, but his claim was met with skeptical har-rumphs by sheep whose herd mentality held that the long line must be the right line.

Standing sentry over a color-coded map of Palace Valley at the check-in table was a Paul Bunyan look-alike whose name tag, fittingly, read Tree.

"Utility bill, please," Tree said to the man in line in front of Ben. The man handed Tree a water bill paper-clipped to a one-hundred-dollar bill. Tree explained that payments were taken inside and tried to hand back the money, but the man winked and held up his hands as if to say *No backs*. Tree breathed a knowing sigh and checked the address on the man's utility bill.

"You are in the East Side district, not Palace Valley."

"Yes, well I, along with my friend Ben Franklin there, thought you might make an exception."

"Sorry, sir. No exceptions."

"My kid is a puss."

"Excuse me?"

"I love the little guy to bits, but it's true; he'll get eaten alive by those East Side thugs."

"If it means that much to you to play here, you might consider moving into the district."

"Ha! Have you heard of this little thing called the recession? We've had our house on the market for two and a half years. We've dropped the price six figures—twice."

"I'm sorry I can't help you."

"You can have sex with my wife."

"Excuse me?"

"What?"

"What did you say?" Tree asked.

"What did you think I said?"

"I think you said I could have sex with your wife."

"I did not say that," replied the man. "But you can. She's already diddling our neighbor, so what the hell."

Tree handed the man his hundred dollars and his utility bill and sent him on his way, but not before the man fired off a warning. "When one of those peewee East Side gangbangers with the Oakland Raiders logo shaved into his buzz cut and *puto* tattooed across his neck shivs my kid in the dugout, his blood will be on your hands!"

Ben received the coveted *PVYBL* stamp without incident along with two new player registration packets, which were thicker and more involved than any home mortgage, car loan, college admission, or job application Ben remembered ever having to fill out. Two questions into it he had to call home. "Jili, what size shirt and pants do the boys wear?" He thanked her, hung up, completed the first page, turned to the second, then called her back. "What is the pediatrician's name? And when were their last tetanus shots? And does your father's side of the family have any history of heart disease, diabetes, cancer, gonorrhea, or syphilis?"

"Gonorrhea or syphilis?" Jili asked.

"I'm kidding about those two, but you should see this registration packet."

With completed packets for both boys in hand, Ben made his way to the registration table, only to have his path blocked by a woman who shrieked, "Ben Holden!"

It was the nightmare scenario Ben dreaded about moving back home: bumping into people he used to know who recognized him but whom he could not pick out of a lineup of one.

"Wow. Hi. Wow." It was the best Ben could muster, though luckily for him she was working sign-ups and wearing a name tag. But the instant his eyes slid away from hers she slapped her hand over her name tag.

"Don't tell me you don't remember me!" she cried.

Ben chuckled as he struggled to place her.

"I'll give you a hint," she said revealing the first letter.

L . . .

She seemed to be enjoying this just as much as Ben was not.

LI . . .

Ben politely feigned it was on the tip of his tongue while trying to imagine her without bottle blond hair, coffee breath, and crag-riddled chipmunk cheeks.

LIZ . . .

There was a one-in-twenty-six chance the next letter was an *A*, but what were the odds that she was Liza Heston?

"Lizzie Fessenkreider!" she squealed, revealing the *ZIE*.

"No *A*!"

"Yes way!"

So relieved was Ben that she was not Liza Heston, he wrapped Lizzie Fessenkreider in a big hug despite still not having the slightest clue who the hell she was.

Ben's paperwork all looked to be in order except for Tommy's birth certificate, which he explained got misplaced in the move.

"I am sorry," said the guy behind the table, "but your boy cannot register without proof of age."

Ben stared at the guy, dumbfounded. "Herb, you're my next-door neighbor. You know Tommy is six. You and your daughter, Wendy, were at his birthday party. Remember, the one with all the sixes on the hats and the balloons and the paper plates? In fact, I am pretty sure it was you who ate Tommy's piece of cake with the big, red number six."

"Frosting is my Kryptonite. But without a birth certificate . . ."

Tom Doyle stepped in and initialed Tommy's form. Tom was president of the league and one of Ben's oldest friends. The two stepped aside to catch up, but trying to talk to the league president at registration was like trying to talk to the groom at his wedding reception.

"Who is in charge here?" interrupted a mother on a mission. Ben's expression clearly said *Don't look at me*, so the mother turned on Tom. "My son is twelve and playing in Majors, and I want to request a coach."

"I understand, and I appreciate your coming to me with this," he replied in the mollifying tone of someone who'd had extensive experience dealing with overbearing parents. "But we have a draft—"

"Yeah, yeah, yeah, that's what the little man at the table said, but if I cannot request a coach, then I want to request my son *not* play for Del Mann."

"I hear what you are saying, and let me say this to you: let's see how things go and once the teams are formed and the children start playing ball, if your son has an issue I will be more than happy to address it."

"Fine," said the mother, pacified, at least temporarily. "But Del Mann is an asshole, and why you let him coach in this league in the first place is a wonder."

"Del Mann?" Ben cringed. "As in *Promgate* Del Mann?"

"You think?" asked Tom. "I still say it was Chris Vonjensen."

Prior to Clyde King's bludgeoning his wife, *Promgate* was the most salacious crime in the history of Palace Valley. On Sunday, April 26, 1987, the night before the start of Spirit Week at Palace Valley High, someone or someones nabbed three dozen goats from Mr. Pellegrino's farm and let them loose in the main hall at PVHS. Stray laxative wrappers suggested the perpetrators intended for the animals to clear their bowels, and the goats complied. The volume of excrement was astounding, though one particular clump was especially disturbing. It was deposited right smack in the middle of Principal Middleton's desk, not by a dexterous goat but by a calculating human with a dark heart and a belly full of corn.

Martin Middleton was a beloved figure in Palace Valley, a selfless man who dedicated not just his career but his life to educating, mentoring, and helping children. His generosity touched generations. He was an unfailing presence at every game, concert, play, debate, car wash, crab and pasta feed, walk-a-thon, and on and on. He got to school early on the Saturdays when students took the SAT and made certain every kid had a protein bar and a sharp pencil. He ate with the kids, more often than not forgoing his lunch for a child who would otherwise go without. You couldn't not like Mr. M because, if nothing else, you knew he cared, which is more than a lot of kids could say for their own mother and father. He loved the kids, and he lived for Spirit Week, which made the act all the more heinous. It was offensive beyond reason, but it was the symbolism that crushed Mr. M.

"I am a dinosaur," he began as he addressed an assembly of the full staff and student body. "Time has passed me by. Where I come from, not only would nobody do this, nobody would ever even *think* to do this. That may be a sad commentary on our times, but in my heart of hearts I cannot help but feel like I failed you by not being able to foster an environment where this sort of violating act would exist beyond imagination. I say that I feel like I failed you because while this prank was meant to appear to be the handiwork of students from our rival East Side High Billy Goats, it was, in fact, the callous and malicious act of Palace Valley students who sit amongst us today."

Mr. Middleton had to wait for the murmuring to subside before he could continue.

"You know you did it, but here's the thing: I know you did it. I know the individual who is responsible. You may be bold, but you are not clever. I know who did it, and I can prove it."

Calls for the offender's name were met with the wave of a hand.

"Exposing and expelling the student would be easy, but in this case, as in life, the hard thing to do is inevitably the right thing to do. Plus, it would not rectify the underlying issue that this incident has caused me to face the fact that, as I say, time has passed me by. I believe in kind words and big hugs. I am simply not a baseball bat and bullhorn kind of guy.

"I know each and every one of you. And I know you well enough to know that not one among you is cold enough not to let this affect you. You will see the folly of your ways—maybe not today, maybe not tomorrow, maybe not until you send your first child to his or her first day of high school, and maybe not even then. But regret is a powerful emotion that only intensifies with time. And if I have learned one thing in my many, many years as a school administrator, it is that any discipline I dole out pales in comparison to the punishment that comes from within, from living with the consequences of your actions, especially when those consequences extend beyond the imagination that it took to conceive the act in the first place."

Mr. M took a moment and a sip from a glass of water to clear a lump in his throat.

"This morning I tendered my resignation as principal effective immediately—"

The assembly erupted in deafening disbelief and opposition.

"What's done is done," Mr. M said over the din. "Though let me say this: do not mistake my demeanor as stoic; I simply have no more tears left to cry." The same could not be said for many of the students and faculty. "I am an old man, and I may be doing yard duty on that great playground in the sky when you are ready to say you are sorry. If so, know this: I forgive you. But know this too: I am sorry, so truly sorry, that I failed you."

Suspicion fell on a group of four slackers: Phil Winston, Duane Shafter, Chris Vonjensen, and Del Mann. Conventional wisdom held that one of the four would crack, especially when Vice Principal Thornton cranked up the peer pressure by canceling Spirit Week and announcing that if the offender did not come forward—or was ratted out, which was not said but was unequivocally implied—there would be further consequences. Veronica Burr turned herself in, but it turned out she was just looking for an excuse to finish high school a month early so she could get a jump start on the rest of her miserable life. Plus, she was allergic to corn. The further consequences were never specified but, proving Mr. M prophetic, they extended beyond anyone's imagination when Vice Principal Thornton came on the intercom and made a momentous announcement.

The timing was ill-fated, as at that very moment Ben was standing face-to-face with Liza Heston. He'd faked a stomachache to get out of the last few minutes of Mr. O'Neill's history class and made a beeline for his locker, where he popped a cassette tape in his Walkman and listened to the theme song from *The Karate Kid, Part II,* "Glory of Love" by Peter Cetera, with the volume fully cranked. By the time the song ended, class had let out. Feeling a surge of confidence, Ben marched down the hall straight to Liza Heston's locker, tapped her on the shoulder, looked her in the eye, and said, "Liza Heston, will you go to the pro—"

The reverb of the school's ancient intercom drowned Ben out.

"This is Vice Principal Thornton, and I am sorry to report that because of the actions of one student who chose not to take responsibility for his or her actions, Senior Prom has been officially canceled."

"I still say it was Chris Vonjensen," Tom Doyle said.

"My money is on Del," replied Ben.

Tom got pulled away to answer a question about the dimensions of the bleachers and whether they could accommodate two exes with a restraining order stating they must stay fifty feet apart from one another. Ben and Tom promised to get together for a beer, then Ben turned to leave but was chased down by his neighbor.

"One more thing," said Herb. "I need to mark on your registration forms what you want to volunteer for. Snack bar, field prep, scorekeeper, team parent, umpire, game monitor?"

"What is a game monitor?" asked Ben.

"Game monitors are impartial observers who sit in the stands and make sure parents don't get out of line."

"Undercover cops at Little League?"

"Pretty much."

"Would I get to pack heat?"

"Excuse me?"

"Do I get to carry a weapon?"

"Uh, no."

"Then no thanks."

"Coach?"

"I beg your pardon?"

"Do you want to coach?"

The consequences of what you suggest extend beyond the imagination it takes to conceive such a ludicrous notion.

He thought about hitting Herb with a deep, philosophical answer but felt it best to keep his nice and neighborly.

"Anything," said Ben, "except that."

Monday morning Ben went to see Dr. Kennedy. There was not an open seat in the waiting room, which was a good thing because anytime Ben was forced to seek medical attention, his discomfort seemed to rise or fall based on the apparent well-being of others in the room. Last autumn he visited the emergency room after accidentally clipping his finger in a hedge trimmer, which seemed quite dire relative to the wheezing infant of freaked-out first-time parents, an elderly woman who gargled citronella torch fuel she mistook for mouthwash, and a teenager too stoned to notice or mind that his right foot pointed back instead of front, the result of a *Jackass* copycat stunt gone bad. But Ben's acute pain in his finger suddenly abated with the arrival of a farmer impaled by a pitchfork.

In the corner of Dr. Kennedy's office, an old man wearing a jumpsuit with an elastic belt sewn into the waistband looked pallid and twitched uncontrollably as he curled in a semi-fetal position in his chair. If not for the twitching, he looked positively dead, which made Ben feel better about his own situation and sparked a note to self never to wear a jumpsuit.

Once in the exam room, Ben sat on the edge of the examining table stripped to his boxers and draped in a gown. As he waited he spotted a plastic model of the male reproductive organ sitting on the counter. Ben chuckled recalling the day in sophomore biology class when Pat Weeks stealthily erased and replaced the substitute teacher's name on the blackboard, only to see earnest Emily Burlingame raise her hand and ask a question of Mr. VasDeferens. Considering the model more closely, Ben thought the penis ought not be quite so long, as an anatomical model implied a standard of normalcy, and patients who did not measure up might be made to feel inadequate. This dovetailed with Fred's theory that a man should always buy his woman a vibrator to preempt her from buying a unit that is bigger than his. But size was not Ben's problem.

"I get this sharp pain when I touch this certain spot on my testicle."

The doctor motioned for Ben to drop his drawers. He squeezed Ben's fruit like he was comparing avocados.

"How long have you had this?" he asked.

"Since I was born."

"Not your balls," the doctor said, unamused. "The pain."

"Sorry, just trying to make light of an uncomfortable—*ouch!*"

"How long then?"

"Saturday night, my wife—*ouch!*" Ben gritted his teeth as the doctor poked and prodded.

"Do you think it could be a hydrocele?" Ben asked.

The man whose name appeared on the Harvard Medical School diploma hanging on the wall looked over his eyeglasses at Ben. "Interesting theory, Doctor, but given the presence of pain and the absence of swelling, I am inclined to think otherwise. Any dizziness or nausea?"

"No."

"Any discomfort urinating?"

"No."

The doctor held Ben's scrotum in one hand and stroked his inner thigh with the other.

"Are you checking my cremasteric reflex?"

The doctor slid his rolling stool across the room and rummaged through his cabinets. Unable to find what he was looking for, he turned back to Ben and grumbled, "That's not good."

"What? What's not good?"

"Well, you obviously did your homework, but I am fresh out of little gold stars." The doctor tossed Ben his pants. "It appears to simply be irritation or inflammation, though it could be mild testicular torsion, where the spermatic cord that provides the blood supply to a testicle gets twisted. But you already know that. Common risk factors in adults include strenuous physical activity and trauma. Do you do heavy labor or play contact sports?"

"I make furniture and ride my bike."

"Did your wife kick you in the nuts?"

"Excuse me?"

"Earlier you said 'Saturday night my wife' and then you yelled *ouch*."

"That's because you were squishing my gonads."

"Don't look so surprised; you'd be amazed at the crazy shit I see. A guy came in here last week with second-degree burns after dipping his dice in hot . . ." The doctor shuddered and waved away the thought as if it were too painful to recount.

"So you don't think it's epididymitis or orchialgia?"

"I think you should get a urine test and an ultrasound." The doctor scribbled on his prescription pad and handed the slip to Ben. "And stay off the Internet."

Ben got an appointment for an ultrasound that afternoon. He breathed a sigh of relief when a squat, homely man entered the exam room, because while he was waiting Ben could not help but wonder how he might react if the tech were a striking redhead with translucent green eyes and full lips like the woman in the lab coat who sauntered in and said, "Mr. Holden?"

"Who are you?"

"I am the ultrasound tech."

"Then who is he?"

"He's the vending machine guy." She winked at Ben and whispered, "He gives me free Twix, and I let him take rubber gloves home to his kids."

The vending machine guy smiled, then left with a couple dozen gloves in each pocket.

"You like Twix?" she asked Ben.

"Actually, it's my favorite."

"Well, then we have something in common." She opened the wrapper, handed one to Ben, and slid the other in her mouth, slowly, sighing with delight, then licking clean the tips of her fire engine red fingernails. "You are here for a scrotal ultrasound?"

"You are really the ultrasound tech?" Ben had talked to Fred following the doctor visit, and he would not put it past his brother to hire a hottie to impersonate the tech.

"I really am," she said, flashing a smile as bright as her eyes. She leaned close to Ben and presented the hospital badge pinned above her ample breast, but Ben's eyes involuntarily gravitated past the badge to her red lace bra.

"Have you ever had an ultrasound before?"

"I haven't," Ben answered, "but I was in the room with my wife when she had hers with each of our kids."

"How many kids do you have?"

"Three; a girl who's fourteen, a boy who's twelve, and a boy who's six."

"I have a son who's twelve too," she said, though Ben thought that hardly seemed possible, unless she'd had the baby when she herself was twelve, as he had pegged her for her midtwenties. She flipped back Ben's gown, catching him by surprise but missing the last lingering effects of the chubby he'd sprouted while watching her savor her Twix. She matter-of-factly cast aside his penis as though it were garnish and frosted his balls with gel. "This is going to be a little cold," she warned a little late.

Ben fixed his eyes on the vent in the ceiling above him and tried to focus his thoughts on the intricacies of the hospital's duct work rather than the adorable young woman juggling his jewels, though it became all but impossible to deny her entry to his imagination once he caught a whiff of her. With one hand working the transducer and the other the computer, she had to flip her hair out of her eyes, and with each fetching whip her essence wafted downwind. Fresh pineapple, he thought, and as he did he felt a jolt in his loins—though not the sharp, shooting pain. With each thought Ben had of her, he grew a little more, like Pinocchio telling a lie. He picked up the scent of vanilla—*schwing!*—and sensed a hint of almond—*schwing!*

"Looking good," she said with a sexy rasp to her voice and her eyes fixed on the monitor.

I bet she can purr like a kitten.

Ben did not mean to think it. He tried not to think about anything but halting the southbound flow of blood, but he was rising faster than a Thanksgiving Day balloon that's late for the Macy's parade. He shut his eyes and thought of acorn squash, the vilest food ever. His mother used to make him eat it, but it was beyond gross, even when she tried to sweeten it with warm honey. *Warm honey.* Ben changed mental channels and pictured Ms. Carlisle, the elementary school lunch lady with the festering boil. He thought about the month-old curdled milk he found in a sippy cup under Tommy's bed, and the time he accidentally dropped Coach's car keys into a Porta-Potty and had to fish them out, and dissecting a cow's eye in biology class, and the rat that Bear recently regurgitated on Ben's pillow, and the gunk that accumulated in Jili's bathroom drain, and the most foul matter in the universe: other kids' vomit. It was bad enough when his own kids upchucked, but another kid's yak was exponentially more repulsive. Ben tried to conjure the pungent stench in his mind, certain that would extinguish his flaming totem pole, but a final flip of her ruby tresses tickled Ben's nose with an intoxicating aroma. Gardenia.

"Natália," he mumbled, not realizing he'd said it aloud.

"I wish. I buy the knockoff perfume online because the real stuff is like fifteen hundred dollars an ounce. But you have a very impressive . . . nose." The pause and breathless gasp came as she turned from the monitor back to Ben, standing at rigid attention.

When Ben shuffled out of the exam room, he found her waiting in the hall. His cheeks were as red as her hair.

"The doctor should have the results before the end of the day."

"Thank you," Ben replied sheepishly. "Sorry about that," he said, pointing back toward the exam room.

"You have nothing to be ashamed of," she said, biting her lip. "Nothing at all."

The multitude of parents milling around the Palace Valley Big Time Ballpark & Sports Complex for tryouts reminded Ben of sign-ups, only multiplied exponentially given that each parent brought one or more—or seven in the case of Danny O'Sullivan—kids along. Every child carried a glove and every adult a Starbucks cup. For as many children as the league needed to accommodate, it was a surprisingly well oiled machine: grouped by age, kids started in left field of mini Wrigley Field, where they were given three fly balls. From there, they were to hustle, interpretations of which ranged from sprinting to slogging, over to shortstop, where they fielded three ground balls and threw across the diamond to an adult manning first base. Moving to wee Yankee Stadium, each kid got three swings off the pitching machine, ran to first base, and then slid into second. Based on their performance, coaches rated each child on a scale from one up to five; at the player draft, all the fives were selected first, then all the fours, then the threes, and so on in an effort to strike a competitive balance and keep coaches from stacking their teams. But human nature, compounded by the übercompetitive nature of Little League coaches, inevitably proves that where there's a will, there's a way.

Tommy's group was up, but first he had to pee. Andrew parked himself in the bleachers and buried his nose in a book. Tommy had an aggravating propensity for failing to plan ahead for routine bodily functions. Just as Jili was guaranteed to nod off in the passenger seat, Tommy was a lock to have to relieve himself within the first five minutes of a car ride, movie, church service, or trip to Home Depot, where, upon graduating from diapers to big boy underpants, Tommy once lifted the toilet seat on a floor model and made his mortified daddy proud.

"I can go by myself, Dad," carped Tommy. But Ben's years in New York City had left him with an ingrained mistrust that saw him still lock his car even when he parked in his garage, so he followed Tommy into the big stall in the back of the bathroom.

"I thought you had to pee?"

"I did, but now I gotta go number two."

Knowing this could take a while, Ben dashed Jili a text.

want 2 retard kids

???

want to TRADE kids, sorry, still new to texting
will give u back rub if u trade kids

20 minute back rub?

fine

unreciprocated?

ok

2nite?

yes

deal!

sweet. where r u?

bra shopping w/ Kate

never mind

weak.

"Here, take this," Ben heard a voice say in a hushed tone from the other side of the stall. Peeking through a slit he spied a man hand a boy a baseball glove, though he could not see their faces.

"But this glove is for a righty, and I'm a lefty," cracked the pubescent voice of a teenager.

"I know you are a lefty, but I am *the only one* who knows you are a lefty. You are new to the league, no one knows you, but if the other coaches catch sight of that cannon arm of yours, you'll be rated a five for sure, and if you are rated anywhere above a three, then there is no chance I can draft you. And if I don't draft you, then you are going to wind up playing for one of these goody-two-shoes dads who's out here 'to have fun,' and that not only does me no good, it will almost surely cost you a spot on All-Stars and on the summer travel team."

"Wait, so you want me to try out righty?"

"Damn, Logan, it's a good thing you've got your brains to fall back on should anything ever happen to that golden arm of yours."

"I know, right?"

"That's enough thinking for you for one day, now get out there and suck."

"Whatever you say," said the teen on his way out.

"And don't you forget it."

Cleaned up and zipped up, Tommy pushed open the stall door, startling the man at the urinal.

"Benny Holden?" The man peered at the big stall, then stepped toward Ben, sizing him up with body language that said *I don't know what you heard, but you didn't hear anything.*

"Hello, Del."

Del Mann projected an intentionally imposing presence, favoring attire that was all black and a size too small so as to sharpen the definition of his muscles. Twenty-three years since Ben had seen him, and Del still favored a pornstache and a scowl. Del stepped closer still. A notorious close talker, his habit of invading one's space seemed a transparent bully tactic, but at least his breath smelled spicy fresh thanks to the cinnamon toothpick, an ever-present trademark dangling from the side of his mouth since middle school.

"This one yours?" asked Del as Tommy dried his wet hands on Ben's pant leg.

"This is my son, Tommy. Tommy, this is Mr. Mann."

"Nice to meet you," Tommy said, looking Del square in the eyes. "I'd shake your hand but you didn't wash after you peed."

"I see you have a boy playing Majors too."

"Yes, Andrew."

"Well, here's hoping he takes after Uncle Fred."

"Excuse us," Ben said, ushering Tommy out.

Del checked his visage in the mirror, then left without washing his hands.

When his name was announced, Tommy anxiously ran out to left field. He caught the first two fly balls with ease, but when the pitching machine fired the next ball over his head, the guy working the machine shouted for him to let it go. But Tommy hopped on his horse and ran it down, making a Willie Mays–robbing–Vic Wertz over-the-shoulder grab that drew *oohs* and applause. Tommy raced to shortstop and fielded the first ball cleanly but was so amped up that he airmailed his throw over first base and into the stands. He chewed his own butt out, then calmed down and made solid plays on the next two balls. At the plate, Tommy did indeed appear to take after Uncle Fred. After raking a pair of line drives back up the middle and lacing a ball deep to the opposite field, Tommy scampered down the first base line, then slid into second, hopping up and pointing skyward, just like Homer King on TV.

"Way to go, Holden!" Ted Watson congratulated Ben as they waited for their sons to come off the field. Ted and Ben were fierce tetherball rivals in grade school and ran track together at PVHS. Ben had no trouble recognizing him.

"You actually look younger," Ben said, sincerely.

"What can I say, that's the power of *Joie!*"

"Pardon?"

"JoieJuice!" Ted pointed to the lightning in a bottle embroidered on his denim shirt. Ben scratched his head, though he was pretty sure that the custom-painted Hummer emblazoned with lightning bolts he parked next to belonged to Ted. "When I heard you moved home from back east, I didn't realize you'd been living on another planet! JoieJuice is nothing short of the fountain of youth in a bottle! It's made from the roots of Arctic sedge tussocks, aged sea buckthorn berries, and marrow from female reindeer antlers, which is totally humane because female reindeers—the only species of deer in which the females carry antlers as well as the males, FYI—shed their horns each spring after the birthing season."

"What does it taste like?"

"Shit."

"Really?"

"No! It sounds like it would, but it tastes like berry heaven. And the benefits—have you got all day? We're talking Mother Nature's nectar!" Ted whipped out his iPhone. "We are hosting a tasting party next Wednesday; give me your cell number."

Ben grudgingly gave Ted his number, then they were joined by their sons. Ben introduced Tommy, and Ted introduced Tristen. Dressed in bleach-stained sweats and the replica Homer King jersey he got for his birthday, Tommy looked like a ragamuffin compared to Tristen, decked out in new baseball pants, an authentic Homer King jersey, eye black, sweatbands, and a cap that read *PVYBL All-Stars*.

"Nice to meet you," Tommy said, shaking Ted's hand and looking him in the eyes.

"Tristen, can you shake hands with Mr. Holden?"

Tristen spit at his father's feet.

"His tryout didn't go the way he'd hoped," explained Ted. "Don't worry about it, pal, the coaches all know what you can do."

"Shut your piehole! You don't know anything. You never played baseball. You were good at tetherball, *whoop-dee-doo!*"

They were joined by a boy who appeared to be Andrew's age and was trailed closely by six adults. "'Sup, T!" Ted's attempt to high-five the boy was met with a discomfited glare, and his subsequent look for a knuckle bump fared no better. "Ben," said Ted, "this is my son Troy, and this is his hitting coach, fitness coach, mental coach, nutritionist, chiropractor, and videographer."

Troy pulled Ben into a bro hug, then tousled Tommy's hair. "That was some dope stroking, Li'l Bambino. Maybe you should go to Triple-A and Kristen, er, I mean Tristen, should go back to Single-A."

"Bite me, loser. I'm not the one who gave up a grand slam last year—to a girl!"

Ben and Tommy left the Watsons to their squabbling. As they held hands and walked around the ballpark, Ben marveled at the sights and sounds. The kid trying out in cowboy boots was only slightly less curious than the kid in rain boots. One boy wore a sailor cap; another, a parka; another, a boa. Ben overheard a parent say, "You deserve to be drafted as a number two because you played like number two." Another asked, "If I staple-gun a note to your face, will *that* get you to quit pulling your head when you swing?" One father disregarded his child, saying, "It's blood, not battery acid for chrissakes," while a dismissive mother barked, "Do not walk next to me because after that tryout I don't want people thinking you are my kid."

Ben and Tommy watched from the stands as the boy trying out before Andrew took a fly ball off his face. Ben ached for the kid, who lacked skill, depth perception, and apparently coagulants, as his nosebleed spewed like a gusher. When Andrew caught the first fly ball, Ben breathed a sigh of relief. Andrew dropped one he should have had, then he caught the last fly and trotted to shortstop, where he bobbled balls but did not let them past. His throws lacked zip but hit their target. Following Andrew, a boy named Logan Winters dropped three routine pop-ups and threw the ball like he had his elbow surgically attached to his ass. When it came time to hit, Andrew swung and missed at his first pitch, then put the next two balls in play. It was an average performance made to look exceptional by Logan, who flailed at the first pitch as though he were chopping wood, then golfed at the second. He hit the outfield fence on the third pitch, though not with the ball but rather the bat, flinging it like a whirlybird to the warning track. Everyone watching gasped in horror, save for a beaming Del Mann.

6.

She came to him in his dream. Slipping into the exam room, she locked the door be-
hind her. With each step forward, she left behind a piece of clothing. By the time
she reached Ben she was a vision in red——hair, bra, panties, fingernails, lips. She
kissed him, long and deep, purring as she climbed on top of him. She shuddered
with anticipation as his hands explored her every curve. She overflowed his senses,
inducing fits of euphoria and semiconsciousness. Her lace lingerie floated in slow
motion like a snowflake and melted on his tongue. She bit her lip and gazed at him
anxiously, giving him one last out, but he remained silent, and her happy smile
invited him to have her completely.

Ben had had thoughts of other women, and he was not naïve enough
to believe that Jili had never thought about other men. He took her at
her word that she had been true to her vows, as had he. Ben's ponder-
ings were born not of anything he did not have with Jili but rather of everything he did not have before her. Ben had never been with another
woman. He never got laid in high school——though not for lack of trying; it was more a case of circumstance and opportunity. He never had
a high school sweetheart, not like JiliandKeith, and despite carrying a
condom everywhere he went lest his big chance with Liza Heston come
when he least expected it, when Ben unexpectedly got inside Terri Hil-
debrant's grass skirt at the Senior Luau, he found himself unexpectedly
unarmed after Tom Doyle nicked the rubber from Ben's wallet when
Tom got the chance to do the naked hookie lau with Laurel Immhoffer.

Ben's curiosity was natural and understandable. Having only danced with Jili, he could not help but wonder: was he a good dancer or was he just a good dancer in Jili's eyes? Ultimately the latter was all that mattered, but then there was this: was he really good in Jili's eyes, or when her eyes rolled back as she climaxed, did she ever imagine another lover? She said all the right things, made all the right moves, but Ben had nothing to compare himself with. He did, however, make certain Jili had something to which she could compare him. Heeding Fred's advice, Ben had driven an hour to Vacaville to buy his wife a vibrator, fairly ensuring that he would not be recognized by any former classmates and guaranteeing that she would not purchase a unit that was bigger than his.

On the subject of cheating, Ben and Jili agreed that there was once and there was two-through-infinity. Something could happen one time, something regrettable, something that would never, ever happen again and could be worked through over time. But two was the same as a thousand, and no time heals those wounds.

"Screw up once and I may forgive you," she told Ben. "But I will stick your pecker in the blender."

They differed on the hypothetical of if you were going to cheat, would it be with someone you knew or a total stranger? The topic had arisen recently after they'd polished off a bottle of St. Francis Old Vines Zinfandel truth serum; Ben held that it would have to be a total stranger, otherwise the risk would be too great and the emotions too real. (This is what baffled Ben about Tiger Woods: with all his fame and money, why wouldn't he boink a famous actress who knew a thing or two about discretion, or high-priced call girls whose job it was to open their legs but keep their hearts and their mouths shut?) Jili countered that it would have to be someone she knew because there would have to be some connection beyond the purely physical.

"I see plenty of hot guys," she said, "but I don't feel the urge to do them."

"Where do you see 'plenty of hot guys'?"

"At school, at the gym, at the grocery store. For a Podunk town, PV is not lacking nice-looking men."

Which of our friends do you think is hot?

Ben knew better than to fall into the trap of asking a question to which he did not want the answer.

"You're telling me you don't ever see a hot mom around town and let your imagination wander?"

Ben shrodded.

"Liar."

Ben's dream about the ultrasound tech was different. It overrode his limbic system, seeping deep into his brain, and stuck with him throughout the day; however, it was just a dream and he could not be held accountable, in the same way he could not be held accountable for slaughtering the Brady Bunch when Ben dreamed that he fire-bombed the TV family's suburban abode based on bad intel that Osama bin Laden was holed up and hiding in Greg's groovy attic loft.

Ben and Jili never discussed the subject of marriage until the summer after their graduation from Brown. They were trolling the midway at the Rhode Island State Fair when Ben spotted the game where you shoot water from a pistol into a clown's mouth, which inflates a balloon, and the first person to pop their balloon wins a prize. In the summer of 1982, at the Sacramento County Fair, twelve-year-old Ben Holden could not be beat, parlaying a black light poster of Blue Öyster Cult into a San Francisco 49ers AstroTurf doormat that graced the hall outside his bedroom. Ben did not know that the carneys tweaked the water pressure in order to hook the person who looked to be the biggest sucker, nor did he realize that he'd wound up spending forty-six dollars to win a prize he could have purchased for nineteen at the team store, had he actually wanted a San Francisco 49ers AstroTurf doormat. All Ben knew was that, given a water pistol and a clown's mouth, he was invincible.

"How do you play?" Ben said, playing dumb.

"It's easy," Jili replied. "Care to lose?"

"What have I got to lose?" Ben feigned ineptitude by grabbing the wrong end of the gun. "What are we playing for?"

"Ten-minute back rub?"

"Make it twenty," he said, his eyes taking on a steely resolve.

"You're on, cowboy."

Channeling his inner Clint Eastwood, Ben growled, "I'm gonna beat you like a three-legged mule."

On the sound of the bell, Jili turned on Ben and squirted him in the ear. Stunned, he dropped his gun and she won easily. He cried foul play, so the first round was called a draw. She beat him straight up the next round. He insisted they switch guns, but she beat him again. They stayed until they'd played every combination of guns, but Ben never caught on that the carney kept tweaking the pressure to keep his sucker coming back for more. They walked away sixty-four dollars later with a three-foot stuffed Pink Panther.

On a warm summer night illuminated by a setting sun and the glow of carnival lights, Ben sat at a picnic table across from Jili and watched her, transfixed. Her eyes were as bright blue as the cotton candy she enjoyed with the rapture of a little girl. She wore no makeup. Her hair was pulled back in a ponytail. Mustard marked the corners of her mouth, remnants from a playfully seductive bite of his jumbo corn dog. As she bopped to the honky-tonk beat of Johnny Lobster and the Crustaceans, Ben reached across the table and took her hand.

"Will you marry me?"

He just said it. For the first time in his life, Ben bypassed his mind and spoke straight from his heart.

Jili reached across the table and took away his beer. Ben walked around the table, got down on one knee, slipped an onion ring on her finger, and asked her again.

"Jili, will you marry me?"

"That's your belly full of brave juice talking."

Ben stood, turned, and stalked off. Jili hopped up on the picnic table, expecting to see him reappear any second on the far side of the stage. When he did not, she panicked and took off after him.

"Hold your horses, Jili!" Johnny Lobster shouted into the microphone.

"Thank you, Mr. Lobster," Ben said, taking the mic. Jili froze, stunned. "Ladies and gentlemen, I just asked the love of my life to marry me." The crowd cooed in unison. "She didn't say yes," he reported, as the coos turned to boos, "but she did not say no." All eyes and a spotlight turned to Jili. "She said she thinks I've got a belly full of brave juice, and I'll admit I had a mighty fine time in the microbrew tent tonight, but she and I have known each other since the first day of kindergarten, and she knows in her heart of hearts that after the trauma I suffered in our elementary school production of *Cinderella*, when she accidentally kicked me in the mouth and knocked me out cold—"

"Hey!" shouted a toothless granny in the front row. "You're Prince Charming from *America's Funniest Home Videos*!"

"Yes, ma'am, I am. And my Cinderella here knows that no amount of alcohol could get me back up on a stage." Ben got back down on bended knee. "Jili, before the witnesses here assembled, and before the reality of my being on stage sets in and I either faint or soil myself, will you marry me?"

The cute couple who got engaged at the fair made the newspaper the next day, though the story reported that the betrothed slunk off before anyone could get details. Backstage, Ben and Jili sealed the deal with a kiss, then ran hand in hand to the Ferris wheel, but not before Ben swiped a large nut and a heavy bolt off Johnny Lobster's trailer.

As they climbed skyward on the Ferris wheel, Ben dropped the nut at the feet of a couple sitting a few carriages below. The next time around he dropped the bolt into the same carriage. The couple screamed bloody terror, certain the ride was falling apart. The ride came to a halt, as planned, with Ben and Jili enjoying a panoramic view. And while the operators scrambled to secure the ride, Ben and Jili enjoyed memorably wild monkey sex atop the Ferris wheel.

THESIS

A sociological examination of the disintegration of mores and manners exacerbated by aggressive/regressive behavioral patterns in adults participating in the selection rite of children playing ball.

One could write a PhD dissertation on a Little League player draft. When the managers and coaches gathered, playground personalities quickly surfaced. The organizers, the rule followers, the bullies, the subversives, the peacemakers, the incessant question askers, the feck-less wonders—every archetype was present and armed with legal pads and spreadsheets, pens and highlighters, pencils and erasers, anxiety-inducing beverages, and some form of nervous activity snack like sunflower seeds or smokeless tobacco.

The depth and breadth of scouting was astounding. Most coaches worked laptops loaded with software that ran calculations of complex formulas and recommended the best player available based on the metrics of player ability and team need. Woe was the guy who had a job and a family and came to the draft with just the notes he made at tryouts. Chicanery was a draft night tradition, and despite the board's best efforts to make the draft fair for all, there were those who became so invested in Little League that draft night set the tenor for their entire year to come. It wasn't just important, it was all-important. Nothing could be left to chance. The lengths to which people went were at once comic and tragic, the most egregious example being the thrice-divorced board member who married an illegal alien so that he could assure himself of having her six-year-old pitching prodigy on his team for years to come.

It used to be that kids stayed with their Majors team for as long as they played in that league, allowing for the time-honored practice of coaches stocking their ponds by picking good young ten-year-olds who were not ready for Majors now but showed promise for the future. Those kids did not play much, did not develop, and often lost interest; their options, however, were limited to sit or quit. PVYBL began to see a decline in the number of ten-year-olds who returned as elevens, so the league's board of directors had voted to redraft every team in every league every year.

Every coach received a printout of the available players grouped by their league age and tryout ratings, fives down to ones. Majors drafted first. If a manager had a child on the team, as most did, that child was slotted in as the team's first pick regardless of his or her tryout rating. In the second and third rounds, any player could be drafted so as to allow managers to pick their coaches' kids, again, regardless of their rating. After that, all the fives went, then the fours, then the threes, and so on.

Whereas most of the coaches shared tables and information and sunflower seeds and good-natured ribbing, Del Mann holed up in the back all by his lonesome. His son, Dante, was Del's mandatory first pick, and when his turn came in the second round, Del announced, "Logan Winters."

The room fell silent save for the riffling of papers as the other coaches flipped back and forth through their notes. Whispers and murmurs were bandied about before Bobby Jeffries, a ditchdigger with a face like a pug and the physique of a fire hydrant, exclaimed, "That kid was a friggin' mongoloid!"

The name-calling escalated, not directed at the boy but rather at Del. Tom Doyle quickly gained control of the room and addressed Del. "Logan Winters rated a one. Are you drafting him as a coach's pick?"

The player agent handed the boy's registration form to Tom, who noted, "There is no father listed."

"Yeah, but did you see the mother?" asked another coach. "She is reason enough to draft the kid. Hands down the hottest MILF in the league this year."

"Where did he play last year?" someone asked.

"He moved here from San Dimas," Tom confirmed.

"Where does he go to school?" asked another.

Tom sighed.

"Let me guess," shouted Roger Pollock, like Del, a notoriously competitive hothead. "Sacramento County Opportunity School."

"Who is this kid, Del?" asked Tom.

"I'll tell you who he is," Roger interrupted. "He's the spastic, shitty kid that no one has ever seen or heard of who just happens to go to the school for juvenile delinquents where Del just happens to be the vice principal."

"If you are insinuating—"

"I am not insinuating, Del, I am accusing. To your face. And I'd be more than happy to take this outside."

"Let's remember we are drafting kids here?" interjected Tom.

"You pocketed the kid by getting him to tank his tryout," said Roger. "Everyone in this room knows you did it, and I think I speak for most, if not all, of the other coaches in this room when I say what goes around, comes around."

Roger returned to his seat and the proceedings continued without incident until the third round, when a coach who favored hemp clothing and went by the single name Q'urmdoq was on the clock. Q'urmdoq had a son in the league named Terdsoz. Now, when you take a name like Q'urmdoq or give one like Terdsoz, you invite the inevitable question about the origins of the names (which, to hear Q'urmdoq explain it, derived from some unpronounceable indigenous dialect of some extinct civilization in some South American jungle). Or, if you live in Palace Valley, you get comments from rednecks like Bobby Jeffries, who shouted, "What the hell kinda names are Corndog and Turd Sauce?"

Q'urmdoq proceeded to make Curtis Florp the draft's obligatory "tryout pick." It happened every year: a baseball-challenged kid plays out of his gourd at tryouts and gets rated higher than he should. Terdsoz was homeschooled; had he gone to PV Middle School, he would have known that Curtis Florp struggled with the simplest multitasking, like walking and breathing. The consensus was that Curtis had used up the only three hits he had in him at tryouts.

Sparks flew again in the fifth round when Gus Fernandez drafted Kimo "The Throwin' Samoan" Tagovailoa, a ten-year-old who had dominated batters in Double-A the previous season. His father, Faaesea, who stood an imposing six foot four and tipped the scales at three bills easy, took umbrage with the pick, as he had planned to manage his boy in Triple-A. There existed a gentlemen's agreement not to pick the kid of a manager in a lower league, but it was not against the rules. In fact, it kept things honest because some parents sought to manage teams as a means of keeping their child down so that the kid could be a big fish in a smaller pond. Also, with the stocking of Majors ponds eliminated by the redraft rule, coaches had no incentive to pick younger kids unless they were truly ready to contribute now. An all-but-untouchable pitcher in Double-A, Kimo bypassed Triple-A altogether and earned a promotion straight to Majors. Once the pick was announced, Faaesea passed his Triple-A draft notes to the guy he'd planned to coach with, got up, lumbered across the room, and took a seat next to Gus Fernandez.

Andrew Holden and Percy Blumenthal were the last players available among those who rated a three. Del Mann had his pick, and Keith Campbell would get the other.

"If I take Blumenthal, you can be reunited with Jili," said Del. "High school sweethearts together again." Sitting at the next table, Keith did not respond. "Whaddaya think?" Del said. "Both kids suck, so it's six of one, half dozen of the other. Eeny-meeny-miny-mo. One potato, two potato. You got a preference?"

Keith wore no expression, gave no intimation that he had a preference one way or the other, although the thought of being around Jili at practices and games and team parties twisted his innards in a knot. Keith had a family. He was a kind husband to a pleasant woman and an attentive stepfather to her eleven-year-old son. He worked an honest, steady job as a glazier, and they lived a quiet, comfortable, uneventful life. Keith was picking out artichokes a few months back when Jili spotted him from across the produce section. She looked fit and trim and happy and, save for the eyeglasses and the wedding ring, pretty much exactly as he remembered her. She told him he looked great, and he could see in her eyes that she meant it, even though he felt pudgy and stagnant. She wrapped him in a warm embrace, and he kinda half hugged her back, for he did not know the protocol governing public displays of affection for people you'd never quite gotten over. Keith loved his wife, dearly if not desperately, but he loved Jili first and still: not *in love* but *true love*, the kind that burrows deep into the recesses of the heart, the place reserved for people you are better for having loved and lost.

"Do what you're going to do, Del," said Keith. "Just please do it soon because I've got a family to get home to."

The not-so-subtle dig silenced Del. His messy divorce and venomous encounters with his recently remarried ex-wife had provided morbidly gripping entertainment at the ballpark last season—so much so that the end of Little League felt like a TV cliffhanger. People left yearning for next season to see where the storyline picked up.

"No way in hell I'm having a kid named Percy on my team," said Del. "I'll take Holden and hope he's half as good as his little brother."

Ben's ultrasound came back negative. The pain soon subsided, leading to the conclusion that it was, just as the Harvard MD had suggested, simple irritation or inflammation. Ben and Jili celebrated with Grande sex. With their children becoming older and wiser, Ben and Jili took to classifying their encounters using Starbucks verbiage. *Tall* was a quickie, typically without fully disrobing and most often occurring just after the top or bottom of the hour when a new episode had started on the Disney Channel or Nickelodeon. *Grande* was stripped naked but antennae up, a quality roll in the hay but nothing that could not be explained away in the event of an unexpected walk-in. *Venti* was a full-on session with music, candles, wigs, costumes, body oils, extended foreplay, multiple positions, drizzled confections, and, if the kids were out of the house, a change of scenery like the trampoline or the top bunk.

Venti sex was far more frequent back in the early nineties when Ben and Jili graduated from Brown and moved to New York City. While he looked for a job in publishing, she landed a spot as an analyst in a training program with an investment firm on Wall Street. She was banking nearly a hundred thousand a year right out of school while he was freelance fact-checking at *This Old House* magazine part-time and moving furniture the rest of the time for the TriBeCa gallery above which they lived. On a brisk autumn day when the wind zipped through the nooks and crannies of downtown Manhattan, sending leaves fluttering every which way, a rocking chair changed Ben's life.

"Be careful, will ya!" barked Mr. Barrengos, the gallery owner. "You break that and you owe me $5,600."

Ben eyed the half-dozen wrapped pieces in the back of the truck. "Someone actually paid $5,600 for all this?"

"No," the old man said. "Someone actually paid $5,600 for that rocking chair you just smacked."

Fifty-six hundred dollars for a rocking chair. Fifty-six hundred dollars for a rocking chair? Fifty-six hundred dollars for a rocking chair! No matter how he punctuated it, the thought did not compute. Ben was pretty sure Coach and Patty paid right around $5,600 for their first house in Palace Valley. On the drive to the Upper East Side home of Mr. and Mrs. Irving Goldfischer, Ben's curiosity festered to the point where he simply had to see the chair, so he offered to stay and help the Goldfischers unwrap the furniture. They were skeptical at first, but he seemed like a nice young man. Too nice, it turned out, as he politely obliged when they wanted every other piece opened and placed before getting to the rocking chair. An hour and a half later, including a break for tea and rugelach on which Mrs. Goldfischer insisted, Ben removed the brown paper and cardboard from the mystery piece, gingerly, like Charlie Bucket peeling back the Wonka Bar wrapper. The rocking chair was exquisite. Rich, dark wood with sweeping grains and flowing angles, intricate joinery, patterned slats, accented with ebony plugs, and a cushy leather seat. Ben helped himself. He rocked back and forth and stroked the smooth, polished arms and rocked back and closed his eyes and rocked forth and decided this is how he wanted to spend his life. The ride came to an abrupt stop with the Goldfischers standing over him like Mama and Papa Bear staring down at Goldilocks.

"You like Greene and Greene?" Mr. Barrengos asked. Ben appeared both dumbstruck and impatient as he pumped the gallery owner for information about the chair. "Charles and Henry Greene were turn-of-the-century architects and designers. They are the rock stars of the American Arts and Crafts movement."

"Do you have any of their pieces I could see?"

Mr. Barrengos laughed so hard he coughed up a chunk of lung butter. "A couple years back Sotheby's auctioned an original Greene and Greene armchair, not unlike that replica rocking chair. What do you bet it sold for?"

"More than $5,600."

"Try $913,000." Mr. Barrengos disappeared into his office and returned with a book for Ben: *The Art and Craft of Greene & Greene.* "That rocking chair you delivered was made by this old Swede out in Brooklyn named Olle Ollesson. What a character."

The next morning Ben took the subway out to Williamsburg and rapped on the unmarked door of a nondescript commercial building per Mr. Barrengos's instructions. Peering inside, Ben could see lights on so he knocked again, then again. Hearing the tumblers unlock, Ben checked an index card tucked in his palm before the door flew open in the hand of a sturdy little gray-haired Viking.

"Vem fan är du och var brinner det? Jag var på toaletten."
Who the hell are you, and where is the fire? I was on the toilet.

"God morgon, jag heter Ben Holden och jag beundrar ert arbete mycket."
My name is Ben Holden and I greatly admire your work.

"Du mumlar nar du snackar."
You talk like you have marbles in your mouth.

"Gungstolen du gjorde var jättefin," Ben said, glancing at the index card.
The rocking chair you made was exquisite.

"Din Svenska är skit dassig."
Your Swedish is shit.

"Jag vill jobba med dig. Jag vill lära mig."
I want to work with you. I want to learn.

"Du försökte lära dig några enkla fraser på Svenska från en bok och du låter som en fårskalle. Du är väl inte ens medveten om att jag just kallade dig en fårskalle? Det spelar ingen roll. Varför skulle jag ha någon anledning att tro att du kan lära dig min konst?"
You tried to learn a few simple phrases in Swedish from a book and you sound like a horse's ass. You don't even know that I just called you a horse's ass, do you? It doesn't matter. Why would I have any reason to believe you could learn my art?

"Pratar du Engelska?"
Do you speak English?

"Yo hablo un poquito español. Je parle un peu français. Ich spreche ein wenig Deutsch. Parlo un po 'l'Italiano. Ik spreek een beetje Nederlands. Яговорю немного русский. 私は言葉はほとんど日本語. And yes, I speak English, you boob."

Ben talked his way inside, and once in the door he proved to be a quick study. He helped Olle Ollesson increase production such that within six months the old man was actually able to pay him. Ben and Jili could easily live off her paycheck; they were just happy that Ben had found his calling. Jili completed the two-year training program, at which point most of her brethren went to business school to get their MBAs. But a senior partner who took a liking to Jili bypassed convention and hired her to do something with bonds. Ben never quite understood exactly what she did—acting as some sort of go-between for financial institutions or pension funds or insurance companies borrowing money from one another with the investment bank taking a cut of the action. She'd explained it a thousand times, but like high school calculus and the appeal of the Grateful Dead, Ben just didn't get it. All he knew was that her bonus alone was triple his annual take-home pay, which allowed him to continue making furniture.

Olle liked Ben. He liked that the boy was cheap, eager labor, but he liked his work too. Early on, the old man's fingerprints touched everything Ben did, but in about the time it took Jili to make VP, Ben's solo pieces were soon fetching handsome prices. Olle taught Ben the art and craft of fine furniture making. He also taught him to appreciate jazz music, play Norrlandsknack, and drink akvavit, all of which they enjoyed together at the end of most days given that Jili worked eighty-hour weeks and Olle had no wife or children. He lived alone in a studio apartment two blocks from his shop and rarely ventured into Manhattan, though he did accept Ben and Jili's annual invitation to Christmas Eve and was always delighted and humbled that they would go to the trouble to prepare a traditional *Julen smorgasbord*.

Olle taught Ben to speak Swedish. Forced was more like it, as work was an ersatz immersion program: Olle spoke only *på Svenska*—except when he cursed. He would not disgrace his mother tongue, so he'd learned to swear in Spanish, French, German, Italian, Dutch, Russian, Japanese, and English. He offered compliments the way he spooned *socker* into his *kafe*—sparingly. A good old-fashioned pat on the back was high praise indeed. He aimed to teach Ben the value of saving by withholding and depositing into a bank account twenty dollars of his pay every week (unaware that Jili made more in the time it took to walk from the elevator to her office). A stickler for punctuality, Olle would lock the door and crank up the jazz at precisely eight o'clock in the morning. So when Ben arrived for work one nothing-special Tuesday in 1996 at seven minutes past eight and found the door ajar and the studio quiet, Ben knew his friend had died.

Olle left everything to Ben—his shop, his tools, his collection of jazz LPs, his record player, and the old Royal *skrivmaskin* on which he typed all his invoices and correspondence. As he collected Olle's effects from the apartment, Ben came across a bankbook with an old plastic Dymo label affixed to the front that read, simply, BEN. Inside, the record showed a series of regular deposits, twenty dollars, every two weeks for over five years, plus interest, and a current balance of $2,652. Ben managed to hold his emotions in check until he spotted, taped to the fridge, the one and only photograph in Olle Ollesson's home: a beaming Olle holding one-month-old baby Kate on Christmas Eve.

Jili's brother Fritz made a boatload of money in the Internet boom, which afforded him the wherewithal to fulfill his dream of opening his own brewpub. McShane's was, first and foremost, a venue where Fritz and his blues band were guaranteed a live audience. The fact that the business grew into such a cash cow was gravy, thanks largely to Fritz's wisely overpaying a Scotsman named Euan Patterson to leave Gordon Biersch in San Francisco and move to Palace Valley to be the brewmaster. McShane's microbrews were available nationwide, even in the Korean bodega in the Williamsburg section of Brooklyn around the corner from the nondescript commercial building whose formerly unmarked door now read,

HOLDEN | OLLESSON
FINE FURNITURE

The Internet changed everything. Fritz set up Ben with a website back when the only people who said "www" were stutterers. Fritz nabbed dozens of domains, including misspellings of popular companies so that if someone typed in mircosoft.com or epsn.com, they would be directed to Ben's site. He optimized search engine keywords so that Holden│Ollesson appeared atop results for furniture, Arts and Crafts, Greene and Greene, rocking chairs, armoires, and Tom Cruise. Anticipating big box office for the 1996 releases of both *Mission: Impossible* and *Jerry Maguire*, Fritz cybersquatted TomCruise.com. The matter was settled before going to court, but by then the plan had worked to perfection: the story had become news, traffic skyrocketed, people got a look at Ben's work and liked what they saw enough to rack up six-figure sales and build both a database and a waiting list.

Jili's promotions to director in 1997 and managing director in 2004 were both followed, nine months later, by the births of Andrew and Tommy, respectively, both conceptions the result of celebratory Venti sex. Ben cut back his schedule to three days a week, which allowed him to be home part-time with the kids and also resulted in a sharp increase in the demand for his work. They lived comfortably, traveled frequently, donated generously, and saved wisely, banking enough for all three kids to attend Ivy League schools if they so chose. They had everything money could buy and happiness to boot, but the life they had come to know and love came to a jarring halt when Jili's mother went missing.

7.

The call came as the family was sitting down to Friday night dinner, so they let it go through to the answering machine.

"Hello, I am trying to reach the Holdens." There was an unmistakable undertone of trepidation in the voice of the man who wished he were not making the call. "If you have not already heard, your son Andrew has been drafted by the Angels. This is his coach, Del Mann, and we are going to have a mandatory team meeting and family barbecue tomorrow at noon at the home of Mike and Christine Yamagata, Seven Willow Lane. Do not be late. Please." The "please" came as an afterthought, blurted into the phone as Del was hanging up.

"*Promgate* Del Mann?" Jili stared pie-eyed at Ben. "You've got to be kidding."

"Why, what's wrong with Del Mann?" asked Andrew.

"Nothing is wrong with Del Mann," Ben answered with a bullshit smile.

"He is a bag of doosh," offered Tommy.

Wide eyes and slacked jaws all turned to the six-year-old. Under the table, Kate surreptitiously posted on Facebook:

> omg, my 6-yr-old bro just called some guy a
> "bag of douche" at the dinner table, LOL!

"What is a bag of doosh anyway?" Tommy asked.

"Where on earth did you hear that?" said Jili.

Tommy pointed at his father. Ben had no clue what Tommy was talking about until he explained, "We saw that guy in the bathroom at baseball tryouts, and after we left, Dad called him a bag of doosh."

It was true on both counts: Ben had said it, and Del was one.

"What is a bag of doosh?" Tommy implored. Jili looked to Ben. Andrew, clueless, also looked to Ben, who realized he had been lax in bringing his seventh grader up to speed. He'd vowed to do better by his kids than Coach's "just put the pencil in the sharpener and grind awhile" advice. Andrew was now the same age Ben was when Coach caught him shucking his nub to Miss March 1981. He had to imagine that Andrew had taken to sullying his tube socks, but Ben was more concerned about Andrew getting bad information from middle school blowhards—like Derek Zimmerman, who had led an impressionable young Ben to believe that redheads were called "fire crotch" because if you had sex with a redhead, the friction caused by the grinding of your pubic hair and hers could cause her patch to catch fire.

"It's douche bag," said Kate. "Women use it to clean their—"

"Enough!" Jili glared long and hard at Ben, while the siblings ducked below their mother's gaze and finished the conversation using the sign language of children spoken with facial tics.

Clean their what?

Their you-know-what.

Ewww.

"I am not going to that lame barbecue tomorrow," announced Kate.

"Oh, you're not?" asked Jili. "Thank you for telling us."

Kate coughed up a hairball and rephrased. "May I please not go to that lame barbecue tomorrow?"

"It's not going to be a lame barbecue," Ben said with an even bigger bullshit smile.

Actually, it was pretty lame. Not for families that knew one another or for people who mixed easily, like Jili and Tommy, just for introverts like Ben and Andrew who would rather have their faces gnawed raw by sewer rats than be made to endure icebreakers in the company of strangers.

Del's shrill whistle called the proceedings to order. Players and parents sat together in clusters around the expansive patio while siblings were dispatched to the pool house. Not that they minded, as it was bigger and better equipped than the homes of most of the families in attendance—foosball, Ping-Pong, a pool table, a pinball machine, a jukebox, a big screen for video games, a bigger screen for watching sports, a full kitchen, a full bathroom, even a laundry room. The players longed to join the fun, but Del demanded their full attention.

"Thank you to Mike and Christine Yamagata for hosting us today. Let's go around and have the players introduce themselves, say how old you are, what grade you are in, where you go to school, and the parents can introduce themselves, say what you do, blah, blah, blah, then we'll get to the important stuff. Dante?"

"I'm Dante Mann, and I'm in seventh grade."

"I'm Melissa Picard," came a voice from the back. "I am Dante's mom, this is my husband Bradley; he is a dentist, and I am the office manager."

"I'm Drake Yamagata, and I'm in seventh grade."

"I am Christine Yamagata and this is my husband, Mike, and we want to welcome you all to our home and to the Angels. Drake has played with Del the past two years, and we are looking forward to another exciting season. I signed on for another tour of duty as team mom, and Mike is assistant coaching, and we are both surgeons."

"I'm Aaron Ashford, and I'm in sixth grade, and this is my mom Laura and my stepfather Grandpa Frank, and my dad Bill, and my stepmother Aunt Michelle."

Ben and Jili exchanged a befuddled glance. Aaron's mother and aunt were identical twins, and his father bore a striking resemblance to his grandpa. Bill interpreted, explaining, "Laura and I split up, then Laura married my father and I married her twin, making me Aaron's father and stepuncle, and making Laura both Aaron's mother and also his stepgrandmother, as well as my stepmother!"

"And if that weren't weird enough," Laura chimed in, "I am my own ex-stepmother-in-law!" Bill and Michelle and Laura and Frank all got a kick out of this, making Jili feel comfortable enough to crack, "I wish I was your therapist!"

That drew a big laugh, over which one of the fathers exclaimed, "I'll do you one better: I was their divorce attorney!" Murray Simon introduced himself, his wife Audrey, and their boy Joshua, a seventh grader.

"I'm Hunter Lopez," said the next boy, "and I'm in seventh grade."

"I am Rubén Lopez, and this is my wife, Maria. I am a butcher, and I am going to be assistant coaching the team again this year."

"I am Ailsa Patterson, and I am in seventh grade," said the only girl on the team.

"Cheers, I'm Ailsa's father, Euan," said Fritz's brewmaster from Mc-Shane's in a heavy Scottish brogue. Ben was happy to see there was at least one parent he knew and liked on the team.

"'Sup, I'm T-Roy," rapped a white boy wearing jeans around his thighs with boxers sticking out, a retro Montreal Expos jersey, and a Dodgers-colored Giants cap half backward and half sideways. As Ben tried to imagine what Coach would do if a kid showed up for baseball looking like that, Ben placed the Eminem wannabe as Ted Watson's son Troy, whom Ben met at tryouts. "I'm doin' time in seventh grade," said T-Roy, "and I played All-Stars with Big D-Mann and Li'l D-Mann last year. I've played All-Stars every year, so I am jacked to get back, and dat's a fact."

"My name is Tiffany Watson," said T-Roy's mortified mother. Ben pegged her as Ted's wife when he spotted her denim shirt embroidered with lightning in a bottle. "My husband Ted is over by the barbecue setting up a tasting table for JoieJuice. We are regional distributors, number one in our network and number twelve in the nation, and if you have not yet tried JoieJuice, well, it is nothing short of the fountain of youth in a bottle!"

"I'm Duncan Baxter, and I'm in seventh grade."

"I am Duncan's mom, Janet," said a rotund woman who smiled self-consciously as her eyes met Ben's. Seated on the opposite side of the patio, a dad with a store-bought tan and capped teeth shared, "I am Duncan's father, Butch, and this is my beautiful wife, Trixi."

"I'm Conor Moran, and these are my parents, Lucy and David."

"I'm Logan Winters, and this is my mom, Cynthia."

Ben liked the economy the introductions had taken on. He elbowed Andrew to speak up. Andrew shrodded and whispered, "Later." In the interest of keeping the brisk pace rolling, Ben piped up, "My name—"

"Excuse me, friend," interrupted Conor's father, standing. "I just wanted to take a moment to say thank you to Christine and Mike for opening their lovely home. Thanks, too, to Rubén for providing the gourmet sausages from his butcher shop for the barbecue today."

"Now you know why I keep drafting their kids!" Del meant it as a joke, and half of the parents halfheartedly laughed; however, people around the league who knew Del could not help but question his motives. Drake Yamagata was a one-dimensional catcher whose parents had the killer team party pad. Hunter Lopez hadn't had a base hit—*ever*—but his father gave Del free steaks and a side of beef as a year-end gift. Murray Simon had handled Del's divorce practically pro bono. Euan Patterson was a brewmaster, Butch Baxter was a car dealer, Bill and Frank Ashford were jewelers, and while Del received no present or potential benefits from Troy, Conor, Blaine, Logan, or Andrew's fathers, their moms were all easy on the eyes.

"I have to admit," Conor's father continued, "that going all the way back to Single-A I've never liked playing against you, Del. But I respect what you have accomplished in this league, and I have always admired the passion you bring to the game, the knowledge you bring to the kids, and the commitment you bring to the team, so I just want to say thank you for taking our kids under your wing—and go, Angels!"

Could you please repeat that because I could not make out what you were saying with your lips pressed so firmly against Del's ass.

Ben thought it but kept his mouth shut. So did Andrew. When it came his turn to speak, Andrew clammed up. Jili gave Ben a stern look suggesting he not let Andrew off the hook, but fearing the ramifications of his son's getting off on the wrong foot with Del, Ben intervened. "I am Ben, this is my wife, Jili, and our son Andrew, who is a seventh grader at PVMS. Right, pal?"

Andrew nodugged.

"Andrew comes from fine baseball stock," Del said as he handed each player a three-ring binder. "His grandfather coached generations of Prospectors at PV High, myself included—but not Ben. Ben's brother Fred looked to be a stone-cold lock for the big leagues until, well, no need to rehash that story."

"What story?" Andrew whispered to Ben.

Feet spread, spine straight, and pecs flexed, Del struck a pose like a drill sergeant. "People say Little League is 'all about the kids.'" Del added air quotes for derision. "Well, it's not. It's all about winning. There, I said it. So sue me. Baseball is all about winning. That's why we keep score. In baseball, like in life, people win and people lose, and winning is fun, and losing sucks, and whoever said 'it doesn't matter whether you win or lose, it's how you play the game' either never actually played the game or was the parent of a kid who sucked."

The parents whose kids had previously played for Del seemed only slightly less incredulous than the astounded newbies like Jili and Ben. Ben scanned the patio for hidden cameras, hoping they were unwittingly starring in a prank TV show with a title like *How Big of a Douche Bag Can Your Kid's Little League Coach Be?*

No such luck. So zealous was Del that he had drafted his own Ten Commandments, presented on the first page in the binder in ink-jet calligraphy on fake parchment for added effect.

    I.   Thou shalt not be late.

   II.   Thou shalt come prepared.

  III.   Thou shalt play hard.

   IV.   Thou shalt practice harder.

    V.   Thou shalt practice after practice.

   VI.   Thou shalt put the team before themselves.

  VII.   Thou shalt not e-mail the coach.

 VIII.   Thou shalt not question the coach.

   IX.   Thou shalt not keep the coach waiting.

    X.   Thou shalt have fun.*

Amy Solomon and her son Blaine arrived just in time to be made examples of.

"Sorry we are late, I—"

"Don't care," Del cut the mother off. "No excuses. You are on time or you're not, and if you are not, you sit on the bench. Simple as that. Commandment number two: come prepared to practice and to games. Eat ahead of time, go to the bathroom ahead of time, and do not forget any part of your uniform for games. And for chrissakes learn how to wear a baseball hat." Del plucked Troy Watson's bassackwards cap off his dome and flung it like a Frisbee into the swimming pool. "Regarding uniforms, the league issues these knockoff shirts and hats, but we have the option to wear these authentic jerseys and caps." Del tossed aside the replica sample and held up the real deal. "Unless anybody has any objections, I can go ahead and order those. Number three—"

"How much do those uniforms cost?" asked Jili.

"We get a discount through the supplier. Number three—"

"OK, but how much do they cost?"

"Thirty percent off."

"Thirty percent off is still seventy percent on."

"For the authentic jersey and cap it's $125."

"For the team, right?"

"No, per player, but these are the authentic uniforms the pros wear."

"These aren't pros," said Jili. "These are kids."

Del had not anticipated her roadblock to his railroad.

"A hundred and a quarter seems awfully steep," said Joshua's father.

"Especially if they already get a uniform," said Aaron's mother/step-grandmother.

"The replicas look right enough," said Euan.

"What's the difference?" asked Logan's mom.

"If you can't tell the difference, then just forget it," Del carped. "Clearly, not everyone shares my level of commitment, so whatever."

"But thank you for sharing this option with the team, Del," said David Moran.

"Number three," Del continued. "Play hard. If you walk, you sit."

"But what if you are up to bat and you draw a walk?" asked Conor.

"I accept your apology for interrupting, young Mr. Moron, er, Moran, but there is no such thing. You are referring to a base on balls. On this team we run. If you walk, you sit." Conor's father glared at the boy incredulously.

"Number four: between now and the start of the season we will practice every Monday, Wednesday, and Saturday, take batting practice in the cages on Thursdays, and have conditioning on Tuesdays and Fridays. Technically we are not allowed to practice on Sundays, but if you happen to show up at my house at noon and my pitching machine happens to be fired up, and you ask me if you can take one hundred cuts, I will not turn you away and, technically, that is not an organized practice." The word *optional* was neither uttered nor implied.

"Excuse me, Del, are you suggesting—"

"Excuse me, Ben, do you have a question?"

"I wanted to ask—"

"Did you want to raise your hand?"

"Do you want me to raise my hand?"

"That is a courtesy that I would expect, yes."

Ben raised his hand.

"Let's hold questions until the end, although if you read through the materials thoroughly, everything is explicitly clear."

It could've been that Del was peeved Ben did not show him the level of respect or fear that fueled Del's superiority complex, though a more likely explanation for his authoritarian approach was a career spent surrounded by teenage reprobates as an administrator at the Sacramento County Opportunity School. He had no forbearance for insubordination of any kind from any quarter, on the job or off, real or perceived. It was a credit to his ex-wife that she only divorced Del and did not go all Clyde King on his ass.

"Number five: in the back of the binder are home practice logs that you are to complete, have your parents sign, and turn in every Friday at practice. If you don't, you sit." Ben flipped to the back of the binder, where the detailed spreadsheet called for a weekly regimen of one hundred grounders, one hundred fly balls, and on and on. "Number six: team before self, so no skiing, snowboarding, skateboarding, paintball, tree climbing, or any other funny business during baseball season. If you do, and I find out, you sit."

Ben leaned close to Jili and whispered, "It's like he's goading some of these kids into quitting before the season even starts." In fact, he was. Back when Del coached Double-A, his "garbage pick," Del's moniker for the final kid he was forced to draft, was a boy named Joey Maddox. Joey had been rated a one at tryouts, and that was awfully generous, like spotting a kid 600 on the SAT just for filling his name in the bubbles. While waiting for his parents to pick him up from the first practice, Joey broke his leg playing hopscotch. Del was steamed at first, but as he fiddled with possible lineups, he realized that he was better off playing with eleven players instead of twelve because the league mandated minimum playing time of three innings in the field and one at bat for each child, and the way the rotation worked out, the six best kids played all six innings, and the seventh, eighth, and ninth best players split "three-and-one" time with the tenth, eleventh, and twelfth players. Del did the math, and before the hopscotch accident Del's no. 7 would get as much playing time as his no. 12. But with his "garbage pick" gone, no. 7 would now get as much playing time as no. 1. Over the course of an eighteen-game season, which saw ten teams all play each other twice, it added up to an extra eighteen at bats and one-hundred-sixty-two outs in the field for no. 7 versus no. 12.

Del's no. 7 that year, Richie Carlson, had a batting average of .398, an on-base percentage of .472, twenty-seven runs scored, seventeen stolen bases, and only four errors in the field. Those were not bad numbers for the ninth-best nine-year-old on the team, and hands down better than even God could have expected from the klutz who somehow broke his fibula while hopping on one foot.

Invigorated by this dark enlightenment, Del managed, in each of the two subsequent seasons, to furtively persuade one of his weak links to quit. The way Del saw it, he was doing both the kids and the parents a favor by helping to point them in a more appropriate and potentially enriching direction. He was banking on free steaks and a side of beef, so Hunter Lopez was safe, but Del was convinced that by opening day he could rid his roster of Duncan Baxter, Joshua Simon, or Andrew Holden.

"Number seven: do not e-mail me. I will not answer your e-mails because I will not read your e-mails. If you have something to say, say it to my face. These young men are old enough to speak for themselves."

"And the young lady," said Jili.

"Her too. The point is this: you can jolly well tell me to my face if you choose to attend another activity rather than fulfill the commitment you've made to your team.

"Eight: in a democracy you get to vote. This is not a democracy. I am standing here and you parents are sitting there because I stepped up to manage a team and you did not. If you truly cared about what position your kid plays or the amount of playing time they get, then you would have signed up to manage. But you didn't. I did.

"Regarding positions, everybody gets a chance to play every position—in Single-A. This is Majors. I set the lineup. You will play where you are told and say thank you. If you want to pitch or try a different position, ask me before practice; ask me during a game and you sit." Del pulled three crisp twenty-dollar bills from his pocket. "Number nine: I charge sixty dollars an hour for babysitting. It's outrageously expensive because it is meant as a deterrent. If you are late picking up your child from practice, I will charge you a dollar a minute, and you will pay, or your child will sit."

Do you pay us a dollar a minute when practice runs long?

Ben thought it. Everyone thought it. But only Del's ex-wife had the nerve to actually say it. Del stood silently before the parents and the players for a long moment as he pictured himself taking Melissa by the nape of her neck and shoving her Botox-frozen face into the big bowl of Jili's delicious guacamole and holding his ex-wife there as she writhed and kicked and suffocated on avocado that filled her throat and nostrils as she gasped for air until her liposuctioned body went limp and she fell, smacking her head and her new breast implants on the corner of the wrought iron table before hitting the ground, where a pack of rabid hyenas that had emerged from behind the pool house licked the guacamole clean then dragged her lifeless carcass into the woods, removing any and all traces of evidence.

A menacing grin crossed Del's face and he continued. "The tenth commandment is the most important," he told the players. "I want you to have fun. But I put an asterisk by this because if you signed up for baseball so that you could get outside, breathe some fresh air, have some laughs, and play with your friends—then go play soccer. Otherwise you are wasting your parents' money and my time and—"

"And with that, why don't you all go join the other kids in the pool house." Jili had heard enough. The Angels all scattered in a blink. Del seethed, but his puffed-up chest quickly deflated when Jili hit him, swift and strong, with a look that said *Do not mess with the lioness.*

Jili sat in a boardroom gazing out at the Statue of Liberty and pretending to listen to a discussion on option strategies, arbitrage, and technical and fundamental analysis for institutional equity derivatives when an invisible wave hit her blindside. She excused herself and left in such a rush that her managing directors could not help but conclude that Jili was pregnant and making a mad dash to the nearest wastebasket to throw up. That, they agreed, would not be good for next quarter's earnings. But dread, not morning sickness, had caused Jili to bolt the boardroom. It felt like that quick, consuming fear when you realize you left the stove on or the bath running or the baby in the taxicab, only this pierced deeper. Jili felt it in her bones.

She bobbed and weaved through the maze of colleagues and cubicles as the wave intensified behind her, gaining ground like the beast in a bad dream that you cannot outrun. Like a rocket jettisoning boosters, Jili kicked off her heels and sprinted to her office.

"Answer the phone. Answer the phone. Answer the phone." Jili repeated it and repeated it and repeated it until she heard the voice of an older woman.

"Hello?"

"Mom, thank God." Jili heaved a sigh of relief.

"Jili?"

The wave cut Jili's legs out from under her and she fell into her chair. Mitzi had never called her daughter anything but Jillian. "It's Louise, dear. Here is Fritz."

"Jilsie?"

"What's happened?"

"How did you—"

"What the hell happened!"

Her shriek echoed across the forty-third floor.

"Mom has gone missing."

Within the hour Jili was wheels up on a plane bound for California. All anybody knew was that Mitzi did not meet Louise for their weekly walk around Pembroke Lake. Louise called Fritz, who went by his mother's house and found everything in order. Her purse hung, as always, from the handle of the entryway closet. The only thing missing was Mitzi and her car. Highway Patrol discovered her Dodge Dart three days later, abandoned at a gas station near Bakersfield, some 250 miles south of Palace Valley. Officers found a faulty starter but no signs of foul play, nor did they find any clues.

Mitzi had experienced her share of senior moments, and while Jili and Fritz had noticed an increase in frequency, the episodes seemed perfectly harmless—confusing the grandkids' names and ages, making gin rummy moves while playing bridge, brewing a fresh cup of tea while one was still steeping. Her recent memory was clouded, but her recollection of the distant past remained crystal clear, which led Jili and Fritz to share with authorities that their mother may have been headed back toward her childhood home in Los Angeles. The good news of a legitimate lead was tempered by the fact that Mitzi had grown up in South Central.

Crenshaw was a white working-class neighborhood when Esther Clark moved there in the 1930s. Young, uneducated, unwed, and the mother of a baby girl she named Miriam but called Mitzi, Esther met and married a dry cleaner named Arnold Radford, who adopted Mitzi and moved the family north to Palace Valley shortly after the Supreme Court's 1948 ban on racially restrictive covenants on property deeds that barred blacks and Asians from owning property in the area. Crenshaw changed, and in time the neighborhood where Mitzi grew up became among the city's most inhospitable.

Day after day after day, Jili, Fritz, and a volunteer army of friends and neighbors worked the phones calling hospitals and shelters from Santa Barbara to San Diego to Palm Springs and all points in between in search of Mitzi, but to no avail. Ben dearly wanted to be with Jili; however, they agreed it was best for the kids to remain at home and in their regular routines. As far as they knew, Mama was back home visiting Grammy. But after a week had passed, they agreed that Ben should get on a plane with the kids and come home.

Jili, Fritz, and Patty were waiting at the gate when they landed in San Francisco. The moment Jili saw her family, she burst into tears. She kissed the kids, then hugged Ben and pulled him close. "They found her," she sobbed.

"Where?"

"In Arizona. She's OK."

As best as they could piece together, Mitzi was driving to meet Louise when something must have short-circuited in her brain. She got onto Highway 99 going south and did not stop until she hit Bakersfield, four hours later. When the car conked out, aid came in the form of a kindly trucker. The little old gal had no identification and no money, and while she seemed confused about why she was in Bakersfield, she was adamant about two things: her address was 212 Crenshaw Boulevard in Paradise Valley, and her name was Esther Clark.

The trucker plugged Paradise Valley into his GPS and found the suburb of Scottsdale, Arizona. Two twelve Crenshaw Boulevard was five hundred miles from where they stood, and since he was headed home to Tucson, the trucker figured Esther Clark was safer with him than sitting alone in a gas station in Bakersfield, so he offered her a ride home. Seven and a half hours later, the truck pulled up to 212 Crenshaw Boulevard in Paradise Valley, Arizona, only to find an In-N-Out Burger.

"Well, this can't be right," she said.

The trucker took Esther home to Tucson, where he lived with his infirm father. The trucker did not call the police for fear that she would wind up in some godawful institution, the kind of hellhole he'd recently seen on a *Dateline* exposé on TV. Instead, he set her up comfortably in the guest bedroom and figured her memory would come round in a day or two. He did not figure to become attached to Esther. His father could not speak, and it was nice to have someone to talk to. She liked to play gin rummy, and she baked chocolate chip cookies that were out of this world. She seemed happy, and he was happy; it was like finding a stray puppy: he knew her family would be worried—if she had one.

One afternoon they were watching a rerun of *Murder, She Wrote* in which the heroine, Jessica Fletcher, is on a bus to a convention in Boston when a wicked storm forces the passengers to seek shelter in a remote diner, where one of Jessica's fellow travelers is murdered. The episode guest starred Rue McClanahan, post-*Maude* and pre–*Golden Girls*, as a woman named Miriam Radford.

"Hey," the trucker's houseguest exclaimed, "she's got the same name as me!"

Jili, Ben, and Fritz hopped a flight to Tucson while Patty drove the grandkids back to Palace Valley. Mitzi and her children were reunited by sundown. As Jili and Fritz walked Mitzi to the car, the trucker stopped Ben in the doorway. "Say, I don't know if there was any kind of reward or anything, but if I could just get her chocolate chip cookie recipe, I'd be mighty grateful." To this day, on the first of every month Jili still sends the trucker a tin of otherworldly homemade chocolate chip cookies.

Every point on the long list of reasons why they should not move back to Palace Valley was valid and reasonable and justifiable but ultimately trumped by caring for Mitzi. The fact that the kids would grow up knowing their grandparents and their aunts and uncles and cousins came into play, but by then the deal was sealed. Jili said she was willing to stay in New York and fly back and forth, and she was sincere; she did not want to be the one who dictated the move. Kate announced that the family was free to move but she would be moving in with the

Finkelsteins in 4G. Andrew shrodded. Tommy was happy to move so long as he could have a pet llama. Ben would have preferred a move to Crenshaw over back home, but he had never forgotten Principal Middleton's sage advice that regret is a powerful emotion that only intensifies with time. The seed of regret grows roots of resentment.

They bought Billy Mendes's old house and moved Mitzi into a comfortable assisted-living home not ten minutes away. Ben could drop Kate at the high school on his way to work, Andrew could walk to the middle school, and Tommy planned to ride his pet llama. Ben set up shop on the south side in an area known as the EaGle District. Bordered by Gleason, Dickson, Gaylord, and Killarney Streets, the hip trend of naming gentrified neighborhoods by combining a direction with a street name left city planners with a choice between NoDick, SoGay, WeKill, and, the winner by default, EaGle. The developers went for industrial chic with residential loft space above a bistro, a wine bar, a coffeehouse, a futon shop, a photography studio, an independent bookstore, and a candle shop whose overpowering scent gave Ben a headache when he was next door browsing jazz LPs in the funky record store owned by a Jewish Rastaman named Ari. Ben sublet a display window from a fly-fishing shop, in which he rotated a different piece of his furniture every few weeks. Gold lettering on the glass read simply:

HOLDEN | OLLESSON
FINE FURNITURE
WWW.HOLDENOLLESSON.COM

Ben's shop occupied space on the back side of the EaGle District between a screen printing operation and an outfit that sold souped-up boat parts. He arranged the shop exactly as Olle had, right down to the record player and the old Royal *skrivmaskin*, though Ben relied on an iMac and an iPod for his business and his music. With his unmarked door locked and his jazz blaring, Ben could make himself feel, if only for a short while, that he hadn't actually moved back to Palace Valley.

8.

The team meeting is like the first day on *Survivor*. Everybody is happy to be on the island, the conversation is breezy, easy smiles and pleasantries are exchanged, and the air is moist with anticipation. But once the games begin, it's pretty much all the parents for themselves. Over time, jealousies fester, factions form, alliances emerge. Cheering takes on a subtext. "Just hit the catcher's mitt!" is a common refrain intended to focus a struggling pitcher—lest the child be intentionally aiming at the umpire's elbow. "Just put the bat on the ball" suggests to hitters that in the ten-second span between pulling a bat from the rack and entering the batter's box, they somehow blanked on the fundamental concept dating back to when cavemen first put stick to rock. Encouragement that begins with "Just . . ." communicates that you know damn well they cannot succeed, so in the absence of competence *just* limit the damage.

This does not seem to happen in soccer, where calls of "Nice try!" and "Good idea!" are commonly heard on the sidelines. Perhaps it is because soccer is a fluid sport constantly in motion, whereas baseball takes a break between every pitch, giving parents time to think too much. Also, soccer does not come with a stigma-rich lexicon. Soccer players are called for a penalty, whereas baseball players are more grievously charged with an error. Fail to reach base and you are out. Make the third out and your side is retired. Make the third out with teammates on base and you have left them stranded.

• • •

"Thank you for cutting Del off." A young mom wearing Lucky jeans, a Juicy shirt, and a nouveau military-style baseball cap approached Jili as she shoveled ceviche into her mouth.

"Mmmm, sorry, I can't get enough of this, it's outrageous."

"Thank you, I made it."

"You seriously have to give me the recipe."

"I'd be happy to. I'm Logan's mom."

"Andrew's mom. And don't mind Del, he can be a bit over the top. Been that way since kindergarten."

"We just met him. We moved here from Southern California. Logan goes to the Opportunity School. Del seemed nice at first, but once he found out Logan played on a travel All-Star team down south, he kinda turned into Dr. Jekyll."

Logan's mom seemed sweet, and she had a killer ceviche recipe that Jili was not willing to jeopardize, so she opted not to mention that it was the good Dr. Jekyll who turned into evil Mr. Hyde.

Ben stayed within his circle of comfort and chatted with Euan, though he could only understand about every third word the Scotsman said.

"Baseball is Ailsa's bloody idea. I told her I'd buy her a horse, a piano, dance lessons, anything. But she loves baseball. I don't understand it for shite. It's worse than cricket, truly. And I hate cricket, I do. Though in cricket you don't get penalized for not swinging at a crap ball. But it is an insufferable game, cricket, tedious as hell. What kind of bampot dreams up a game that can go on five days without producing a winner? I will say this for baseball: at least you're on the clock and you know when the affair is going to end."

Ben looked at Euan askance. "There is no clock in baseball."

"What's that you say?"

"A tie game could, theoretically, go on longer than five days."

"There's no two-hour time limit?"

"There is in Little League but not in professional baseball, no."

The Scotsman glowered at Ben. "Baseball's one saving grace—gone. Brilliant."

Euan stalked off to the beer tub, while Ben turned and faced a face he knew he should know. The problem was the woman was twice the size of any girl he'd known in high school. Unlike Lizzie Fessenkreider, she showed Ben a measure of mercy.

"Jan—"

"Janet Darnell," Ben said, deftly throwing in an "of course."

She smiled, genuinely touched that he remembered before she offered, "You would not have been the first person not to recognize me. Years of fertility drugs and prednisone will do that." A plate filled with baked Brie balls and a McShane's Hairy Porter will too, but that was neither here nor there. Ben hugged Janet, his outstretched arms getting only as far as her scapulas. He remembered embracing her fully when they went together to the turnabout dance senior year. Ben had heard rumors that Liza Heston might ask him, but when Janet did ask him, Ben did the gentlemanly thing and accepted. At that time Janet was average in size and most every other way—looks, smarts, fashion sense, sense of humor. All things considered, Ben could never have imagined that she was off the charts when it came to oral sex. After the dance, in the back seat of his 1979 Mercury Capri, overlooking the twinkling lights of Palace Valley from atop Higgins Butte and to the memorable strains of Aldo Nova's "Fantasy," Janet Darnell blew Ben's mind. Then it was her turn. Janet sat back, found a cushy spot in the Naugahyde, settled in, let down her hair, hiked up her dress, and presented Ben with the pot o' gold at the end of her rainbow.

What do I do now?

He didn't actually say it, but then he didn't have to. Gawking gave him away. Janet encouraged him—never using the word "Just . . ." As with the fine art of furniture making, Ben proved a quick study. The tutorial would serve Ben well; Jili was duly impressed when she first experienced his prowess, but Ben was not one to cunnilingus and tell.

Janet and Ben took turns filling in twenty-three years' worth of blanks. (This exercise might have been abbreviated had Ben joined Jili at either their tenth or their twentieth high school reunions, but he was perfectly happy hanging with the kids and letting Jili fly off for a weekend with her girlfriends.) Ben explained how he and

Jili got together quite unexpectedly in a pub during their freshman year at Brown, graduated, moved to New York City, got married, she worked on Wall Street, he got into making furniture, they had three kids, girl-boy-boy, Kate, Andrew, Tommy, high school freshman, seventh grader, kindergartener, then Jili's mom got sick, so they moved home last summer. Janet recounted going to Chico State and meeting Butch, who'd also grown up in Palace Valley but went to East Side High. They got married, and he took over his father's car dealership. They tried to get pregnant for ten years, during which time she took every fertility drug available in North America plus one in Australia that had worked on kangaroos. That did the trick and they had Duncan, but the pregnancy triggered an autoimmune disease for which she takes prednisone, which caused the weight gain, which did not sit well with image-conscious Butch, who did shit like hiding her jewelry and threatening to sell it on eBay unless she lost the weight and making cracks in public like, "Just remember I brought the BMW, not the flatbed."

The ultimate indignity came two years ago when Butch hooked up with Trixi, whose son Chad played on Duncan's Double-A team. The wife is usually the last to know, but in this case Janet found out right along with the rest of the Little League families. Butch was up in the booth announcing the game, and Trixi was up there too, working the scoreboard—though that was not all she was working. As she bobbed his knob and he braced himself for blastoff, he unwittingly flipped the switch on the PA system microphone. It turned out Butch liked the dirty talk and Trixi liked to be spanked. In addition to obliterating what was left of Janet's negligible self-esteem, Butch caused a lot of parents to have premature conversations with their children, who wanted to know what Chad's mommy was gagging on and why Duncan's daddy kept telling her to "tickle my sack."

Jili and Ben reconvened at the beer tub.

"Dibs on drinking," said Jili.

"This is my third beer."

"This is my fourth glass of wine," she said as she drained the happy drips from her glass and poured herself a refill. "Did you try the ceviche? It's orgasmic. Logan's mom is going to give me the recipe."

"She looks really familiar." Ben spied Logan's mom across the patio. "I swear I have seen her before."

"In your dreams," kidded Jili. "Who was that you were talking to?"

"Janet Darnell."

"Shut up!" Jili shoved Ben, knocking him off kilter. "Did you two ever . . . ?"

Ben rolled his eyes and strolled inside the house. Jili followed. The Yamagatas clearly had good—and expensive—taste, but Ben and Jili questioned how a family with young children could keep a house that was so white so clean.

"When's the last time you think the kids were allowed to set foot in here?"

"That assumes they ever have."

The family room was more in line with Ben and Jili's aesthetic sensibilities: wood paneling, hardwood floors, exposed beams. Jili perused the furniture and framed pictures while Ben joined David Moran in admiring a high-def flat-screen TV the size of a stadium JumboTron.

"Ohmigod, Ben!" Jili shrieked. Christine and Mike Yamagata entered the den to find Jili stroking their armoire. "Ben, this is yours!"

"I beg your pardon?" said Christine.

"This is Ben's. This is Ben's!"

Ben crossed in front of the Yamagatas to take a closer look.

"I do not know what you are implying, but I assure you that is not stolen property. It is a one-of-a-kind original that we purchased from a highly respected artisan."

Jili flung her arms toward her husband as if to say *ta-da!*

"I make furniture," Ben said sheepishly.

"You made that?" asked an impressed David Moran.

"May I?" asked Ben.

The Yamagatas nodded as Ben slid out a drawer, into the bottom of which a brand had been burned: Holden│Ollesson.

The Yamagatas were duly impressed, as was David Moran. "I'd give anything to be able to make something. I can't put butter on toast without making a mess. That is so cool."

"Thanks, though I am sure what you do is interesting to people who don't share your talents."

"Really? Because I am a recently demoted submiddle manager for a chicken wire supplier who moonlights driving the long-term parking shuttle at Sacramento Airport."

"Well . . ."

"Don't bother, it's OK, really."

"Basic woodworking is not that hard to learn. If you ever wanted to—"

"Build something together?" David's eyes grew wide with excitement. Ben was going to say take a class at Sacramento Community College. "My wife's birthday is in May," said David. "Maybe you could help me make something simple like a jewelry box?"

At least he wasn't asking for an armoire. And it wasn't like Ben got this sort of request a lot. His skills were not subject to emergencies or universal demand. A friend who owned an auto shop once complained that the problem with being a mechanic is that all of his friends owned cars. Plumbers and electricians get the same thing. A doctor friend of Ben's could not attend a social function without fielding queries from parents who just wanted to ask a question. "It's not just a question," the doctor griped, "it's just *another* question." Ben liked that line so much he appropriated it for use with his children: "It's not just twenty dollars; it's just *another* twenty dollars." He never got calls during dinner from frazzled friends having trouble with mortise and tenon joinery, plus David seemed like a nice enough guy.

"Sure, we can make your wife a jewelry box."

Back when Ben played Little League, the coach would hit a few grounders, mix in a few pop flies, then the kids scrimmaged. Del's eight o'clock on a Saturday morning practice at PV Elementary School resembled a three-ring circus. One station had kids hitting off a tee, another had kids taking infield on the blacktop, and a third had kids catching fly balls and throwing to a cutoff man. Assistant coaches Rubén and Mike had menial roles feeding a pitching machine to launch pop-ups and restocking the hitting tee, respectively, and Ted Watson helped out hitting ground balls, but instruction came solely from ringmaster Del.

Throw the hands and accelerate to full extension!

What part of 'deliver the relay to the glove side' do you not understand?

Field a ground ball at the apex of its trajectory, dammit!

Ben arrived a few minutes early to watch the end of practice, joining parents who lingered on the playground while siblings climbed the Megalopolis. A mini city of fun, the sprawling structure looked more like a Disneyland attraction than the monkey bars Ben remembered playing on when he went to school there. The good old swing set had been rendered obsolete by the jungle gym on steroids with the climbing wall, cargo net, rickety bridge, tire swing, and corkscrew slide. The sandbox had been replaced by some sort of eco-groovy vulcanized rubber substitute made from recycled milk jugs.

Everything was better for kids these days, Ben concluded. A generation of dads who played with little plastic Army men now watched their kids carry out covert ops in CGI-rendered 3-D video games. In Ben's day it was cruel and unusual punishment to be sent to your room; nowadays parents can't drag kids out. The whole point of being banished is to be alone, but with computers and cell phones kids are never alone and parents can't know who they're communicating with. It was a traumatic deal for Ben to call a girl's house and risk having her father answer, but it was a life lesson in sacking up. Now kids hook up and break up via IM and txt msgs. Vowels are an endangered species.

To Ben's mind, social networking could not be more antisocial. He had come to loathe Facebook and Twitter, which he believed caused debilitating and sedentary addiction on par with Oxycontin and Quaaludes. People no longer talked; they tweeted and poked and posted to one another's walls. The sound of rapid thumb tapping on tiny keypads and touch screens by people who turned up their MP3 players and tuned out the world around them had largely replaced spirited, thoughtful, pint-fueled discourse emanating from neighborhood pubs—except at McShane's, where Fritz flatly refused to hang a single TV and cell phone users were forced outside alongside the smokers.

"Hey, guy." David Moran winked and fired his finger pistol as he joined Ben by the Megalopolis.

"How are you?"

"I'm happy to see Del has Conor playing second base. It's his natural position. He's a Dustin Pedroia type, small but scrappy."

The reference to Dustin Pedroia, the five-foot-nine star second baseman for the Boston Red Sox who grew up in the Sacramento suburb of Woodland, was lost on Ben. Conor was indeed small, and as Ben watched the boy take infield, he wondered whether his father had said "scrappy" or "crappy." The kid might as well have been wearing ski boots and fielding with a frying pan. He could not get out of his own way. Peeved, Del fired ground ball after ground ball at Conor, purposely hitting sharp one-hoppers to his left and his right, balls that a Gold Glove big leaguer would have a hard time getting.

"Just get in front of the ball!" *Smack!* "Do not let it get past you!" *Smack!* "Knock it down!" *Smack!* "Use your face if you have to!" *Smack!* "Why do you think your parents have dental insurance?"

"We actually don't have dental insurance," David mumbled anxiously.

When practice finally ended—forty minutes late—Conor got an earful from his father on the way to the car. Ben put his arm around Andrew and asked how it went. Andrew nodugged. He presented his tattered baseball glove, which by all rights would barely pass muster as an oven mitt. "I'll make you a deal," said Ben. "I will buy you a new glove if you can dethrone the King of Megalopolis." Standing astride the peaked plastic roof of the lofty watchtower, Tommy did not appear a ruler ready to abdicate.

Ben did not believe it possible to make any one product more confusing to purchase than toothpaste. There is paste, gel, or liquid gel; tartar protection, tartar control, or advanced tartar control; cavity protection, plaque prevention, gingivitis guard, enamel shield, or sensitivity relief; with mouthwash or with baking soda and peroxide; whitening, invigorating, revitalizing, or refreshing; and a cornucopia of flavors including cinnamon, vanilla, citrus, bubblegum, and all manner of mints, from cool mint to winter mint to spearmint to peppermint. But buying a baseball glove proved to be an even greater head-scratcher.

Ben drove downtown to Burdette Bros. Sporting Goods on Main Street, only to find a Starbucks in its place. He generally did his best to avoid the big box behemoths on the north side of town, but the Sports Emporium had squeezed out the competition. They offered everything under the sun, it seemed, except for assistance. Ben stood before a wall of baseball gloves for a good five minutes before a stock boy happened by.

"Can you help me, please?"

"Let me see if I can find the assistant department manager in charge of team sports."

"One person covers all that?"

The stock boy scratched his pimply chin and nodded.

"I just need a couple of baseball gloves for my boys, please."

"Well," said the stock boy, looking over his shoulder to make sure the assistant department manager in charge of team sports was not watching, "there are three key factors to consider when selecting a glove: size, features, and field position." Ben gave the boys' ages, and the stock boy, who had heard the assistant department manager in charge of team sports' pitch enough to have it committed to memory, fit Tommy in a size ten and Andrew in a size eleven.

"As for features, all gloves come with an open or a closed web. An open web makes it easier to get the ball out of the pocket, while a closed web offers more support when catching. Then there is pocket depth. A shallow pocket is better for infielders who need to grab the ball quickly and throw to a base, whereas a deep pocket helps outfielders hold on to fly balls. Lastly, there is the back. An open back features a space above the wrist and a closed back doesn't. That is more a matter of personal preference. The other factor is field position. If they don't need a catcher's mitt or a first baseman's glove, then at their age it shouldn't much matter if they get an infielder or an outfielder glove. Are you looking for full-grain leather, top-grain leather, regular cowhide leather, or premium steer hide?"

"Am I?" asked Ben.

The stock boy handed a glove to Tommy. "This model offers a Dermi-Dri lining that removes moisture from the skin, an Anti/Shox palm pad, a Tri-Welt finger design to maintain a stable pocket, and CrossVent construction that is half the weight and twice as strong as regular gloves, plus it comes already broken in."

"I want this one!" said Tommy, pounding his fist in the pocket.

"How much is that one?"

"That one is $179."

Ben pulled the glove from Tommy's hand and flipped it back to the stock boy. After ten minutes of digging Ben found Tommy and Andrew two perfectly serviceable gloves for less than the cost of the Dermi-Dri Anti/Shox Tri-Welt CrossVent model.

Moving to the bat racks, the stock boy prattled on about BPF ratings, weight drop, flex, sweet spot, break-in time, and the relative advantages and disadvantages of aluminum bats, composite bats that are more forgiving but should not be used in temperatures under seventy degrees, and bats with double-wall construction designed to increase the trampoline effect at contact.

Ben checked the price tag of the bat in Andrew's hands. "Four hundred dollars? Are you shi—kidding me?" Andrew and Tommy giggled at their father's half curse. Ben rifled through the racks, setting bats clanking like wind chimes. He could not find one that cost less than $150. It was the principle more than the price tag. It smacked of collusion, the bat companies getting together and charging ridiculously inflated prices like the robber barons of breakfast cereal who charge upwards of five bucks a box for sugar-caked flakes. And yet, in the brief time that Ben was scouring for a bargain, three different parents plucked bats from the rack, each of which cost over $300.

Two gloves, two cleats, two pants, two color-coordinated belts, socks, and undershirts, plus batting gloves, wristbands, and eye black, and Ben walked out of Sports Emporium $403 poorer.

"What am I going to do for a bat?" Andrew asked fretfully.

"You can use your teammates' bats."

"Del said we can't."

"I will talk to Del. It will be fine," Ben said.

"Don't worry," Tommy said reassuringly. "Dad will take care of that bag of doosh."

Ben shot Tommy a glare that suggested he disapproved, though he never actually said it.

As they climbed in the car, Tommy whispered to Andrew, "And if Dad doesn't, Mom will."

Opening Day at the Palace Valley Big Time Ballpark & Sports Complex rivaled the pomp and circumstance of the ceremonies at most big league parks. Red, white, and blue bunting adorned the backstops of each field. Family and friends gathered around mini Yankee Stadium, where each player ran onto the field as their name was announced and joined their team in the outfield. The president of the United States of America appeared in a video on the CrystalVision scoreboard and led the assemblage in the Pledge of Allegiance.

> *I pledge allegiance to the flag of the United States of America,*
> *and to the republic for which it stands, one nation under God,*
> *indivisible, with liberty and justice for all.*

As always, this sparked a handful of catcalls from dissenters who opposed either the president, God, liberty and justice, or all of the above, but more people got goosebumps than got offended. Following the president, actor Matt Damon appeared on the big screen and led the kids in the player pledge:

> *I thank God for the ability and the opportunity to play this game today.*
> *I will give my best effort, and I will play by the rules.*
> *I will treat my teammates, opponents, coaches, and umpires with dignity.*
> *I will be gracious in defeat or victory.*

Homer King drew raucous cheers when his face graced the scoreboard to lead the parent pledge:

I will offer positive encouragement to the children for their efforts,
support the coaches who volunteer their time,
and respect the judgments of the umpires
regardless of the results.

As a personal favor to Homer, Beyoncé and Justin Timberlake recorded a duet of "The Star Spangled Banner" that stirred such emotion and Internet buzz that it set the record as the most-watched video on YouTube, topping Charlie biting his brother's finger and the drugged-up kid driving home from the dentist. As the national anthem ended, the Blue Angels arrived for a flyover, courtesy of Homer King. The PVHS Barbershop Quartet sang "Take Me Out to the Ball Game" then tradition held that some local personage threw out the ceremonial first pitch. Coach got the nod the year he retired. Other local dignitaries included a soldier just back from Iraq, the family of Principal Middleton upon his passing, and Pirate née Pistol Pete Peterson. This year, in what many saw as a sign of the apocalypse, the first pitch was thrown out by Angie Schmenk, PVHS class of 2004, who achieved notoriety as a reality TV star by making it to the final rose ceremony on *The Bachelor*. The fact that Angie went postal on the guy when she did not get the ring, busting open his lip and scratching his cornea while calling him four-letter names that would make a dockworker blush, evidently did not dissuade the board from bestowing on her the honor.

Opening day was quite the scene, especially for teenage girls who dressed to impress the boys. Kate did not get caught up in all that, which pleased Jili and Ben—to an extent.

"Would it kill you to brush your hair or change out of the sweats you slept in?" asked Ben. She did not dignify his gibe with an answer but instead remained focused on texting, her speeding thumbs a blur. Ben's cell phone rang to the sound of the *Pokémon* theme. Tommy giggled, having successfully switched his unsuspecting father's ringtone.

**whatever happened to "it's what's on the inside that counts"
and "beauty is in the eye of the beholder"**

I am not having a conversation with you by texting Kate

btw, look out . . .

Ben did not see the old man in the motorized cart until his handlebar drilled Ben in the groin. "Get off your goddamn cell phone and watch where you're going, dumb ass!"

Not "I'm sorry." Not "Are you OK?" As Ben mentally massaged his balls—knowing that if he grabbed his throbbing crotch in public Kate would never text or speak to him again—Ben wondered when road rage had trickled down to the crippled scooter set.

Jili had walked ahead with Andrew, who did not dare show up late for fear of incurring the wrath of Del. His game started at 1:15, but Del wanted the team there at noon. What they were going to do for over an hour was beyond Ben. He figured it was the same logic he and Jili employed with his sister Nancy: tell her to arrive an hour early and she may actually show up on time. Ben bought lunch at the snack shack: chili cheese nachos and a slushie for Tommy, a Diet Coke for Kate, a veggie burger for Jili, and a Polish sausage for himself. They joined Jili in the stands at the Majors field, where she was talking with Logan's mom. Ben knew he knew her from somewhere. They had not gone to school together; Logan's mom looked at least ten years younger. It was like seeing your dentist at the movies; he could not put her in context. But he knew he'd seen her somewhere.

"I noticed on the team roster that you only live a couple blocks away from us," said Jili.

"Actually we live on the East Side, but Del said he got us some kind of waiver or something so Logan could play in this league." Actually, Del doctored Logan's registration form and listed his own mother's in-district address as Logan's home address.

"Are you wearing *Natália*?" she asked Jili.

"I am."

"I love it, but I buy the knockoff perfume online because the real stuff is like fifteen hundred dollars an ounce."

Ben choked on his Polish. His eyes watered as he tried to cough, tried to breathe. Logan's mom leapt past Jili, clutched Ben from behind, gave him the Heimlich, and dislodged the chunk of sausage that had plugged his windpipe, the result of Ben's gasping with a hunk of pork in his mouth when he finally placed Logan's mother.

Jili thanked her as she tended to Ben. "Are you a doctor?"

"No, I am an ultrasound technician."

Her translucent green eyes met Ben's, and suddenly she, too, knew how they knew one another.

"I don't even know your name," said Jili.

"I am Cyn."

"Thank you," said Ben, his face as red as her ruby tresses. "Sorry about that."

"You have nothing to apologize for," she said, biting her lip. "Nothing at all."

To understand the hearts and minds of Americans
you must understand baseball.

—*Jacques Barzun*

9.

Pride, envy, lust, greed, wrath, sloth, and gluttony. The seven deadly sins are all on display at the Little League park, oftentimes all at the same time. Parents cheering while wondering between pitches what it would be like to get jiggy with that mom or that dad, or parents seething over why their kid was not playing here, there, or more. Coaches running up the score and ripping into kids who had not yet grown peach fuzz much less thick skin. Kids who would not run even if you lit a pack of firecrackers in their back pocket, and a herd of heifer-sized men, women, and tubby children grazing on a diet consisting of the four ballpark food groups: pork, processed cheese, fried anything, and candy.

The first game of the season pitted the Angels against the Tigers. As families and friends settled into the bleachers, Laura Ashford beckoned to Jili for a quick word in private behind the stands.

"Thank you so much for inviting Aaron to Andrew's birthday party," she said sweetly. "But it's not going to work out."

"I'm sorry Aaron won't be able to make it."

"Not just Aaron, but all the kids."

"I don't understand," said Jili.

"You scheduled your boy's party for the first Sunday in May, but rainout games are always made up on Sundays in May."

"But there haven't been any rainouts to make up."

"Well, not yet, but if there are, then you can't very well have a birthday party—much less a swim party—on the day of a game."

"The party is at 12:30. If there were a makeup game and if it were a morning start, then kids could come to the party afterwards, and if it was an afternoon start, we could start the party earlier."

"And allow the children to swim before a game?"

"So long as they bring their swim trunks."

With a dramatic and exasperated sigh, Laura handed back her son's invitation, along with a handful more she had collected from other parents on the team.

Logan Winters pitched the top half of the first inning and struck out the side on nine pitches. Del looked pleased. In the other dugout, coach Bobby Jeffries did not. The ditchdigger with a face like a pug and the physique of a fire hydrant had not forgotten Del's draft night shenanigans, and it was no real surprise to anyone who had been at the draft when Del's son, Dante, led off the bottom of the first inning by getting drilled in the ribs. Del marched out onto the field, though not to his gasping son but rather to the umpire.

"I want that pitcher and the coach ejected, right now."

The ump removed his mask and sighed as though he had known he was going to have his hands full. No shrinking violet, Grant Robertson was a seasoned and respected umpire. "Why don't you check on your player, Del?"

"Why don't you check your rule book?" Del never broke his glare, not so much as glancing Dante's way as his son hobbled to first base clutching his midsection, fighting back tears, and struggling to catch his breath. "If a coach instructs his pitcher to intentionally hit a batter, then the coach and the pitcher are ejected."

"The coach and the pitcher *can be* ejected *at the umpire's discretion.*"

"There was nothing discreet about that pitch!"

Bobby Jeffries joined the party at home plate. "It's the first game of the season. My pitcher is rusty and has butterflies."

The ump ordered the coaches back to the dugouts and called for the next batter. The second pitch of the game hit Drake Yamagata in the back.

"Time, Blue!" called Jeffries before trotting out to the mound. "No more curve balls," he told his pitcher loud enough for Del and the ump to hear. Dante took second base, Drake took first, and Logan Winters stepped to the plate. The next pitch caromed off his batting helmet over the backstop and into the stands. The Angels' dugout and bleachers erupted. Del charged back onto the field and made a beeline for the pitcher, but the ump cut him off. Using his booming voice as his gavel, the ump restored order. He removed the pitcher for hitting three batters in a game, per the rules. He warned both coaches that if any pitcher on either team hit any batter going forward, both the pitcher and the coach would be ejected. "You are going to be seeing a lot of me this season," the ump told Del and Jeffries. "Best you not get on my bad side."

The pitcher and center fielder switched positions. The first offering from the new pitcher hit the sweet spot on T-Roy's bat and sailed deep into center field, where the kid who plunked the first three batters made the catch, then threw a seed to home plate to get Dante tagging up from third. "Your boy suddenly seems to have found his control," Del sniped at Jeffries.

Conor Moran drew Del's ire when he missed the bunt sign and grounded out weakly to the first baseman. In the stands, his father reacted with such utter disappointment one would have thought that his son had just snipped the blue wire that triggered the bomb instead of the red wire that would have prevented Armageddon. Euan's daughter, Ailsa, not only laid down the bunt but beat the throw, loading the bases. Andrew stepped up to the plate with the bases loaded and two outs. Jili cheered. Ben sighed.

They were a lot alike in a lot of ways—both were health-conscious and into fitness, savers more than spenders, socially liberal and fiscally conservative, preferred the mountains to the beach—however, Ben and Jili were also a study in how opposites attract. He loved jazz, and she was into hip-hop. He craved rich chocolate desserts, while she went for the fruit tart or cobbler. He was an early bird, and she was a night owl. He gave up running for swimming, then got into biking. She gave up swimming for biking, then got into running. Ben was a serial pessimist, whereas Jili was an eternal optimist. So she was feeling pretty good when the pitcher threw Andrew three straight balls. Andrew peered into the dugout at Del, who ran his right hand down his left arm, then across his chest. That was easy; that was the "take" sign, meaning do not swing. Andrew left the bat on his shoulder and watched the pitcher throw a strike.

"Step out," barked Del. Andrew backed out of the batter's box and watched Del as he touched, in rapid succession, his right earlobe, his left wrist, his nose, his chin, his nose, his chin, his nose, the bill of his cap, his chin, and then clapped three times. "Got it?"

Andrew shrodded and stepped back in the box without the foggiest idea of what Del wanted him to do, but the pitch was coming and it looked high, so he laid off.

"Stee-rike two," bellowed the ump.

"Holden," barked Del. Again Andrew backed out of the batter's box and watched as Del touched his left wrist, his left shoulder, his left wrist, his chin, his nose, his chin, the bill of his cap, his earlobe, his left wrist, and then clapped twice. Andrew was not alone in not understanding Del's complex signs, nor in being deathly afraid to speak up. As if Del's mixed signals were not confusing enough, Andrew got an earful from the Angels parents in the stands.

"Choke up!"
"Protect the plate!"
"The pitcher's got nowhere to put you!"

And from the Tigers fans.

"Just hit the mitt!"
"The pressure is on the batter!"
"He hasn't swung yet, and he's not going to start now!"

Andrew did swing. And he missed, badly, at a pitch that was up above his eyebrows and would have been ball four. Instead it was strike three, inning over. Ben heard someone mumble something snide about Andrew swinging like he was casting a fishing pole.

"It's all right," shouted Jili. And in the grand scheme of things, she was right: it was all right. No one had lost life or limb, but Andrew had lost face, and in that moment, making the perp walk back to the dugout, pummeled by Tigers fans cheering his misfortune, Andrew felt no less alone and exposed than if he were trudging off the field buck naked. When one of his players failed to deliver in a pinch, Coach used to say, "You can't hit a home run if you're not up there swinging." Del had a decidedly different take. "Hey, Paul Bunyan," he shouted at Andrew. "If I wanted you up there chopping wood, I would have given you an axe instead of a bat. Sit your ass down."

It was hard for Ben to sit in the bleachers, in part because it pained him to see his son struggle, but also owing to the assault on his eardrums by the incessant screeching of Blaine's mom, Amy. The woman never sat down and never shut up. Jili commented to Ben that it was like the time they went to see Bruce Springsteen and the E Street Band at the Nassau County Coliseum on Long Island and the Jersey chick in her fifties sitting right behind them spent the entire four-and-a-half-hour show shouting, *"Bruuuuuuuce! Bruuuuuuuce!"* For kicks, Ben and Jili tried to see who could come up with the most apt comparison for Amy's shrill yelp. Jili likened it to a duck in a trash compactor. Ben countered with a velociraptor scratching his talons across a chalkboard. Jili won with an orangutan getting a titty twister while its barbed-wire-wrapped gonads are crushed in a vise.

When Jili got up to go get Andrew a Gatorade from the snack shack, Ben found himself with an unobstructed view of Cyn's hind side. Tattooed on the small of her back was the tail end of a rattlesnake. Ben could not help but wonder where it went from there. Sitting in the row behind him, Euan leaned close to Ben's ear. "They call it a whale tail."

"A whale tail?"

Euan nodded toward Cyn, whose red thong underwear rode up and out of her tight shorts. It took a moment for Ben's eyes to pass the image through the rods and cones, invert it, project it onto the retinas, then transmit it via the axons of the ganglion cells up the optic nerve to the brain for processing.

"Whale tail," Ben said. "Got it."

Ben had been so transfixed by the rattlesnake tattoo that he had hardly noticed the red thong. Jili had tried a thong once but complained it felt like ass floss. She had not graduated to granny panties but preferred cute, skimpy cotton undies—when she wore underwear at all. Jili was a fan of going commando. Plus, she still rocked the bikini while most women her age had transitioned to the tankini or succumbed to the one-piece. Last summer on the beach at Lake Tahoe, Ben could not help but notice the number of fortysomething women who had given up and gone the route of the matronly one-piece plus skirt that draped over their butt, which seemed a bit like trying to hide a Christmas ham with a cocktail napkin.

Ben's and Kate's cell phones chimed simultaneously, his to the theme from *Pokémon* and hers to a hip-hop tune that sang *"Shake your tush, shake your tush, shake your tushie good, girl!"* It had become the soundtrack to her life. Ben had read a statistic in the newspaper claiming that the average American teenager exchanges between 2,200 and 3,200 text messages per month. Since leaving New York Kate never tallied fewer than 6,000 per month, which by Ben's math meant she had to be texting in the shower and in her sleep. Her thumbs existed in a state of perpetual motion. How she was able to maintain multiple conversations without accidentally texting the wrong thing to the wrong friend was beyond Ben. Kate suddenly burst out laughing. She showed her phone to Tommy, who howled and handed the phone to Jili as she returned to the stands.

"Ohmigosh, Ben, did you see this?"

Ben could see that he'd received a video message from his mother, but he could not figure out how to access it. Tommy snatched his father's phone, pressed a couple of buttons, then handed back the phone, which played a clip showing Patty jumping out of an airplane with a handsome young skydiving instructor strapped to her back.

The Angels beat the Tigers 6–0. Logan threw a complete game one-hitter with only forty-nine pitches. There was a spring in Del's strut after the game, for not only did he plan to throw Logan again in the next game, but he also overheard Andrew Holden tell his father he wanted to quit.

She'd come to him in the snack shack. They'd be the last two cleaning up after working the team's assigned shift, and as he wiped down the deep fryer, he'd hear the door lock. He'd turn to find her wearing only a red lace bra, the red thong, and stiletto heels. She'd remove her hair net and release her ruby locks. "I want you," she'd coo. She'd reach back and unhook her bra, unleashing her perfectly pert gazongas. "Inside me." She'd brush her lips against his as she slithered past him. "Now." She'd hop up on the counter, unwrap a cherry Rocket Pop, and lick the hard candy cone. Setting one heel against the cash register and the other against the nacho cheese dispenser, she'd open herself to him, a tattooed rattlesnake's head pointing the way.

This was different. It wasn't a dream for which Ben could not be held accountable. He was lying next to his snoring wife, wide awake with his hand in his SpongeBob boxers. Was thinking of Cyn cheating? Was it cheating to think of her while shaking his bacon? He had not broken the commandment about committing adultery, and the one about coveting thy neighbor's wife could go either way because while Ben was guilty red-handed (rosy palm, anyway) of coveting, Cyn was divorced and lived on the East Side, thus she was neither his neighbor nor anyone's wife.

On the subject of cheating, Ben and Jili agreed that something could happen one time, something regrettable, something that would never, ever happen again. Did this count? If so, should he tell her? Would it be worse if she found out later with the Gaze of Truth? Which raised the tangential conundrum: if Ben could harness the power, would he use the Gaze of Truth on Jili to ascertain whether she had ever pleasured herself while thinking of someone else? Did he really want to ask a question to which he might not want the answer? The thoughts bounced around his mind, swelling his brain like a bag of microwave popcorn. Ben was not quite sure what to make of all this, but he felt pretty certain that if this did count as cheating and Jili did find out, she would likely make good on her threat to stick his pecker in the blender.

The first pitch of the second game drilled Dante Mann in the ribs. Mariners manager Gus Fernandez feigned shock. Dante took first base and Drake Yamagata stood in. Certain he too would be plunked, Drake jumped out of the batter's box on a juicy pitch over the middle of the plate. Drake stood back in and eyed the pitcher, a heavyset kid with a face oozing sebaceous oils that only a blind mother could love. The pitcher winked at Drake, then reared back and hurled another perfect strike as Drake jumped out of the way. Next pitch, same thing, strike three. Del scowled at Drake. "Way to fight, Nagasaki."

Logan did a double take when Del gave him the bunt sign, but he did as he was told; as Del expected, the tubby pitcher waddled toward the ball and could not field it in time to throw out Logan. Del then had T-Roy bunt his way on to load the bases. Blaine bunted in a run, bringing his mother such glee she screamed like she was birthing him all over again. Conor bunted in a run, as did Ailsa, then Duncan, then Aaron. The Mariners parents heckled Del for playing small ball, to which he responded with a smug grin and a nod to the scoreboard. Logan pitched lights out once again, throwing a second consecutive shutout as the Angels won 7–0. Andrew got in the game for the minimum three innings and one at bat, never seeing a ball in right field and striking out at the plate. His request to quit had been denied by his parents, who insisted that he finish what he started and fulfill his commitment.

"You don't always get to pick your coach or your teachers or your boss," said Ben.

"Or your parents," Andrew grumbled under his breath. That remark earned Andrew a week's worth of doggie doodie duty.

The first pitch of the third game drilled Dante Mann in the thigh. The ump wasted no time and ejected Athletics manager Rich Richards on the spot. He seemed neither angry nor surprised as he exited the dugout. By rule, he had to leave the field and could not sit in the stands, so he watched the game on closed-circuit TV in the comfort of the sports grill—but not before crossing paths with Dante's fuming mother. "Try that shit one more time," Melissa threatened. "You throw at one of our kids one more time and I will kick your ass!"

"She's got the weight advantage," cracked Richards's wife, a leathery-looking woman who appeared to have been ridden hard and put away wet.

"Don't think I won't use it on you too." Melissa pointed a French-manicured finger in the woman's face. She slapped Melissa's hand away, and it was on.

"*Time!*"

The ump stopped the game and halted the hissy fit, ordering Richards to leave the field and his wife and Melissa to return to their respective bleachers with a warning that any further outbursts would result in their being ejected too. On the field, Dante Mann and Richie Richards both looked like they wanted to crawl under a base. In the stands, the other mothers were stunned, while most of the fathers were secretly hoping to see a chick fight. Nothing compared to the raw energy of two girls scratching and clawing at each other. Middle school represented the zenith of chick fights, and Jili and Ben still occasionally talked about the day in eighth grade when Sally Martinez and Lynn Harper got into it and Lynn, who had broken her leg skiing, swung a crutch at Sally, catching her with a wingnut right across the forehead and opening a gash that bled like a burst dam.

Logan's pitch count in the previous game prevented him from pitching a third straight time, so Del threw T-Roy for the first three innings, Ailsa in the fourth, and Conor in the fifth. Del had planned to use Dante as his closer in the bottom of the sixth, but his bruised ribs prevented the boy from making a full pitching motion. Del looked up and down his bench, then barked, "Bunyan." Save for his stunned parents, Andrew was as surprised as anyone that Del gave him the ball in the bottom of the sixth inning to protect a 4–3 lead. Del reasoned that while Andrew did not throw the ball hard, he did throw it straight, and with the bottom half of the Athletics order coming up, all he needed to do was throw strikes and trust his defense. Plus, if he failed he might just quit the team after all.

All of Andrew's warm-up pitches were right over the plate, but the presence of a live hitter threw Andrew, and he walked the first batter on four straight balls that were not even close. Jili held her breath while Ben held back explosive diarrhea. Andrew got the next two kids to hit into outs, and Jili breathed a little easier but Ben didn't dare unpucker. The next batter roped a clean single, putting the winning run in scoring position, then the Athletics' eighth hitter dribbled a gift-wrapped grounder to Conor at second base. He could've tagged the runner leaving first base or tossed the ball to the shortstop for the force-out at second. The textbook play called for a quick flip to the first baseman; however, with the batter running slower than a backward turtle, Conor could've easily kept the ball and stepped on first base himself to end the game. Coaches, parents, teammates, family, friends, the scorekeeper, the PA announcer, even the old man who picked recyclables out of the garbage cans yelled mixed messages at Conor.

"Get the force out!"

"Go to first!"

"Throw it!"

"Tag the runner!"

"Get rid of the ball!"

"Run to first!"

"Do something!"

Overwhelmed by the options, Conor froze. He was still holding the ball when a beet red Del called time-out and stamped onto the field and ordered the entire team to gather on the pitcher's mound. "Except you," he sneered at Conor. With the other eleven kids surrounding him, Del said, loud enough for Conor to hear, "Everyone look at Conor. Because that is the last time you will ever see him play second base again."

Del sat Conor and subbed Ailsa in at second base. As Andrew toed the pitching rubber, Jili turned to Ben.

"What are you thinking about?" she asked.

"Depends."

"On what?"

"No, Depends," said Ben, "the adult diaper. I wish I had one."

With the bases loaded and two outs, the Athletics sent their ninth hitter to the plate. Andrew recognized him from school. The kid was suited to sports like a cat to swimming. Slouched at the shoulders and dragging his bat, his body language screamed *Please Lord, get me out of here!* The boy's discomfort and lack of interest could not have been more readily apparent to everyone except the man standing behind the backstop shouting, "Come on, Maurice! Let's go, son. Today's the day!" It was enough that he'd hung the name Maurice on the kid, but it was something else that he continued to force the boy to play baseball. Ben and Jili agreed that exposing children to new and different activities is good parenting. Insisting they keep playing when they did not want to play in the first place, not so much. Ben had half tried to talk Andrew out of signing up. Maurice was never given a choice. When he was five, Maurice played T-ball and did not like it. His father signed him up for Single-A, and he hated it. He was made to play Double-A and despised it. He went on a hunger strike to protest playing Triple-A, to no avail. All the boy wanted to do was dance. He was gifted, a natural performer who felt the music innately, but his father could not bear the thought of his son not playing baseball, and so for four months every year Maurice had to stash his tap shoes and don his infernal cleats.

Today was not the day, and Athletics manager Rich Richards knew it. Watching on closed-circuit TV from the sports grill, he dashed a text message to his first base coach. The coach got it, called time, and pulled Maurice aside.

"If you get on base, we tie the game and our good hitters get up to bat," he told the boy. "There are four ways to get on base: a hit, a walk, catcher interference, or getting hit by a pitch. So here is what we need you to do . . ."

The coach jogged back to the first base box. As Andrew began his delivery, Maurice slid back in the batter's box. His instructions were clear: do not swing at the pitch; instead, hit the catcher's mitt to draw the interference call. Maurice swung and missed Drake's mitt, strike one. He swung at the mitt and missed again, strike two. Andrew's next offering was only halfway to the plate when Maurice turned and took a mighty hack, missing the catcher's mitt but drilling his helmet and knocking Drake unconscious.

"Strike three!" cheered Del.

"Catcher interference!" argued the Athletics coach.

"What the hell is wrong with you two?" scolded Mike Yamagata as Del and the Athletics coach pleaded their cases to the umpire while paramedics tended to Drake. Once he was stabilized and on his way to the hospital, the umpire officially ruled Maurice out for having his back foot out of the batter's box. Del jumped for joy but found no takers for high fives.

Rich Richards got a high five—across the face—from Dante's mom in the parking lot. As he staggered backward, his wife took a swing at Melissa, and the catfight was on. As fate would have it, the nearest sane adult happened to be Ben. As he jumped between the two mothers, one rabbit-punched him in the back of the head and the other clocked him in the jaw. The cops were called, reports were filed, and Ben ultimately decided not to press charges. For Ben, seeing the faces of the children watching their mothers handcuffed and placed in the back seat of squad cars seemed punishment enough.

Ben did not get much foot traffic to his shop. Had he kept a guest book, the sum total of the entries would have included the landlord, the mailman, the FedEx guy, Ari the Rasta Jew who owned the funky record store, Jili, and the kids. So it was always something of a surprise when a knock came at his unmarked door. It was doubly surprising one afternoon when the knock came from a bald dude as big as a polar bear and a jockey-sized man in a pumpkin-colored three-piece suit.

Foghorn Leghorn and the Chicken Hawk.

Ben thought they looked like the Looney Tunes characters, but he did not say it. The Chicken Hawk presented a business card.

"Touché?" asked Ben.

"The accent mark is over the *o*, not the *e*." The Chicken Hawk sighed condescendingly.

"Of course, how silly of me." Ben handed back the card and shut the door.

A heavy rap pounded three times, clearly Foghorn Leghorn, but Ben ignored it. His phone rang, and Ben ignored that, letting it go to the answering machine.

"Please excuse my assistants, Mr. Holden," spoke the lyrical voice of a young woman with a British accent. "Would you please be so kind as to let me in and grant me a moment of your time?"

Ben obliged the voice, which came packaged in a rock-hard body vacuum-sealed in black leather.

"You're not from around here, are you?"

"No, Mr. Holden, I am not."

"And I don't suppose you are here to sell me Girl Scout cookies."

"I am Tóuche," she said, shaking Ben's hand.

"Tooshay?"

"Tushie," she said, jiggling her hiney.

"Got it."

"My fiancé is a tremendous fan of the style of furniture you make, and I am here because I would like to buy your work."

"Which piece?"

"All of them."

"Please, come in."

Tóuche, the Chicken Hawk, and Foghorn Leghorn took seats in the reception area that Ben had arranged but never actually used.

"You don't know who I am, do you?" said Tóuche, as if she found it kinda cute.

"I get the feeling I should."

"Is that your daughter?" she asked, pointing to the screen saver slide show on Ben's computer, which flashed a photo of Kate on the beach at Lake Tahoe—texting.

"Yes, that's Kate, she's fourteen."

"You have a fourteen-year-old daughter, and you really do not know who Tóuche is?" said the Chicken Hawk.

Ben threw up his hands, guilty as charged. The Chicken Hawk shook his head, *tsk, tsk*. Foghorn Leghorn held up his iPhone and pressed a button.

Shake your tush, shake your tush, shake your tushie good, girl!

"That's you?"

Tóuche threw up her hands, guilty as charged.

"I used to like that song."

"And then what happened?"

"And then my daughter set it as the ringtone for her text messages."

"Touché," said Tóuche.

She explained that she had recently become engaged to a famous actor whose name Ben did not recognize, to the Chicken Hawk's added dismay. Tóuche's betrothed adored Arts and Crafts–style furniture, so much so, she said, "that he went to an auction a couple years back and paid over $900,000 for one freaking chair!" As a wedding gift, she wished to decorate the bedroom of their new Aspen home, and Ben had come highly recommended by her dear friend Brad Pitt, a Greene and Greene aficionado who had photographed the brothers' famed Blacker House in Pasadena for a coffee table book.

"I need an entire bedroom set—armoire, dresser, chest of drawers, his-and-hers nightstands, a king-size bed, the thingy that goes at the end of the bed that you put extra blankets in, plus whatever else you think I might need."

"Brad Pitt referred you to me?"

"Mmm, indeed. So how long will that take to make, and what will it cost?"

"It's mid-April now, and you're talking six or seven pieces, big pieces. I could write you up a quote but you're looking at October and upwards of fifty thousand dollars."

"I need it in mid-June."

"There's no way—"

"I'll pay you a hundred thousand."

"June it is."

"Half now and half on delivery?"

"Please, thank you."

She snapped her fingers, the Chicken Hawk whipped out a checkbook, and Tóuche wrote Ben a check on the spot for $50,000.

"Will you excuse me a moment?" Ben asked. He ducked into his shop, out of earshot, and dialed his cell phone. A robot woman said, "Please enjoy the music while your party is reached," then Billy Squire sang "Stroke Me," then Ben got Fred's voice mail greeting and warned his brother, "If this is one of your pranks, I swear to God I will tell Mom it was really you and not Vern who put the pot in the brownies last Thanksgiving."

Ben rejoined his guests. Tóuche stood to go. "Now remember, this is a wedding gift, so you can't breathe a word of this to anyone, OK?"

"OK, sure."

"Thank you so very kindly, Mr. Holden."

"Please, call me Ben."

"Thank you, Ben. You have made me a very happy bride-to-be, and to show my appreciation I will arrange tickets at will-call for you and your daughter for my concert tomorrow night." Tóuche wrapped Ben in a hug and kissed him on the lips. She smelled fantastic, like dark cherry and cinnamon.

10.

Jili prided herself on making home-cooked dinners. Not to make up for time lost or meals missed when she was working crazy long hours on Wall Street, nor to fulfill any vision or expectation of what so-called stay-at-home moms do in a place like Palace Valley, but rather because of what too many families no longer do: talk. Granted, a goodly portion of the conversations focused on getting Kate to stop texting under the table and Andrew and Tommy to keep their hands to themselves, but in between the harping a few noteworthy nuggets always emerged.

"At recess today Danny Kessler asked Melanie Hart to kiss his penis," offered Tommy.

"Do you think he knew that was wrong?" asked Jili.

"Probably."

"Then why do you think he did it?"

"I guess because he thought it would feel good?"

Ben and Jili stifled their laughter while exchanging a look that said, *The kid's got a point.*

"I had something interesting happen to me today," Ben shared. "I had a new client stop by the shop who was referred to me by—are you ready for this?—Brad Pitt."

"Shut up!" Jili said excitedly.

"Ha! You said shut up, so now we can say shut up!" chirped Tommy.

"You are such a dork," grumbled Andrew.

"Shut up, you big doofus."

"You shut up, you little dweeb."

Jili pounded her palm on the table, loud enough to get the kids' attention and hard enough to topple the salt and pepper shakers. "Barney!" she ordered.

"But you said shut up first!" argued Tommy.

"You are old enough to know the difference," she said, jerking his chair away from the table, "and old enough to pay the consequences."

Tommy and Andrew grudgingly stood, faced one another, held hands, and began warbling the theme song from *Barney*.

"I love you, you love me, we're a happy family . . ."

It was the perfect punishment: effective and entertaining.

"Please, Ben," Jili said, "continue."

"Evidently, Brad Pitt is a fan of Arts and Crafts furniture and somehow knows of my work because this woman named Tóuche stopped by my shop today, and she said I had come 'highly recommended' by her 'dear friend Brad Pitt,' who is into Greene and Greene . . ." Ben's voice trailed off when he noticed both of his sons, his daughter, and his wife all staring at him agape.

"Did you just say Tóuche stopped by your shop today?" Jili asked.

"I didn't even know who she was until we were sitting there talking and her bodyguard played that song that Kate has on her cell phone."

Tommy jumped up and started dancing and singing, *"Shake your tush, shake your tush, shake your tushie good, girl!"* Kate reached for her cell phone, but Ben snatched it away. "You can't tell anyone I am doing work for her."

"What! Why?"

"I gave her my word, but if it's any consolation she put two tickets at will-call for her concert tomorrow night."

Kate said something about the concert having sold out within ten minutes and tickets going for $500 on Craigslist, but she spoke in such a high-pitched squeal it was hard to understand her over the dog's baying.

"Mom, can I take a friend and you can drop us off and pick us up?"

"You are not going to that concert without one of us," said Jili, "and

I am busy." The specter of Ben's taking Kate to the Tóuche concert struck father and daughter at the same instant. Both pleaded their cases to Jili as they cleared the table, but she refused to budge. Andrew and Tommy both had baseball games and she had snack shack duty and that was that.

Kate slogged off to her room, while Ben and Jili did the dishes. "And I thought I had a big day because I washed *and dried* my hair," she joked.

"At one point I excused myself and called Fred to make certain it wasn't a prank."

"Are you sure it wasn't?"

"After they left, I called her bank to verify funds and the banker actually laughed as he assured me she could cover a $50,000 check."

"What do you think about using some of that money to take the kids to Hawaii this summer?"

"Not before the middle of June, as I am going to be holed up round the clock making all her furniture. But in the meantime, I was thinking that if you took Kate to the concert, I would buy you that—"

"No deal."

"I'll work the snack shack."

"No."

"Why not?"

"For one, you already bought me a gift certificate for a facial so that you didn't have to work the snack shack."

"Keep the facial, I'll work my shift, and you take Kate."

"No."

"I'll throw in a mani/pedi."

"I don't want a goddamn bribe," Jili shouted as she slammed the dishwasher shut. "I want you to spend time with your daughter. I want you *to want* to spend time with your daughter, but maybe that is asking too much."

"She doesn't want to go with me."

"Maybe that's because she knows you don't want to go with her."

"Kate and I have nothing in common."

"You might if you made an effort with her."

In his defense, Ben could only muster a sigh.

"I never really knew my father," said Jili. "Your sister didn't have any sort of relationship with your father. Is that what you want for you and Kate?"

The drama in Majors was mercifully absent in Single-A. Ben much preferred Tommy's games, where the teams did not keep score, coaches lobbed fat pitches to the hitters, and every kid got a chance to play every position. Parents got into the games, though the emotional investment was penny-ante compared to the high stakes in Majors. The energy in the stands became so intense at Andrew's games that Ben abandoned the bleachers for a patch of solitude and tranquillity along the left field line. He'd have preferred the sunnier right field line, but that is where Del had banished Andrew for his requisite three innings, and Ben's presence would only make his son all the more skittish. As a result of having to take Kate to the concert, Ben missed seeing Andrew make a diving catch in right field to seal the Angels' third straight victory, as well as Tommy's first career home run. Jili saw both highlights, having arranged to pay the older sister of one of Tommy's teammates twenty bucks to work her snack shack shift.

Ben and Kate, it turned out, did have at least one thing in common: a love of Mexican food. Sitting across from one another in a taqueria near the arena, Ben stared intently at Kate as she texted her envious friends back east. *What happened to her beauty mark?* he wondered. Kate was born with a little brown speck to the left of her nose beneath her eye, but now it was gone. It was not hidden under makeup, as Kate wore little if any after a brief goth phase in middle school. Perhaps all the tears over the move from New York and the adjustment to Palace Valley and missing her friends and teenagery in general had washed her beauty mark away. Or maybe she had just outgrown it. Ben could not ask, for to ask would be to admit that he had not been paying attention. When had he stopped? What else had he missed? How did they go from being total BFFs to total strangers?

"Thanks for letting me come tonight, honey."

"I said thank you." Defensive had become reflexive for Kate.

"No, I didn't mean it like that. What I meant is I know you'd rather be going to the concert with a friend or your mom, but I appreciate your being cool with my coming because we don't do stuff, together, like we used to."

Their carne asada tacos arrived just in time to break an awkward silence.

"I cannot believe you met Tóuche yesterday."

"What's her story?"

"She was the lead singer of a hip-hop band called Grand Skeleton Cru until one of the band members named Slee-Z got shot and killed by a rival rapper named HellaMen.OP, so Tóuche went out on her own and recorded 'Shake Your Tushie,' which became a huge hit and led to her getting the part in the movie that starred her fiancé, who was married at the time to a former TV star, who was in rehab with a rapper named Dice Bag, who is now clean and sober and opening for Tóuche."

"Where do they come up with these names? How is it that a person comes to call himself Dice Bag?"

"You're a guy, think about it."

"Dice bag. I don't get it."

"Really?"

"Dice bag. Dice bag. What am I missing?"

Kate unfolded a napkin on the table, placed the salt and pepper shakers side by side, took both ends of the napkin in one hand, lifted the pouch, and jiggled it.

"Dice Bag means testicl—"

"Yeah, Dad, it does."

"What would my name be? If I were a rapper, what would my name be?"

Kate thought for a long moment. "Wonder Bread."

Standing in the will-call line, Ben marveled at how provocatively so many girls were dressed. They probably left home looking perfectly respectable, got dropped off by their parents, then changed into their little vixenette costumes in the Porta-Potties, he surmised, but as more and more scantily clad Tóuche wannabes made their way from the parking lot toward the arena, it became clear that half the vixenettes were actually vixen mommies dressed sluttier than their daughters.

Ben slid his driver's license through the will-call slot to a woman who looked him up in the system, then excused herself saying she needed to get her supervisor.

"Don't they have our tickets?" asked a panicked Kate.

"I'm sure they do. I'm sure it's fine."

The will-call agent returned with a husky man sporting the electric orange blazer worn by arena management. "Mr. Holden, will you please meet me at the first door on your left."

"Dad, what did you do?"

"I didn't do anything, honey," he reassured Kate while wondering to himself what he had done. The first door on the left swung open and the man in the orange blazer said, "Please follow me." Ben took Kate's hand. He had half a mind to run, but they would not be too hard to find considering the man in orange still had his driver's license. Walking through the bowels of the arena, Ben felt a bout of explosive diarrhea brewing until he spotted Foghorn Leghorn and the Chicken Hawk.

"Enjoy the show," said the man in orange as he handed back Ben's ID.

"Come, come, we have to hurry," squawked the Chicken Hawk. Ben and Kate took off after him, up some stairs, down a hallway, through a door, and into the green room.

"Ben, there you are!" hollered Tóuche, greeting him like an old friend with a hug and a kiss. "And you must be Kate!" Tóuche hugged Kate, who was too awestruck to hug back. "I am so glad you made it. Anything you want to eat or drink, just help yourself."

"May I please take a picture?" Kate asked, holding her cell phone.

"Only if you are in it with me. Ben, take a picture of us girls so Kate can text it to all her friends!" Tóuche pressed her cheek against Kate's and got her to mug for the camera like best friends in a photo booth. As Ben snapped photos, the Chicken Hawk tapped his watch.

"OK, gotta go, but I hope you enjoy the show." Tóuche draped one of her signature silk scarves over Kate's shoulders.

"Omigosh, thank you!"

"Thank you for coming. That's a pretty special dad you've got, hooking you up with backstage passes and VIP tickets." Kate smiled at Ben for the first time since he could not remember when.

As Kate helped herself to the chocolate fountain, Ben turned and faced Tóuche. "I don't know how to thank you."

"I thought you were messing with me when you said you had a fourteen-year-old daughter and didn't know who I was. When I realized you were serious, well, that's just wrong."

"We used to be so close and then, I don't know what happened."

"I'll tell you what happened: she sprouted boobies and got her period and it freaked you out. But you've got to know that it's freaking her out too. Believe me. I remember going through all those changes, and all I wanted was for my daddy to hold me close and tell me everything was OK."

"She will never forget tonight," Ben said. "And neither will I."

"OK, Kate, I am going to be watching you and your dad to make sure that you . . ." Tóuche broke into song, *"Shake your tush, shake your tush, shake your tushie good, girl!"* Everybody in the room danced and sang along, and when Ben tried to slink away, Tóuche grabbed his hand and pulled him back. *"Shake your tush, shake your tush, shake your tushie good, girl!"* Kate had the moves from the video down cold. Ben improvised. Had this happened fifteen minutes earlier, Kate would have been mortified if her father had even thought about shaking his tushie in public, but somehow suddenly everything was OK.

Tóuche styled them with tickets to the VIP section up against the right side of the stage. On the other side of the barrier, fans stood crammed like rush hour riders on a Tokyo subway. Ben had been right there, front and center, many a time in high school—the Police, Van Halen, Springsteen, the Who, Styx, Journey—and yet as with bunking in hostels, eating ramen, and drinking Mickey's Big Mouths, he could no longer fathom subjecting himself to such indignities of youth. What a difference a day makes. Yesterday Ben had never heard of Tóuche and could not have imagined him and Kate having fun together again, much less at a hip-hop concert.

Kate finagled her way up against the stage while Ben hung back in the corner and danced like the white boy he was, arms waving, head bobbing, legs flailing. During the encore one of his flails accidentally kicked a woman in the butt. She wheeled around, pissed off, then broke into a bright smile. "Ben!"

"Cyn?"

"Of all the places I figured to bump into you, this is not one of them." Ben motioned as if to say he could not hear her over the loud music. She sidled up next to him and put her lips to his ear. "Fancy meeting you here."

As she pulled away he could have sworn she licked his earlobe. Cyn grabbed his hand and dragged Ben out of the corner to dance. Dressed in black leather knee-high boots, a miniskirt, and a sheer blouse with a plunging neckline, her outfit was just this side of slutty. Ben did not associate her with the vixen moms he'd seen outside, though he could not think of another occasion for which her getup would be appropriate. She kept her eyes firmly fixed on him, but looking at her gave him a woody, so he diverted his eyes to the crowd. He watched the ways other guys danced, arms at their sides, head groovin', feet shuffling, no flailing, no overbite. They played it cool and let the ladies do their thang, which appeared to Ben to largely consist of dry humping doggie-style.

Ben first learned of freak dancing from the high school newsletter that came home before last fall's homecoming dance. The principal made unequivocally clear that freaking would not be allowed, though chaperones had a hard time policing the dancing when a mass of students created an impenetrable force field around kids who were essentially, if not actually, having sex. Ben and Jili discussed with Kate the fact that it was submissive and degrading to women, though after she left the room, Ben told Jili he had to tip his cap to the guy who started the fad by talking his girl into turning around and buffing his belt buckle.

As Ben pondered how his life might have been different had there been freaking when he was in high school, Cyn backed up against him. Grinding like a pestle against his mortar, she polished every inch of his loins, then stood and vertically spooned him. With her bare shoulder tucked under his chin he had a bird's-eye view of her braless, sweat-glazed breasts. She smelled edible. He tried to back away, but she reached around him and grabbed his butt and pulled Ben and his raging stiffy up against her hind side. He pulled away, and she pulled him close. He pulled back, and she pulled him forward. Back and forward, back and forward, then he pulled back and she let him go and Ben pushed himself hard up against her. The encore ended with a pyrotechnic blast and the house lights came on and Kate came running up to Ben.

"Omigosh, Tóuche is so amazing!" Kate acted as though she had not witnessed anything, to Ben's great relief.

"Kate, right? I'm Cyn. My son Logan and your brother Andrew are on the same baseball team." Cyn spoke as if nothing had just happened, as if they had shared nothing more than a dance. "Your dad brought you to the Tóuche concert? How cool is that."

"We got to meet her backstage before the show."

"What? How?"

"My dad knows her."

"You know Tóuche." She phrased it not as a question but as a statement of impressed disbelief.

"She was very kind to take care of us tonight."

They exchanged polite good-byes and parted company. Ben and Kate did not talk on the walk back to the car. She posted mobile uploads to her Facebook profile while he wallowed in regret. He pushed. It was all semidefensible until he pushed.

Andrew's game-saving catch in the last game earned him a spot in the starting lineup for the next game, and he made the most of the opportunity, getting on base in each of his four at bats. One was a clean hit, the other three aided by Marlins errors. The Angels played equally sloppy defense, which infuriated Del because it not only kept the Marlins in the game but it kept Dante on the mound and ran up his pitch count. The league mandated pitch count limits by age; the maximum number of pitches equaled the player's age multiplied by seven, which meant that Dante, league age twelve, could throw no more than eighty-four pitches. He was at seventy-one heading into the top of the sixth inning when the Marlins came to bat trailing the Angels by one run. The game looked to be in hand after Dante logged two quick outs, but a flurry of foul balls, a walk, and two Angels errors loaded the bases.

"That's eighty-four, Del." It was Mike Yamagata's job to track the pitch count, even though Del was like Rain Man when it came to the game's minutiae. "Dante has reached his limit."

Del shushed Mike and snatched the pitch counter from his hand. Checking to see that the Marlins' third base coach had not overheard Mike, Del signaled Dante to throw a curve ball. His thinking, while twisted, was clear: the Marlins were just one hit, walk, error, wild pitch, or passed ball from tying the game. Were that to happen, the impact on Dante's fragile psyche might well open the floodgates. The Marlins still had their pitcher available, and the Angels had the bottom of their batting order due up. Del had no one to go to. T-Roy had started the game, and Logan was not available after pitching the last game. So he left Dante in, and he called for a curve ball.

Dante's older brother, Dylan, sat in the stands and watched. He pictured himself back on that field, toeing the rubber on that mound, and pitching the Angels to the brink of the championship in Majors. Dylan had taken a no-hitter into the sixth inning, only to see the curve ball Del called for come up six feet short of home plate. Something went *pop*. That was four years and three elbow surgeries ago.

Del never learned. Not from Dylan, and not from Coach, who had refused to allow his players to throw curve balls. Ever. Coach had also crusaded against kids playing baseball—or any sport—year round. The day of the three-sport star had given way to the age of the single-sport specialist, and just as troubling as the sharp rise in repetitive stress injuries was an unmistakable loss of passion for the game. Kids used to be excited to come out for baseball in the spring after playing football or soccer in the fall and basketball in the winter. But with the proliferation of summer All-Star tournaments and fall ball and winter travel teams, Coach had lamented that kids today never had a chance to miss the sport. They showed up for tryouts looking like factory workers punching the clock. Sighs replaced smiles. The game became more of a chore than a joy to play. Given the choice, kids might have preferred to mix things up, but they were not given a choice by Svengali coaches who viewed the desire to play other sports as a lack of commitment. Compounding the problem were high school coaches who ran the off-season pay-to-play programs as for-profit feeders for their varsity teams, as well as college scouts who increasingly focused their attention and recruiting efforts on All-Star tournaments and travel teams.

The stakes were raised because this was Dante's last season in Majors and Del's last chance to win a championship on the big field after Dylan failed to deliver. The wear and tear to Dante's arm was a risk Del was willing to take—along with the automatic one-game suspension he knew he would receive for allowing a player to surpass the pitch count limit. The fact that the next game was against Q'urmdoq and the last-place Astros surely factored into Del's decision to leave Dante in and call for a curve ball, but the strategy backfired when Dante hung a pitch that the batter smashed deep to right field. Ben could not watch. He heard the cheers when he opened his eyes, and for a second consecutive game Ben missed seeing Andrew make a game-saving catch.

After the game Del called the Majors commissioner and the league president and turned himself in for the pitch count transgression. His feigned ignorance fooled absolutely no one, and Del accepted his mandatory one-game suspension. Prior to that next game, against the Astros, Rubén approached Ben as he stood, blissfully removed, on his patch of solitude and tranquillity.

"Would you like to coach?" Rubén asked.

Ben laughed out loud. Had he been consuming a beverage, it would likely have shot out his nose.

Rubén didn't get the joke. "With Del suspended we need a third coach in the dugout."

"You're kidding, right?"

"No. I heard your dad was a baseball coach and I thought—"

Ben raised his hand, stopping Rubén right there. "My apple fell far from that tree."

David Moran eagerly filled in, and despite his driving Rubén, Mike, and the kids all crazy with his nonstop motormouth, the Angels easily beat the Astros. Two more games passed without Ben bumping into Cyn at the ballpark. He felt unsettled about seeing her after the incident at the concert, although Ben wondered whether it could be considered an incident if he were the only one who considered it so. He wondered if Cyn might be avoiding him, but then he overheard one of the other moms say that she had taken on overtime at work. When they finally did see one another for the first time since the concert, Ben was sporting a gnarly golf-ball-sized knot between his eyebrows.

The other dads immediately figured he'd done something stupid and Jili had let him have it, but the culprit was a bumblebee that flew into Ben's helmet as he was riding his bike to the ballpark. Ben's attempt to simultaneously stop, dismount, and remove his helmet resulted in his slamming his head into a mailbox and driving the bee's stinger deep into his forehead. Ben arrived late and woozy to find Cyn and Jili chitchatting in the stands about ceviche. Jili said that Cyn said she'd seen him and Kate at the concert, but Ben sensed that Cyn had not said anything incriminating, because if she had, Jili would've cracked Ben in the nuts and dropped him right then and there.

Ben wanted to retreat to his patch of solitude and tranquillity along the left field line, but he worried about leaving Cyn and Jili to talk; plus Fred showed up. He greeted Jili with a hug, Ben with a noogie, and Cyn with a chivalrous kiss on the back of her hand. "Hello there, I am Fred, Ben's smarter and better-looking younger brother." Modesty was not one of Fred's strong suits. Nor was subtlety. "Which one of the kids on the team is your brother?"

"Logan, my son, is pitching."

"And which is your husband?"

Cyn presented her vacant left ring finger.

"Boyfriend?"

"You are assuming I prefer boys."

"Kinky. Me likee."

"What about Krystal with a *K*?" asked Jili.

"Yes, well, that situationship ran its course."

Ailsa led off the bottom of the fifth inning with the Angels leading 2–1 over the Royals. Just as she stepped into the batter's box, Del called time. He called Ailsa back to the dugout and spoke to her until the ump yelled, "Let's go, batter!" As she walked slowly to the plate—a curious violation of Del's no-walking rule—Del reached down and untied one of Andrew's shoes. Andrew bent down to retie it, but Del barked, "Leave it."

The first pitch to Ailsa was a called strike. Working quickly, the catcher fired the ball back to the pitcher.

"Step out!" shouted Del. Ailsa stepped out as Del ran through an extended series of signs.

"What time did the game start?" Fred asked.

"Right at 5:30," said Jili.

"What a jackass," Fred grumbled. He checked his watch and yelled at the umpire, "He's stalling, Blue."

"What's going on?" asked Ben.

"And what is bloody blue?" asked Euan.

"Blue is a nickname for the ump, and Del is stalling," answered Fred. "It's a pansy-ass move. See, there is a two-hour time limit, so they can't start a new inning after 7:30. It's 7:24, so Del is trying to slow the game down because if the third out is made after 7:30 the game is over and Del wins. It's the equivalent of milking the clock in football or basketball."

The second pitch to Ailsa was called strike two.

"Step out!" shouted Del again, and again Ailsa stepped out. Del ran through his signs, then Ailsa walked behind the umpire and stepped into the opposite batter's box.

"Why the hell does he have her batting left-handed?" questioned Euan.

"Del is just messing with the pitcher, trying to get him to throw a ball, run up the count. I guarantee you he told her not to swing." The next pitch was a ball, but the pitcher came right back and struck out Ailsa looking.

Del looked dead serious when he told Andrew, "Do not swing, and do not tie your shoe unless *I* tell you to." As Andrew approached the plate, the ump said, "Tie your shoe, batter." Andrew looked back at Del, standing stone-faced in the dugout. "Hurry up, batter. Tie your shoe." Andrew again looked back at Del, who called time and ambled out of the dugout and toward home plate.

"What seems to be the problem?"

"I instructed the batter to tie his shoe, and for some reason instead of listening to me he keeps looking back at you."

"What's your problem, Holden? Tie your shoe and let's play some baseball."

"This is not my first game behind the plate, Del. Delay of game is grounds for forfeiture, so I suggest you tell your team to pick up the pace."

Stepping out between pitches and never taking the bat off his shoulder, as instructed, Andrew watched three perfect strikes and went down looking. The ump checked his watch as Blaine Solomon stepped into the batter's box at 7:28. As the pitcher came set, Blaine stepped back out of the box. The rattled pitcher's throw sailed high and outside.

"Strike one!"

Del shouted something unpleasant at the ump, but he got drowned out by Blaine's furious mother. The woman was a human air raid siren.

"Damn," Fred commented to Ben, "imagine the size of the pillow you'd need to stuff in her face to keep her quiet during sex." Tact was not one of Fred's strong suits either.

Del signaled for Blaine to switch sides and bat lefty. The pitcher threw a fastball for strike two. The ump checked his watch: 7:29.

As Del ran through an absurdly long series of signs, the ump said, "Stand in, batter."

Blaine stood in.

"I'm not finished giving my player signs. Step out."

Blaine stepped out.

"Stand in, son."

Blaine stepped back into the batter's box.

"Time out!" shouted Del.

"Time is not granted," said the ump. "Play ball."

"Blaine, step out!"

"I suggest you stand in, son."

"Step out—or else."

There was a dark undertone to Del's threat that rippled through the bleachers. Blaine stepped out. With the pitcher still holding the ball, the umpire declared, "Strike three! The batter is out. The inning is over. We are playing the sixth."

Del blew a gasket. He knocked Dante to the ground as he raced out of the dugout and ripped into the ump. Like a parent refusing to engage a child throwing a tantrum, the ump remained perfectly calm, sipping from his bottle of water, which infuriated Del all the more. Once Del started to go hoarse, the ump recited the rule that states if a batter will not take his or her place in the batter's box during their appointed at bat, the umpire shall call a strike on the batter without the pitcher having to deliver the ball. Raising his voice above Del's, the ump explained that the umpire in chief can disqualify and eject a manager for objecting to the umpire's decisions and/or the ump can forfeit the game in favor of the opposing team if a manager intentionally delays the game.

"I am officially protesting this game," declared Del.

"You can't."

"Oh yeah? Watch me!"

"A game cannot be played under protest over a decision involving an umpire's judgment."

The Royals scored two runs in the top of the sixth inning, then set the side down in order to hand the Angels their first loss of the season. In his postgame ass-chewing, Del blamed the ump, the Royals manager and coaches, the Angels ineffective hitters and lackadaisical defense; everyone shared the blame for the loss—except Del.

Gathered around the snack shack, the Royals families were all in giddy spirits, while to look at most of the Angels parents one would think that nuclear bombs were descending on Palace Valley and they were all about to be vaporized. And yet while the adults struggled to know how they could move on from this, the kids from the Angels and the Royals all jostled and joked together in the snack shack line. The parents were mere bystanders and they were crestfallen, while the kids who actually did battle, the winners and the losers, were already over it.

The following week, Jili took Ben out to dinner for his birthday. Even though it was his birthday, they went to her favorite sushi place because she had a favorite place and he did not. Whenever it was up to Ben, he inevitably picked McShane's. Jili loved Fritz and loved McShane's, but it was loud and difficult to carry on a conversation. As they sat tucked at a quiet corner table devouring Sushi Sam's samurai platter, the topic turned to fantasies. Ben reiterated his long-held belief that all guys have the same fantasy: as a kid, it is to make it with the hot mom; as an adult, it is to have a threesome—with another girl. No dudes allowed. Jili crinkled her brow as though she would not rule it out entirely, which he assumed she did to tease him, but it was still hot. Jili contended that women did not share a universal fantasy, but hers was to steal away and have sex at a party. She copped to being super horny at Andrew's baseball team mixer and even found a guest room where she wanted to do it, but Del put the kibosh on that when he gathered everyone for his inspirational team speech.

As ever, the discussion inevitably worked its way back to the kids. Inspired by the Tóuche concert, Kate had decided to audition for the high school's spring musical, which they hoped would expand her circle of friends and give her something she could call her own. Andrew seemed to be having fun playing baseball, a conclusion they collectively inferred considering Andrew never said anything one way or the other. Tommy was tearing up Single-A and loving every minute of it, although after his last game his coach took Jili and Ben aside to have a word.

"Tommy's a very talented young player, but Single-A is a developmental league and I've had to ask him on more than one occasion to tone down his competitiveness a notch."

"I'll give you that this is a developmental league," said Jili, respectfully. "But these kids see the older kids on the bigger fields, as well as the pros on TV, and they grasp the game's inherent competition, so while you may choose not to emphasize it, you can't pretend it does not exist."

"Of course, and I am not suggesting that we don't try to score runs or make outs, but we are working to foster an environment of learning over winning, and what we, as coaches, are asking of you is to help reinforce this message with Tommy."

"I value your desire to teach, and I, that is, we, appreciate the time and effort you are giving the kids, but I trust you will agree that you can only go as fast as your slowest child, and if Tommy is, as yourself said, very talented, then he—"

"Your son ripped into one of the little girls on our team today, telling her to 'go big or go home,' for not bowling over the other team's catcher at home plate."

"That was not nice," Jill granted. "But it was not wrong; the runner is entitled to the base path, and if the catcher blocks the plate, he does so at his own peril."

"I wonder where Tommy gets it," Ben said, tongue planted firmly in cheek as he and Jili both eyed the last piece of sashimi. "Do you want it?" he asked.

"You can have it." He pinched it between his chopsticks and lifted it toward his mouth. "Unless you want to roshambo for it?"

"You can have it."

"No, no, it's your birthday."

"Are you sure?"

"Yes, yes, of course. I'm not going to just take it. But if I were to win it . . ."

"Like I said, I wonder where Tommy gets it."

He threw paper. She threw rock.

"You are so predictable, always leading with the heavy artillery. You are a bully. A predictable bully."

"Fine. Two out of three," she declared.

"You can't win."

"Why can't I win?"

"Because I've already won."

"How do you figure?"

"Because you are going paper and I am going scissors."

He could tell by her expression that not only was he right but she was cheesed.

"Your problem is you play emotionally instead of rationally. See, I shamed you for throwing rock, knowing that you would not go rock again, even though you wanted me to think that rock was still in play, but it wasn't, and you and I both know it, and so you were down to paper or scissors. And because you were not going rock again, you assumed, fallaciously, that I would not go paper again, which, to your mind, left me with rock or scissors. Now, because the loser of the first throw typically abandons what did not work the first go-round, the winner of the first throw is tempted, no, baited into picking up the loser's castoff and attempting to vanquish the opponent with his or her own failed weapon. You lose with rock, you ditch rock, I pick up rock with the intent of not only defeating you but also humiliating you. It's an ego play, a trap. The typical American can't resist it; however enlightenment in roshambo can only be achieved by sublimating one's id. I don't expect you to understand this given your pitiful showing here tonight, but—"

Jili reached across the table and popped the last piece of sashimi in her mouth. "I win."

After dinner Ben and Jili strolled arm in arm along Main Street. He asked what she wanted to do, and she said it was his choice, it was his birthday. He suggested a movie, but the 7:20 show had already started and she hated walking in late after having missed the beginning. She suggested ice cream, but it was cold and he was full. He suggested

McShane's, but she wanted to be with him and not have to socialize. She suggested they go dancing.

"Homeboy don't dance."

"That's not what I hear."

"What are you talking about?"

"At the Tóuche concert."

Ben shit his pants. Just a little, but enough to make him visibly uncomfortable. She knew. Cyn told her. She told her, and Jili had been toying with him, letting him think he'd gotten away with it, waiting all week for just the right moment—on his birthday and in the middle of Main Street—to eviscerate him.

"Oh, I heard all about you, you dancing fool."

"Jili, you've got to believe me. I didn't expect it, I didn't initiate it, I resisted, but she grabbed me, and she pulled me." Ben looked to Jili with pleading eyes. "I know that is no excuse, but I swear it will never happen again."

"That's too bad because I would've loved to get in on that action."

She was diabolical.

"Did you really think I wouldn't find out about you shaking your tush with Tóuche? Kate said your moves need some work but you did not embarrass yourself." Jili broke into song, *"Shake your tush, shake your tush, shake your tushie good, girl!"*

She had the moves down cold.

II.

Following an otherwise ordinary Yankees game on an otherwise ordinary Wednesday in April, Homer King followed his normal routine of showering, putting on a suit and tie, and then addressing the media in the press room. But on this day, before the beat writers could ask a question, Homer announced he would be holding a press conference the following day at noon at a midtown Manhattan hotel. And with that he ducked out and was gone. Seeking answers, the media swarmed the team's PR personnel, who sought answers from Homer's manager, coaches, teammates, trainer, and agent, but no one had a clue.

Speculation ran rampant on the evening news, the morning news, sports talk radio, and the Internet. Every television network and major cable channel went live at noon on Thursday when Homer stepped up to a podium in the Grand Ballroom. The hotel had initially made arrangements in a spacious banquet room, but the media throng swelled to such massive proportions that the hotel moved the setup to the ballroom; when fire marshals quit letting people in, the hotel staff scrambled to set up monitors and speakers in two adjoining meeting rooms to accommodate the overflow crowd.

The absence of agents, publicists, attorneys, team officials, and the ubiquitous backdrop with a million little sponsor logos was conspicuous. Homer looked very much alone. He took a single sheet of yellow legal pad with handwritten notes from the breast pocket of his conservative blue suit, cleared his throat, and looked directly into the cameras.

"I am gay."

The silence was deafening. Then, like a supersonic jet breaking the sound barrier, the consequent boom rattled the chandeliers. Homer stood silently at the podium until the frenzy quelled.

"I was taught to live by two words: 'Live true.' But somewhere along the way, in my quest to achieve success and to please others—the fans, my teammates, my manager and coaches, the team owners, and the organizations with which I am associated—I lost sight of those two words.

"Live true. Those two words affected me so profoundly that I had them tattooed as a mirror image across my heart so that I see them every time I look at myself in the mirror. The recent death of Coach Harvey Holden, the man who taught me those two words, forced me to take a long, close look in the mirror, and lately I have had a harder and harder time facing myself. And so today, and from this day forward, I choose to live true.

"I have never spoken with the media about my private life, nor will I going forward. I understand that some people will be upset that I did not tell them in private before sharing this news publicly, but I wanted you, all of you, to hear it straight from me.

"I have not changed. I will continue to play the game with one hundred percent effort one hundred percent of the time. I will continue to play with honor and integrity. I will continue to represent my team and this city proudly and give back to our community tirelessly. I take seriously my responsibility as a public figure, and I will continue to strive to be a positive role model. I have not changed. Maybe your perception of me will change, but there is nothing I can do about that."

Homer set aside his notes and spoke from his heart. "Coach used to say that God made windshields big and rearview mirrors small for a reason, so we focus on what is ahead instead of what is behind us. I choose to look ahead. I choose to live true. Thank you."

Homer did not field questions, though if he had, the ignorance and audacity would not have dignified a response.

"Are you being blackmailed with a gay porn sex tape?"

"Who else is a gay in baseball?"

"Is Natália a lesbian?"

"Did your high school coach molest you?"

Tabloid headline writers had a field day.

"Homer Switches Teams."

"He's Out!"

"King's a Queen."

"HOMERsexual."

That night, in the clubhouse before their game, Homer addressed his teammates. "I have not changed" was all he said. A thick cloud of uneasy uncertainty hung over the room. Finally the team's All-Star catcher stood, crossed the room, and got in Homer's face.

"What do I tell my kids? Huh? Last night I was tucking them into bed, and they told me they want to see a Broadway musical. What the hell do I know about a Broadway musical? Nuthin'. So I'm asking you: what do I tell my kids? What do you recommend?"

The ice broken, he called out the rest of the team. "You can relax because if gay Jackie Robinson here was to have a crush on anybody in this room, it would be me because I am so much more handsome than all y'all. Truth be told, considering some of the slump-busting mongrels you have let play rodeo on your baloney ponies, you should be so lucky. But you've got to look at the bright side: with Homer out of the picture, all those fine, foxy ladies that are always trying to get with him are now gonna have to settle for the rest of you mutts, which means more Vitamin P for all of you!"

The home crowd greeted Homer with a mixed bag of cheers and jeers the first time he stepped to the plate as the first openly gay superstar athlete in the history of major American sports. The first offering he saw came in fast and tight, a message pitch. Homer had a message of his own, as he turned on the ball and blasted it over the fence and deep into the night.

• • •

PVYBL rules state that if a Majors team cannot field a full team of nine players it may fill its roster using pool players. The pool consists of Majors players who sign up to fill in when another team is short. The team that is short does not get to handpick players from the pool, but rather players are assigned by a board member who serves as the pool coordinator. This year that was Darrell Peart, brother-in-law of Roger Pollock, manager of the Orioles, who only had six players available for the game against the Angels. Del thought it curiously convenient that not only were the six missing Orioles all three-and-one kids, but the pool players assigned to the Orioles were all returning All-Stars.

The Angels were down three players and a coach, as Mike Yamagata stayed home with Drake, who still felt woozy from getting his bell rung. Aaron left after barfing during warm-ups; he'd been up all night barfing, but his mother reasoned that since he had nothing left in his stomach, he ought to load up on ibuprofen and try to play. And Dante was a no-show. Del suspected Melissa made him late on purpose just to piss off Del, but when Del had dropped Dante at the curb in front of his mother's house the night before, he had driven off with his son's baseball bag in the bed of his truck. While Del stewed in the dugout wondering where the hell Dante was, Dante was searching frantically for his bag, which at that moment hung on a hook in the dugout. Upon arriving at the ballpark, Del found it lying in the back of his truck and cursed his son for forgetting his gear.

The Angels had already taken the field when Dante showed up crying just moments before the first pitch. Del greeted his son with a warm "Quit your goddamn bawling and grab your glove." Del called time and pulled Joshua Simon in from third base.

"So much for 'If you're late, you sit,'" Joshua's father remarked.

In the dugout, Dante pleaded, "No, Dad, please, I don't want to go in yet."

Del looked at his son, tears streaming down his cheeks. "Get out on the field, or get out of the dugout." Parents in both bleachers ached at the sight of Dante standing at third base, sobbing. Del trained his focus on Orioles manager Roger Pollock, standing in the coach's box.

"Go figure that on the day you play me, the entire bottom half of your lineup can't make the game," said Del.

"Go figure." Pollock had a well-deserved reputation for being every bit as competitive as Del. Their rivalry dated back to the days when they both played PVYBL, and it was not a stretch to say that Pollock would consider his season a success if he lost every other game but beat Del.

"And what are the odds that the three players your brother-in-law draws from the pool are the three best players in the pool?" The words were barely out of Del's mouth when one of Pollock's pool players jacked a homerun over the center field fence. "What did you do, buy your six shittiest players and their families tickets to today's Giants game?"

"No," scoffed Pollock. "Six Flags."

The Angels had last ups. Trailing by a run, Aaron grounded out to the shortstop, then the Orioles pitcher issued consecutive walks to Andrew and Duncan. Pollock called time and gathered his squad on the mound. From his patch of solitude and tranquillity Ben texted Jili in the bleachers.

> do u think he is telling the kids to just relax and have fun,
> it is only a game?

The Orioles pitcher walked Joshua to load the bases. Pollock called time and switched pitchers. Jili texted Ben back.

> pretty sure he just called that boy an asshole.

The new pitcher started Dante off with three straight balls. Infuriated, Pollock called time yet again and stomped out to the mound to talk to his pitcher. Dante looked to Del, who ran through a series of signs, then turned and called for Joshua, Duncan, and Andrew to hustle over. As Del huddled with his base runners, Dante did a double take, then looked to Rubén in the first base coach's box with an expression that asked, *Did I just see what I think I saw?* Rubén nodded, as if to say, *Yes, I saw it too.*

The ump signaled to the pitcher. Dante glanced back at Del, who nodded confidently. The pitch was high, but Dante swung, hitting a dribbler back to the pitcher, who threw home to the catcher, who threw to first base, double play, game over. The Orioles poured on the field as if they had just won the World Series. Rubén gave Dante a pat on the back as the boy choked back tears. As Dante picked up his bat at home plate, his father was waiting for him wearing a look of stunned betrayal.

"Are you happy?" Del shouted at his son. "Are those happy tears that you just lost your team the game? What the hell were you thinking, swinging on a 3-0 count?"

"You gave me the swing sign."

"I gave you the take sign."

"You gave me the swing sign!"

"I gave you the take sign!"

Rubén tried to intervene. "Del, you gave him the swing sign, I saw it too."

Del shoved Rubén. "Stay the hell out of this."

"You gave me the swing sign," said Dante, brushing past his father.

"I'll give you a swift kick in the ass if you dare turn your back on me." He wasn't kidding. Del went to give Dante a swift kick in the ass, only when Dante turned back around as ordered, he caught his father's kick square in the crotch. In all the hullabaloo of showing up late, the boy had never put on his cup. As the crowd let out a collective gasp, the boy crumpled to the ground in a heap.

The board of directors meeting drew a standing-room-only crowd. Every board member, every manager and coach from every Majors team, and every Angels parent attended, as well as a throng of rubberneckers keen to see Del finally get his due. Jili arrived early and snagged seats up front, but as the room quickly filled, she had to give up the one she saved for Ben, who had not arrived by the time the meeting was called to order. PVYBL president Tom Doyle explained that the board would hear from Del and any others who wished to speak before issuing its decision.

Del stood and removed his hat. He seemed contrite as he apologized for his actions. He had made amends with his son and personally apologized to his players and their parents. He regretted not only that it happened but also the poor example it set. As to the action the board would take, Del asked that they take into consideration the fact that in seven years of coaching in the league he had never once been reprimanded, ejected, disqualified, or suspended—save for the recent pitch count violation, which Del spun by stating it was an honest mistake that other coaches, including board members, had also made that season, and by noting that, upon discovering the error, he had stepped up and brought the infraction to the attention of the Majors commissioner. Del offered to participate in a positive coaching course if the board deemed that beneficial. He promised nothing like this would happen again, stated he would put that in writing, and said he would accept whatever decision the board made.

When Tom opened the floor to comments, Jili was the first to stand. "An adult coach in this league kicked a child. That it was in full view of dozens of witnesses, that the child was his own son, and where he kicked the child are irrelevant. The bottom line is that an adult coach kicked a child. What more is there to say?"

Evidently nothing. Tom called for others who wished to speak, but Jili had pretty much said it all. That being the case, Tom outlined the options: suspend Del for some number of games or relieve Del of his duties as manager of the Angels. Were Del to be relieved, the board would either approve a suitable and willing replacement manager for the team, or if a suitable and willing replacement did not step forward, then the Angels would be disbanded, their games forfeited, and the players would be reassigned to other Majors teams.

Del kept a straight face, but he liked his odds. He knew that none of his parents represented a suitable replacement, and as he ran down the roster, he could not fathom that a single one would be willing. Just as Del expected, the other Majors managers vehemently opposed absorbing Angels players, stating that it would further dilute playing time, disrupt team chemistry, turn coaches from teachers into babysitters, unfairly benefit teams that inherited the Angels' good players, and hinder teams that got "the dregs," as Roger Pollock so tactfully put it. Suspension seemed a safe bet, and with nine games down and nine left in the season, Del figured no more than four, which was inconvenient but not debilitating because the way the schedule shaped up, the next four games were against the four worst teams in the league.

Tom asked Angels assistant coaches Mike Yamagata and Rubén Lopez if they would take over the team, but Rubén could not because he owned his own butcher shop, and Mike declined, citing his own busy work schedule and the fact that Drake was still recovering from his recent concussion. Tom asked if any of the Angels parents would be willing to step up. He asked assistant coaches from other Majors teams. He asked board members who were not already coaching in other leagues but got no takers. He asked the Triple-A commissioner if he knew of any coaches in that league who might be interested in moving up. He got no takers.

"In that case," said one board member, "I make a motion to relieve Del Mann of his coaching duties, disband the Majors Angels, record their games as forfeits, and reassign in random fashion their players to other Majors teams." The motion was seconded. Tom instructed board members to write yea or nay on slips of paper and drop them in the passed hat. Tom counted the votes.

"The motion fails."

An undercurrent of incredulity welled up in the room, largely in the voices of disgruntled mothers. Tom struggled to maintain order, then Jili ended the cacophony with a piercing whistle. It was a source of great frustration to Ben that he had never learned how to whistle like that. That and juggling. And doing a flip off a diving board. He'd never done a flip off a diving board.

"I make a motion," said the Majors commissioner, "that Del Mann be suspended for three games." Tom did not get a chance to call for discussion before the questions and comments started flying. Amid the chaos, Del's façade cracked. His expression of earnest penitence could not contain his true colors, and like a sun that cannot be stopped from rising, Del broke into a smug little grin.

Tom's ears pricked up, and in the absence of a gavel he removed his size thirteen cowboy boot and banged the heel on the table. "What? I heard that! Who said that?"

"I'll do it," said a voice from the back of the room. "I'll manage the Angels."

"Yes!" cheered Tom. "Thank you!" The league president didn't do a very good job of masking his bias. "I need a motion."

"Bullshit!" yelled Del, toppling his chair as he jumped to his feet, his face contorted like one of those squeaky dolls whose eyes bulge out of its head when you squeeze its belly. "You can't do that!" Del could not make out who'd dared rise up against him, but he was talking to Tom. "You've got a motion on the floor for a three-game suspension. You have to take the vote."

"Not if it is not seconded," said Tom. "And not if the motion is withdrawn."

All eyes turned to the Majors commissioner. "I withd—"

"I second the motion," interrupted Del.

"You can't second the motion," said Tom.

"Hell yes, I can. I am a member in good standing of this board of directors, and I second the motion for the three-game suspension. Now you've got to take the vote."

Tom huddled with the vice president, an attorney with a working knowledge of Robert's Rules of Order. With a heavy sigh, Tom announced, "Board members please write yea or nay on slips of paper and drop them in the passed hat." The board had a policy that members could neither vote on nor be present during a vote on any matter that affected them directly, though there was nothing that said members could not second a motion that affected them directly. Del left the room. The hat was passed. Tom counted the votes. Del returned.

"The motion fails," Tom declared. "Unanimously," he added.

Del glowered at each and every board member, saying with his scowl that he would not soon forget this, but it was a classic case of reaping what you sow. At some time or other, in big ways or small, publicly or privately, unwittingly or callously, Del had slighted, insulted, marginalized, provoked, or wronged each and every member of the board. When what went around came around, Del's goose was cooked.

"I make a motion," said the Majors commissioner, "that Del Mann be relieved of his managerial duties effective immediately, that he not be allowed to attend the Angels' next four games, and that the board approve, as manager of the Angels, Ben Holden."

The motion was seconded and passed—unanimously. In the back of the room Ben's cell phone rang to the sound of the *Pokémon* theme. It was a text from Jili.

WTF?!?

The Homer King story continued to monopolize newsstands, airwaves, and cyberspace, much to the chagrin of people with lives but to the delight of supermarket rag readers and the degenerate celebrities whom Homer bumped from their covers. Oceans of ink were wasted overanalyzing a narrative that required but three words—*I am gay*—to sum up the beginning, middle, and end of the story. Whoring entertainment news shows and their bubblehead presenters shamefully kept trying to breathe new life into a dead horse by granting the superstar's purported lovers fifteen seconds of fame even though none could produce a single letter, photo, phone recording, text message, or other shred of proof that they had ever been any closer to Homer King than in the same stadium at the same time.

Crowds on the road gave Homer a harder time than usual, littering center field with gay porn magazines and holding up homemade signs that read things like "YANKEE POODLE PANSY." Homer never gave them the satisfaction of the reaction they wanted, though it bothered him to see kids getting in on the taunts. Grade schoolers didn't come up with lines like "Bronx Queer" on their own; it was learned behavior likely bestowed by a giggling parent painting HOMO KING IS A HALL OF FLAMER in big letters on bright neon tagboard.

The initial support that the home fans showed Homer quickly cooled—not because he came out, but because he was one-for-thirty-five since he came out. Save for the home run he belted in his first at bat after announcing he was gay, Homer had gone hitless in nine straight games, far and away the longest slump of his career.

ESPN incessantly ran a clip of Homer King striking out to end a game, then snapping his bat like a twig over his knee. Tommy saw it then tried it after he struck out, but his aluminum bat did not give and he wound up sitting out the next two games with a deep thigh bruise.

12.

Braces and zits. Ben could not get over how many kids had braces and zits as he faced his twelve adopted preteens for the first time. Had he thought before he spoke up at the board meeting, Ben would have talked himself out of it, but he could not abide Del's smug little grin. He could not sit back and watch Del get away with it. Not again. Not after *Promgate*. Ben remained resolute in his belief that Del dropped the dookie on the principal's desk, costing Ben his shot with Liza Heston.

Stepping into the dugout felt to Ben like the dream where you walk into a classroom only to find the teacher handing out an exam.

I am completely unprepared for this.

Ben did not say it, though he sensed the kids all knew it. Asking them which team bats first was a bit of a giveaway. "You are halfway through the season, so by now you know what to do. I just want you to go out there and have fun playing baseball."

"Coach?" Ailsa had a question, but Ben cut her off.

"Ben. Call me Ben, please."

"You have me and Logan both playing second base and no one in center field."

Mike Yamagata sorted out the lineup. He was back, thankfully, and Drake had been cleared to play. "Logan at second, Ailsa in center, Hunter, Conor, and Andrew in the dugout," said Mike, taking the top copy of the triplicate lineup sheet and handing the others to Ben. "Give one to their manager and one to the ump."

Ben wished he'd had time to prepare, maybe hold a practice or at least get with his coaches, but the day after stepping up to manage the Angels, Ben got thrown to the Tigers. He trotted across the field to the other dugout and exchanged lineups with Bobby Jeffries.

"Thanks, Coach."

"Ben. Call me Ben, please." He jogged to home plate and handed the ump the lineup.

"Thank you, Coach."

"Ben. Please, just Ben."

Dante, fully recovered from getting chonged by his father, led off the game. He set his back foot in the batter's box and looked to Ben in the third base coach's box.

"Start us off, Dante!" shouted Ben.

"Let's go, Pujols!" Blaine yelled from the dugout.

"Listen up," said Ben, addressing the entire team. "Rule number one: no insults."

"What are you talking about?" said Blaine. "That was a compliment."

"Poo hole is a compliment?" asked Ben.

"*Pujols,*" Mike Yamagata interjected. "Albert Pujols is an All-Star with the St. Louis Cardinals. He's Dante's favorite player."

Ben laughed it off as if he were only kidding, only the kids were not buying.

Dante asked for time. The ump granted time out and Dante ran back to Ben. "Aren't you going to run through the signs?"

"The signs, right, of course." Again Ben addressed the dugout. "All right, listen up: I've got no signs. If it looks like a strike, swing. If it looks like a ball, don't."

As Dante returned to the batter's box, Ben overheard Logan say to Andrew, "I didn't think there was any way that anyone could know less about baseball than you."

"Time, Ref," shouted Ben.

Amid chuckles from the bleachers, Blaine's dad, Rick Solomon, reminded Ben, "There are no refs in baseball!"

Ben turned and faced the dugout. "In case you missed it: Rule number one is no insults. Ever."

As Ben returned to the coach's box he overheard Logan mumble, "The truth hurts."

"Time, Ump," shouted Ben.

Fans in both bleachers groaned and Bobby Jeffries threw up his hands. Were this football, Ben would have been flagged for delay of game. Ben apologized with a wave as he ran to talk to the ump. After a brief tête-à-tête, the ump turned to the scorer in the skybox, who announced over the PA, "Changes to the Angels lineup: Conor Moran starting at second base in place of Logan Winters."

Ben got an earful as he passed the Angels bleachers. Taking his place in the coach's box, he turned and faced his stunned dugout. "No insults. Ever."

When the game finally got under way, the Angels jumped out to a three-run lead. When it was the Tigers' turn to bat, T-Roy took the mound and Bobby Jeffries marked his territory in the coach's box with a dark dart of tobacco spit.

"Are you allowed to chew tobacco out here?" Ben asked. He was genuinely curious, but Jeffries didn't appear to take it that way as he pulled the nasty brown plug from his cheek and dropped it on Ben's shoe.

T-Roy's first pitch was a strike.

"Hop on that!" Jeffries chided his batter. "Or did you forget that this is the pitcher who gave up that game-losing grand slam in last year's championship game—to a girl."

T-Roy heard this. So too did insulted mothers in both bleachers and Ailsa in center field, but they were collateral damage to Jeffries's intended target. T-Roy visibly deflated. Jeffries would never have made a crack like that with Del standing behind him—the payback would've been a monster bitch—but with Ben in the dugout it was a whole new ball game. The Tigers scored four runs in rapid succession and chased T-Roy from the mound before he recorded a single out.

Ailsa exacted a measure of revenge by clobbering a three-run dinger in the fourth inning to retake the lead, 6–4, but in the bottom of the fifth a series of ill-advised throws by the Angels that more closely resembled pinball than baseball allowed the Tigers to clear the bases off a bunt. With the Angels down by a run heading into their last ups,

Andrew drew a walk to start things off. He advanced to second on a passed ball, then made it to third base when Joshua grounded out to the first baseman. Conor hit a ball to the outfield, and on the crack of the bat Ben yelled, "Go! Go! Go!" to Andrew, who went. The Tigers' left fielder made the catch and threw the ball to the third baseman to get the easy out on Andrew, who had done as Ben said but failed to tag up. Double play. Game over.

"I take full responsibility for that," Ben told the team afterward. "I am trying to make the best of this situation. The main thing is that you have fun."

"Winning is fun," said Logan. "Losing sucks."

"Who is on the hook?" T-Roy asked. Ben did not know what he meant. "After every game Del chooses the person who played the worst and that person is on the hook to clean the dugout."

It sounded like the kind of gag snarky students would play on a substitute teacher. Only no one laughed. "You're joking, right?" said Ben. Evidently not. "OK, rule number two: everybody cleans the dugout. Go."

As the kids slogged off, Ben passed Rick Solomon, reeking of weed. "If you'd kept your big mouth shut last night, we'd have won that game today." Ben turned to have a word, but Rick slunk off like a cockroach from the light.

"Tough loss, Coach," Butch Baxter said.

"Ben. Call me Ben."

"I don't expect you will make that mistake again, Ben."

"I spaced. I knew he needed to tag up, I just got caught up in the excitement of the moment and sent him too soon."

"I didn't mean the tag-up. I meant not starting Logan."

"Yeah, well the kid's got quite an attitude—and a mouth."

"He's also got quite a bat—and an arm. We do not expect you to know Xs and Os like Del, but we do expect you to play to win."

"When you say 'we' . . . ?"

"We families that have supported this league for many years and with thousands of dollars all for the promise that our kids would play competitive baseball when they got to Majors."

"That's why you did it, all those years and thousands of dollars, so that you could watch your kid compete?"

"No duh!" laughed Butch.

"Not teamwork or respect or integrity or discipline?"

"I'm talking about the meat," said Butch. "You're talking about potatoes." Ben was not sure quite what to say, but he was quite sure that it wouldn't be anything nice, so he didn't say anything at all. "So we'll see Logan back in the starting lineup on Saturday?"

"Yes," said Ben. "We'll see."

After the game, Ben nursed a cold McShane's while taking a long soak in the hot tub. Jili appeared on the patio.

"You want another beer?"

"Sure. Nah. I dunno."

It was more of a rhetorical question. She knew he'd take it if she brought it, and she figured he could use it so she'd already opened it.

"Is Andrew OK?"

"He was fine five minutes after the game ended. All the kids were."

"I let him down."

"You stepped up. I hate to agree with Del about anything, but none of those parents signed up to manage a team in the first place and none offered to take it on besides you, so they have no right to complain."

That did not stop them. Before going to bed Ben checked his e-mail to see if the Chicken Hawk had confirmed receipt of the paperwork for Tóuche's order. Ben did not see that e-mail; however, he did get a half dozen others from parents on the team with titles including:

"FW: Rule 7.08(d) Tagging Up."

"Today's debacle."

"What were you thinking?!?"

"Learning from our mistakes."

Ben opened the last e-mail first because the titled sounded sympathetic, only to find that his gaffe had already been posted on YouTube and viewed 106 times.

While Patty ticked another box on her bucket list and *laissez les bon temps rouler* at the New Orleans JazzFest, Ben went crawling around in her attic. He wriggled past the holiday decorations, climbed over the luggage, tossed the wooden tennis rackets onto the canvas camping tent, then paused beside the stuffed chicken. To atone for the collateral damage caused by flying shrapnel on the night he fed Fred's baseball spikes through the wood chipper, Coach had taken Ben's pet rooster to the taxidermist. Behind Clucksie sat a footlocker filled with Fred's stuff, including his collection of 45-rpm records. Ben sent himself a text message to see if songs like "The Rubberband Man," "Dream Weaver," and "The Lion Sleeps Tonight" were available on iTunes. Under the 45s Ben recognized an old issue of *Playboy*. Opening to the centerfold, he gazed wistfully at Miss March 1981, resplendent in nothing but a fur coat and knee-high leather boots. He thought about rubbing one off real quick, just to finish what he'd started before Coach burst in on him all those years ago, but he had to get to practice. Behind the footlocker Ben spotted an everyday object he had seen every day of his childhood but had never had any interest in until today.

Inside Coach's briefcase Ben discovered a spiral notebook. The precision penmanship belonged unmistakably to Coach, but the content may as well have been hieroglyphics to Ben. He knew what his father did; however, he had no idea what it entailed until he held in his hands these reams of numbers, like some sort of binary Da Vinci code. Might these contain answers to the mystery of who his father was and why he was the way he was, and might they in turn also shed light on deep-seated questions Ben had been increasingly asking of himself since his father's death, questions about why he was the way he was when his father was alive, and why he had tried so earnestly *not* to emulate a man who had been so admired and revered by so many?

Three-quarters of the way through the stack, Ben found just what he'd been hoping for: Coach's practice plan. He didn't exactly comprehend it, but it was more than he had to work with five minutes ago. Ben set Clucksie to stand sentry atop Coach's briefcase, then he climbed back down from the attic. As he did, an old, yellowed, key-sized manila envelope fell from the notebook and landed on the hardwood floor with a jangle. Ben bent down, squeezed the sides, and peered inside.

"I'll be damned."

MINUTES	ACTIVITY
:05	Jog
:15	Stretch
:15	Throw
	DEFENSE
:20	Skills
	- infield grounders / 3B bunts, 6-4-3, C throws
	- outfield grounders / throws to cutoff
	- pitcher / picks to 2B, picks to 1B
:20	Team
	- 1st & 3rd with signals from C, OF backup
	- sac. bunts—runner on 2nd (3B positioning)
:10	Team situations
	- set field / R on 2nd & 3rd—all hits to OF
	OFFENSE
:25	Drill stations
	- bunting
	- 1-2-3
	- short toss
	- tee
	- tire
:20	Team hitting
	2 groups live—pitcher drills & throw pen (25 pitches)
	(coaches throw short & off hitters in position)
:15	Conditioning
	- leadoffs from each base
	- home to 1st
	- home to 2nd
	- home to 3rd
	- home to home
	- pitchers sprint the foul poles
:05	Comments/Questions

After a quick stop at the post office, Ben scooped up Andrew and headed to baseball practice. He arrived brimming with enthusiasm that was lost on his disconsolate squad. Their long faces and listless body language suggested that they had seen the future and were throwing in the towel. Ben persevered. He tried to sell his plan with the chipper tone of a cruise director laying out the day's activities on the Lido Deck. "We are going to start off with a quick jog, then do some stretching and throwing. Then we are going to work on defensive skills and team defense. After that we'll set up different stations and work on offense and finish up with some conditioning. Any questions?"

"Yeah," groused Logan. "What's the point?"

Ben flipped through the spiral notebook. Coach's grand plan did not account for insolent brats.

"Coach?" said Aaron. Ben thought to correct him and ask all the kids once again to please call him Ben, but it was a losing battle, so he let it go. "Coach, I don't feel so good."

"Are you too sick to practice?"

"I think so."

"Then why did you come to practice?"

"Because my mom said I had to."

Ben sent the rest of the team on a jog, then called Aaron's mom, Laura. He still had trouble connecting the dots between her marrying her father-in-law and her ex marrying her identical twin, but she was always friendly and engaging and sweet as could be.

"Thank you for calling me," she said over the speakerphone. "May I please speak with Aaron?"

Ben handed Aaron his cell.

"Hi, Mom."

"For chrissakes, you big sissy, what the hell is wrong with you now?"

Ben, Mike, and Rubén shared a collective cringe as they realized that Laura did not realize that she was on speakerphone.

"I don't feel well, Mom. I have a headache and I feel dizzy."

"Honest to God, Aaron, you act like you are on your period. I gave you Tylenol before practice. Maybe I should have given you a tampon too. Don't be such a pussy. Go play baseball and try not to let the ball hit you in the vagina. Now put your coach back on the phone."

Aaron handed back the phone.

"Uh, hello?"

"Aaron really wants to tough it out," she said. "He'll be fine."

He wasn't fine. Ben held Aaron out of practice while the rest of the team bungled Coach's master plan like a bunch of drunken zombies in straitjackets and snowshoes. Ben felt his father's omnipotent glare from beyond the grave. He pictured Coach walking up beside him, observing the chaos, removing his cap, scratching his head, furrowing his brow, sighing, and saying, "Benny, you are about as useless as tits on a boar."

Ben yearned for about eight McShane's and a long soak in the hot tub, but he and Andrew had to stay and wait with kids whose parents were late picking them up. Now that Ben was the one made to wait, Del's threat to charge sixty dollars an hour for babysitting didn't seem so ludicrous. Andrew buried his nose in his book. Joshua was the next to last to get picked up, and Ben was bummed to see him go because he had passed the time regaling Ben with little known factoids about crustaceans (lobsters molt—who knew?), segueing into an erudite comparison of cirrocumulus, altostratus, and cumulonimbus clouds. He had just launched into a critical analysis of the interwoven plot-lines of the next Harry Potter film when his mother arrived, leaving Ben alone with Logan.

The boy said nothing. Ben could not tell if he was actually awake behind the closed drape of long hair covering his face.

"So Logan, do you play other sports besides baseball?"

"Badminton."

"Really?"

"No."

Time passed in dog years. Cyn finally arrived twenty minutes late apologizing profusely and smelling like tuberoses and ginger. "See you Saturday?" she said.

"Yes, Saturday, bright and early."

"I can't wait." She petted the hand Ben placed on the car door before her as he nonchalantly leaned in the window to get a bigger, better whiff of her.

Logan chucked his bag in the back seat and flopped in the car without so much as a glance or a good-bye. Imagining what Coach would do if a kid disrespected him like that, Ben pictured Coach politely excusing himself from the mother, marching around the front of the car, opening the passenger door, fishing through the drapes of Logan's long hair for his ear, yanking him out of the car, and hauling him to his feet.

Son, you will look me in the eyes, you will shake my hand, and you will say thank you, Coach.

The boy would inevitably mumble it the first time, so Coach would place him back in the car, shut the door, wait a half a second, open the door, and reach for the kid's ear, only this time the kid would voluntarily spring to his feet. "Thank you, Coach," he'd say, loud and proud, as he looked Coach in the eyes and shook his hand. Behind the wheel, the parent would close her eyes and say a little prayer of thanks for this angel of good manners. Of course, this was back in the days when an adult authority figure could lay a hand on a churlish kid without worrying about winding up on an Internet site with a virtual red flag on his cyber front lawn marking him a child abuser.

"Good-bye, Logan," Ben said. The boy jerked his head, the way kids nod to one another in the hall at school. "You are welcome," Ben said, feeling bold.

Nothing.

"Say thank you," prodded Cyn.

"For what? For getting Del booted and ruining our chances at making the playoffs?"

"Logan!"

Logan peeked out from behind his mop of hair wearing a wiseass smile. "Thank you sooooooo much!"

"I'm sorry." Cyn sighed, resigned. "I appreciate you." She squeezed Ben's hands three times, then drove off.

• • •

Ben soaked in the hot tub and flipped through Coach's spiral note-book seeking divine inspiration. Nothing jumped out at him until he turned to the last page: "The Three Single Most Important Keys to a Coach's Success."

Ben wondered how there could be three single most important anythings. Wouldn't it be the three most important or the single most important?

"May I?" asked Jili, not waiting for an answer to join him. "How was practice?"

"An unmitigated disaster."

"Did you keep them late?"

"No, Joshua and Logan's moms were late picking them up."

"Cyn still owes me her ceviche recipe."

Ben set aside Coach's notebook and cracked open another Mc-Shane's.

"What's her story?"

"I don't know. I don't know anything about her."

"I think she thinks you're cute," teased Jili. "She hardly talks to any of the other dads."

She was right. Cyn did pay more attention to Ben than to other dads. Ben had spent an inordinate amount of time at work procrasti-nating on Tóuche's order while trying to decipher Cyn's mixed signals. The first time they met, she sucked seductively on a Twix bar; did she mean to entice him as he sat before her naked beneath a thin gown, or did she just really love milk chocolate caramel cookie bars? Was the dance they shared at the Tóuche concert really nothing more than a dance? If Jili had gone to the concert that night and some guy had grinded up against her and pulled her ass up against his crotch when she tried to pull away, what would she have done? Would she have let him keep pulling? And when he stopped, would she have pushed? When Cyn picked up Logan from practice, she petted his hand and said, "See you Saturday" and "I can't wait," and then squeezed his hand three times. Was Cyn simply looking forward to the weekend? Was she just excited about the baseball game? Had she given his hand multiple meaningless squeezes? Or could she not wait to see Ben, so much so that she had knowingly squeezed his hand precisely three times to signify "I love you"?

Cyn induced a static that interfered with Ben's ability to read Jili. He knew his wife so well he could normally tell from the intonation in a simple sigh if Jili had been run ragged and did not want to cook dinner, or if she needed to get out and exercise, or if she needed a stiff martini. But lately it was as if he were unable to get a clear signal, and as they tangoed around the hot tub, Ben could not tell if she was poking fun or prodding for answers.

"You don't think Cyn is cute?" Ben did not answer. "I do," said Jili. "Maybe a bit much on the lip injections, but she's got an adorable figure. I've seen her in the locker room at the club and the boobs are real." He did not take the bait. "What do you think about her for that threesome fantasy of yours?" she joked. He could taste the warm blood in his mouth as his incisors bored deep into his tongue. Jili crinkled her brow as though she would not rule it out entirely, then she tossed her bikini on the lawn and swam over to Ben.

She'd come to them in the hot tub. Ben and Jili would be engaged in hot and heavy foreplay when she'd appear on the lawn wearing what looked to be a skimpy bikini. It was, in fact, body paint that would melt away the moment she joined them. Jili would slide to one side and share, and they would take turns kissing him. Then Jili would sit back and watch as she straddled him and let the whirlpool move her, her nipples glancing against his. He'd lean forward to kiss her, but she would turn and swim away before backing up against him and finishing their dance.

Jili found Ben underwater and backed up against him. Ben closed his eyes, and as he made love to Jili he pictured himself having sex with Cyn.

Homer King had always received mountains of mail, though the volcano erupted after his coming out. Letters from boys who wrote saying they wanted to grow up to be like Homer had dwindled, and most of those that still came arrived on pink stationery. Hate mail flooded in from right-wingers, while love letters poured in from prisons. Women who had previously written seeking to marry, carry a baby with, or simply service Homer united in the challenge of switching him back. The return address from Palace Valley on a Priority Mail envelope caught Homer's eye. Sitting in front of his locker he pondered a letter that read, simply, "Now you know . . . Best, Ben."

Inside the mailer was an old, yellowed, key-sized manila envelope. Homer pinched the sides and into his palm jangled three buffalo nickels—a legit coin that sported both heads and tails, a trick one that was double-headed, and another that was double-tailed. Homer's mind flashed to the day his freshman year in high school when Coach pulled him off the baseball field in the middle of practice and sat him down in the dugout. He pictured Coach taking a buffalo nickel from his pocket and asking, "Are you going to entrust your future to chance or to hard work?"

Homer shrugged.

"Do you aim to be lucky or good?"

"Good, I guess," Homer answered.

Coach showed Homer the heads, then the tails, and told him to call it. Coach flipped it. Homer picked heads. What Homer did not see then but realized now was the deft sleight of hand with which Coach switched the legit buffalo nickel for the double-tailed coin.

It was tails.

"Two out of three, call it."

"Heads."

"It's tails again."

Homer pictured himself calling heads ten times in a row, and each time it came up tails. He called tails the next ten times in a row, and each time it came up heads. Homer remembered Coach taking a seat on the bench.

"Son, you better get busy getting good," Coach said, looking young Homer square in the eye. "Because you sure as hell ain't very lucky."

"I'll be damned," Homer muttered, jangling the coins in his hand.

He was good all right, but a little luck never hurt. That night, playing with three buffalo nickels in his back pocket, Homer King recorded the first hit in what would go on to be a sixty-four-game hitting streak that broke Joe DiMaggio's record.

Teenage bodies are made to bear children and sleep in. Young girls express shock and dismay when they get pregnant after having sex just once, while thirtysomething women who chose to have a career before having kids should know better than to be shocked or dismayed when they have difficulty conceiving. Young boys need sleep more than oxygen, and Jili had long contended that were she running the world, high schools would start at noon. Both rising with the sun and the Electoral College made sense when people lived out on the prairie, but kids should be excused for being totally useless when they are made to play baseball at eight o'clock on a Saturday morning.

Andrew and T-Roy both dropped routine pop-ups in the top of the first inning. Both complained that the sun was in their eyes, which seemed odd to Ben considering the rising sun was at the players' backs. In the top of the second inning Ben spotted a mother in the Blue Jays' bleachers flashing a mirror into the Angels players' eyes. He called time and told the ump, who confiscated the mother's travel mug when he discovered that she had glued a compact mirror to the bottom so it looked like she was sipping coffee when she was blinding opposing players.

When the Angels batted, Rubén coached first base, Ben coached third, and Mike manned the dugout. The chatter among the team at once amazed and appalled. Rarely did they talk about the game at hand, and when they did, it was not to strategize so much as to slam.

"How many strikeouts is that for you? I lost count at like a million."

The insult remained a staple of the middle school vernacular, though the barbs cut deeper and seemed more insidious.

"If you sucked any more, you would be inside out."

And when they weren't bashing, they were boasting.

"Oh yeah, well, we have PlayStation 3 and Xbox 360 and Wii and a sixty-inch flat-screen."

Lulls in conversation were inevitably filled with talk of girls.

"Dude, your sister is so hot."

"Dude, talk about hot, check out Logan's mom."

"Dude, what is up with your mom's tattoo?"

Ben's ears pricked up when Blaine asked that, but Logan had his iPod blaring. Ben could not begin to imagine what Coach would do if one of his players ever dared be so bold.

Tommy had talked his way into announcing the players over the PA. For his star turn at the mic he adopted the overcooked patois of the voice of *SportsCenter*. "Now batting for the Angels, Dante Mann!"

"You D-Mann!" cheered his mother. Ben had heard tell that Del and Melissa had timed his conception so that his delivery came just after the league age cutoff date so as to get their baby an extra year in Majors, but Ben wondered if they also named him Dante for the nickname D-Mann.

"Next up," warbled Tommy, "Andrew Holden!"

Ben cupped his hands around his mouth and shouted, "Let's go, A-Hol!"

The field fell silent. It took Ben a moment to grasp his gaffe, but on the bright side he learned his lesson before the batting order reached Troy Watson.

Down by two runs in the top of the sixth inning, the Angels recorded two quick outs before Joshua drew a walk. Standing in the third base coach's box, Ben watched in disbelief as across the field Joshua's mother gingerly opened then shut the dugout gate, tiptoed next to Rubén in the first base coach's box, and dug a camera from her purse.

"Joshua, sweetheart, look here and smile."

The boy shut his eyes and wished he could curl up like a snail inside his batting helmet.

"My time!" called the umpire. Stepping out from behind home plate, he glared utterly befuddled at Ben. Ben stared back, equally befuddled.

"Got it!" chirped Joshua's mother before slinking off the field and returning to the bleachers.

When play resumed, Conor Moran drilled a ball into the right field corner. Joshua scored to make it a one-run game, and Conor motored all the way to third base with a stand-up triple. In the bleachers his father, David, whooped and hollered like he'd just won three lotteries. Conor jumped up and down excitedly, but in between up and down he got tagged out in midair by the Blue Jays' third baseman to end the game.

No one felt worse than Conor, save for maybe his father. While the rest of the kids headed for the snack shack, Ben overheard David Moran upbraiding his son. "In all my years of playing and watching baseball, I have never seen such a dimwit move. Maybe that's because no one in the history of the game has ever made such a bonehead play. If you were just plain stupid that would be one thing, but if you are not even going to try, then quit wasting my time."

David tramped off. As Conor walked alone, wiping tears from his dust-caked cheeks, Ben ran after his father.

"David, can I speak with you a moment?"

"I'm sorry Conor cost you the game, Coach."

Ben waved him off. "It was a great hit and a tough break."

"We needed a win. If Conor hadn't got tagged out, and if Logan would have come up to bat—"

"And if my aunt had balls, she'd be my uncle," Ben interjected, "as my father used to say. But what I wanted to say is that if you are still interested in making that jewelry box for your wife for her birthday, why don't you come by my shop this week."

"Her birthday is next weekend. She would love that."

"I am in the EaGle district behind the fly fishing shop. Swing by anytime."

13.

Emergency rooms, morgues, and divorce courts are filled with people who wish they could have five seconds to do over. Ben did not hear Jili enter the bedroom as he contemplated whether to wear his standard issue Banana Republic V-neck T-shirt to Thursday's game or the red polo the kids gave him for Christmas that he had never once worn. It struck her as odd: Ben, who cared nothing about clothes, holding up two shirts, and those two shirts no less, trying to decide.

"I think she'd like the red one," Jili said.

He glanced.

She did not need to see the cringe on his face. The mere fact that he turned his head even one degree toward the red shirt gave him away. He faked an innocent grin, turned and faced her.

"Don't," she said coolly.

He was toast.

The boner at the ultrasound and the dream where Cyn came to him in the exam room were involuntary and subconscious. But thinking about her and rubbing one off while Jili lay sleeping next to him, dry humping her at the concert, picturing her while he made love to Jili in the hot tub—those were all on Ben. If he had five seconds to do over, he would wake up and roll over and tell Jili about the dream, and he would cop to his purple-helmeted soldier standing at attention while she iced his cupcakes during the ultrasound, and Jili would see that it rattled him, and they would kiss even despite their dragon breath. It would all have been out in the open, and Ben would never have pulled the thread that now appeared to be his unraveling.

As he braced for the Gaze of Truth, he saw in Jili's eyes an emotion he had never seen in her before. Fear. She was scared. She had him dead to rights, but she was scared to ask the question to which she did not know whether she really wanted the answer.

A foul ball grazed Ben's ear as he stood in the coach's box, his eyes not on the game but on the bleachers, hoping Jili would show. Mike asked Ben if he was OK.

"I'm fine," Ben lied. Looking past Mike he noticed Duncan Baxter standing in the corner of the dugout with his legs crossed and his face contorted. "Do you have to go to the bathroom, Duncan?" The boy nodded and winced. "So what's stopping you?"

"Del doesn't let us go to the bathroom during the game. He says we need to think of that before, but we were running late and I didn't have time to go."

"Rule number three," Ben decreed to the team. "If you have to go to the bathroom, go to the bathroom."

Duncan made it in the nick of time. Trotting back to the dugout, he spotted and snagged a lime-flavored Gatorade sitting next to his step-mother's unoccupied seat cushion. Upon her return to the bleachers with two cups of ice, Trixi Baxter whispered to her husband, Butch, "What did you do with our margaritas?"

"I didn't touch them."

"I mixed them in a Gatorade bottle that was sitting right—"

Three gulps in, Duncan felt the fire in his throat and erupted like a volcano, spitting a mouthful of margarita all over Ben. The commotion drew all eyes to the Angels dugout, where above the din a child was heard shouting, "That's not Gatorade, that's *tequila*!"

A few parents were rightly aghast, though more were duly impressed by Trixi's ingenuity.

In between innings Rubén took Ben aside. "We've got to do something about Logan. He's not pitching to help the team; he is just being cute and trying to throw big curve balls. He doesn't care if he gets guys out or not."

Ben eyed Logan sitting at the end of the bench with his arms crossed, his hat pulled down over his eyes, and his iPod cranked. Ben walked across the dugout and stood over Logan for a long moment.

WWCD?

More and more, Ben found himself asking himself, *What would Coach do?* The picture long etched in his mind of his father as a brute between the chalk lines gradually blurred as Ben got a taste of the crap Coach had to stomach for half a century. Ben had always pictured Coach and Del as cut from the same cloth; from the outside both were brusque and loud and demanding. Ben never had cause to consider the comparison more closely, but once he'd walked awhile in their shoes, the contrast became startlingly clear. Coach and Del may have shared similar execution, but motivation set them apart. Del was blinded by being a winner, whereas Coach focused on developing winners, on the field and off.

Ben did not recall seeing any entries in Coach's spiral notebook titled "Dealing with Ill-Mannered Little Shits," but he was pretty sure his father would approve of his jerking on Logan's iPod cord and yanking the earbuds from his head.

"Dude, what's your problem?"

"My problem is that I let you act like you're God's gift instead of me acting like the coach. No more. Here's how it is: no iPod in the dugout and no curve balls on the mound. You throw fastballs, you throw them over the plate, and you trust your defense."

"What defense?" scoffed Logan, loud enough for the other kids to hear.

"No one player is bigger than the team," said Ben. "Not you, not anyone."

As the Angels took the field, Logan grabbed his glove, brushed past Ben, and mumbled, "Whatever."

Few words rankled Ben more than *whatever*. It had been a perfectly innocuous pronoun for eons before teens turned it into the verbal equivalent of giving you the finger. Logan did as he was told and threw a fastball—right at the umpire's head. He smirked at Ben and said, "What? It was a fastball over the plate." Logan proceeded to walk the batter on four straight heaters, each of which required the ump to duck to avoid a beaning. Logan started the next hitter off with a big sweeping curve ball.

"Not one more," Ben called from the dugout.

Logan reared back and threw an even bigger hook. Ben called time and marched out to the mound. "Give me the ball. You're done."

"I am not coming out."

"I beg your pardon?" Ben said in a measured tone.

"I am not coming out," Logan said in a mocking measured tone.

Ben called the ump to the mound. "Eject him." Logan and the ump looked equally surprised.

"If I eject him," said the ump, "he has to leave the premises immediately and he will be ineligible for the next game."

"No need," said Logan, dropping the ball at Ben's feet.

Ben blocked Logan's path off the mound and nodded at the ump, and the ump ejected Logan with pleasure. The fans could not figure out what was going on, but the Angels parents sounded none too pleased. Logan stormed into the dugout, threw his gear in his bag, then turned to his teammates and sneered, "Have fun trying to win without me, losers."

Ten of the kids replied, "Whatever." Blaine went old school and gave Logan the finger.

At Fred's suggestion, Ben downloaded a software program for baseball coaches. It was amazing. It did everything. Plug in the names and put in the results and the program calculated and correlated and triangulated and compared and contrasted and spit out recommended batting orders and substitution patterns and situational hitting and pitching. The statistical categories looked like an overturned Scrabble board with numbers and symbols thrown in to further confuse: G, PA, AB, R, H, 2B, 3B, HR, RBI, SB, CS, BB, SO, BA, OBP, SLG, OPS, OPS+, TB, GDP, HBP, SH, SF, IBB, Pos, Inn, Ch, PO, A, E, DP, Fld%, Rtot, Rtot/yr, Rtz, Rtzrd, Rtzhm, Rdp, RF/9, RF/G, lgFld%, lRF9, lgRFG, W, L, W–L%,

ERA, G, GS, GF, CG, SHO, IP, H, R, ER, HR, BB, IBB, SO, HBP, BK, WP, BF, ERA+, WHIP, H/9, HR/9, BB/9, SO/9, SO/BB, Wgs, Lgs, ND, Wchp, Ltuf, Wtm, Ltm, tmW–L%, W1st, Lsv, CG, QS, QS%, GmScA, Best, Wrst, BQR, BQS, sDR, 1DR, RS/GS, RS/IP, IP/GS, Pit/GS, <20, 21–35, 36–50, 51–65, 66–85, GR, Wgr, Lgr, SVOpp, SV, BSv, SV%, SVSit, Hold, IR, IS, IS%, 1stIP, aLI, LevHi, LevMd, LevLo, Ahd, Tie, Bhd, Runr, Empt, IPmult, Out/GR, Pit/GR, PA, Ptn%, HR%, SO%, BB%, XBH%, X/H%, GB/FB, GO/AO, IP%, LD%, HR/FB, IF/FB, DPopp, DPs, DP%, Pit, Pit/PA, Str, Str%, L/Str, S/Str, F/Str, I/Str, AS/Str, I/Bll, AS/Pit, Con, 1st%, 30%, 30c, 30s, 02%, 02c, 02s, 02h, L/SO, 3pK, 4pW, PAu, Pitu, Stru, Inf, Bnt, GSo, vRH, vLH, Hm, Rd, <2,3B, Scr, ROE, PB, SBO, SB, CS, SB%, SB2, CS2, SB3, CS3, SBH, CSH, PO, PCS, BT.

Ben spent the entire day entering data from the scorebook, listening to the ominous silence of the machines that should have been cranking out Tóuche's bedroom set, and replaying in his head his conversation with Jili that morning.

"Did you kiss her?"

"No."

"Did you fu—"

"No."

"Do you want to?"

"No," Ben said sincerely.

The infatuation had festered only because it was clandestine; once exposed, the scenarios he'd allowed his mind to explore evaporated. She started to say something but a wave of emotion cut her short. She gathered herself, looked Ben in the eyes with tears in hers, and asked, "Do you still love me?" Her voice cracked, and his heart broke, for he had made her question the one thing he'd always told her she would forever know for certain.

Late that afternoon a knock came at the door. Ben was already neck deep in shit at home, and he prayed it was not the Chicken Hawk and Foghorn Leghorn come to check on Tóuche's unstarted order. It turned out to be David Moran come to make a jewelry box. He seemed exceptionally excited, like a kid on a school field trip to the creamery all eager to churn butter. He even dressed the part, or what he imagined it to be, in brand-new head-to-toe Carhartt he had purchased just for the occasion. Ben ducked in his office, closed the baseball program, piped in some Dexter Gordon, then led David into the shop.

He let David select some cherry wood, on which they marked the proper measurements. Ben fired up the band saw, they both donned goggles, and Ben demonstrated how to cut the individual pieces. David managed that without too much trouble, but Ben began to get impatient with David as he worked to put a miter onto each end.

"What the hell are you doing?" Ben said condescendingly.

"I'm trying to do what you said."

"How about you stop *trying* and start *doing*."

Ben's exasperation grew as David routed out a niche along the bottom of the insides of the end pieces. "I thought you were serious about doing this."

"I am," said David, taken aback.

"You could've fooled me."

David tried to concentrate, tried to perform, tried to please, but it was debilitating with Ben hovering over his shoulder and breathing down his neck. Ben had seen enough. He shut off the router and tossed aside his goggles.

"This is pointless." Ben sighed.

"I'm sorry," said David, affronted. "I am doing my best. I am not a professional woodworker."

Ben eyed him as if that were a gross understatement. "If you are not even going to try, then quit wasting my time."

David set down his goggles and left. Ben returned to the computer and the addictive baseball software program. As he struggled to comprehend on-base plus slugging average—a trendy sabermetric statistic representing the sum of a player's on-base percentage and slugging percentage, or the ability to both get on base and also hit for power—David returned.

"Please," he said, sheepishly, "please tell me that the way you just talked to me is not the way I treat my son."

"He's doing his best," said Ben.

"I want him to have a good year. This is his last year in Majors. Conor has always been one of the best players on his team, but he's a late bloomer and the other kids are passing him by. Even when he does hit puberty, he is not going to have the size or the speed to compete at the next level. Unfortunately he gets that from me, but I overcame that with pure desire and scrap. Conor lacks the fire. It doesn't burn in his heart like it did—like it does—for me."

"That is all fine and good, except your first two words were 'I want.' What does Conor want?"

"I am afraid to ask," David admitted, "because I know he'd say soccer. He loves it; that is his passion. But he knows that baseball is my passion, and I expect he has been afraid to speak up for fear of letting me down." David thought about that for a long moment, and it did not sit well. "Sitting here now, I realize that I have sucked the fun out of baseball for him and in the process sucked the fun out of it for me too."

"The season is not over yet."

"You're right, it's not. And to your question about what Conor wants, I think he just wants to go out there, try his best, have fun with his friends, enjoy some laughs, run around, and eat a bunch of crap from the snack shack."

"All the things we did as kids," said Ben.

"And there is nothing wrong with that."

"Nothing at all."

David stood and shook Ben's hand. "Thank you, Coach."

That night the doorbell rang during dinner. Tommy leapt to his feet, but Ben sat him back down and answered the door. He wondered if it might be David, prayed it was not the Chicken Hawk and Foghorn Leghorn, but was surprised, and none too pleasantly, to see Cyn.

"Who is it?" called Jili.

"Uh, it's . . . Logan?" Ben barely recognized him as his mother hauled him front and center. His long hair had been shorn to his scalp. In addition to the blunt military haircut, he wore a transformed expression, like Ebenezer Scrooge after a visit from the Ghost of Christmas Future.

"I am sorry for disrespecting you, Coach. I was wrong to act the way I've been acting, and you were right to do what you did." Unlike the parade of repentant-for-the-cameras professional athletes who recite prepared damage control statements, Logan's apology was sincere and far from crafted. The boy had clearly been scared straight and fed a heaping serving of humble pie. "I'd like to rejoin the team, and I give you my word I'll do as you ask and be a good teammate."

"I accept your apology," said Ben. "But as for rejoining the team, that is going to be up to your teammates."

Logan nodded. He seemed to grasp that as difficult as it was facing Ben, that was the easy part.

Jili joined them in the doorway.

"Please pardon our interrupting your dinner," said Cyn. "Let's go, Logan."

Logan extended his hand and looked Ben in the eyes. "I'm sorry, Coach."

Ben was surprised to see Logan standing in the dugout in street clothes before the next game. He was not, however, surprised by the chilly reception Logan received from the other kids or the teasing he got for his GI Joe buzz cut.

"I'm not staying," Logan said softly. "I just came to apologize for the way I acted and the things I said." To his credit, he did not bow his head and mumble but rather faced his teammates and coaches. "I was wrong, and if you'll have me back, I promise to be a team player. I'm really sorry. Good luck today."

Logan left before he had a chance to hear the bashing he took at the hands of his teammates. With the consensus running heavily against letting Logan back, Andrew piped up. "It wasn't very easy for him to come and apologize," he said.

"People deserve a second chance," echoed Dante.

"It's up to you," said Ben. "But I think Logan really is sorry."

The players voted to let Logan return. They could have used him that day as the Twins pummeled the Angels 16–3.

Practice resembled a gathering of disaster survivors. The kids were shell-shocked, and Ben was at a loss. He decided to start with running drills, considering how abominably the Angels had navigated the base paths in the Twins loss. He had the players line up at home plate. One at a time, each was to swing the bat at a phantom pitch, then run to first base and turn toward second, listening to the first base coach while picking up the sign from the coach at third. A windmill motion meant run to second base, while arms held high signaled the runner to go back to first. Rubén coached first base and Mike took third as Ben demonstrated. He borrowed a bat, stood in, swung at a phantom pitch, and dropped the bat but accidentally tripped over it and smacked his ankle. Shaking off the pain, Ben skipped up the first base line and drew raucous laughs from the team. It struck Ben that it was the first time he had seen them enjoy a good, hearty belly laugh since the day he took over the team.

"Let's skip this," Ben said.

"Can we bat now?" asked T-Roy.

"No, I mean, let's do this—skipping?"

"You want us to run the bases skipping?"

Logan snatched T-Roy's bat from his hands, stepped to the plate, swung at a phantom pitch, and skipped to first base as fast as he could. The other kids howled as Mike windmilled him around second, then around third and all the way home. Dante picked up the bat, stood in, swung, and powered around the bases skipping as he went. One after another, every last Angel and the coaches too all skipped the bases.

On the far diamond, Orioles manager Roger Pollock was busy putting his preteens through their tiresome paces when a strange sound wafted downwind, a curious noise as distracting as a fart in Sunday mass. It looked like the Angels and sounded like laughter. The Orioles players all stopped what they were doing and strained to hear what couldn't be, but in fact was, Little Leaguers having fun.

Player introductions took a decidedly different form at the next game. The announcer could be heard chuckling over the PA system before roaring, "At first base, the Wiz!" Duncan trotted out of the dugout, and Ailsa followed doing a wee jig. "Playing second base, Braveheart!"

The Angels' starting lineup took the field: Boom-Boom (Dante), Hurricane (Logan), Money (T-Roy), Hammer (Conor), Snake (Blaine), and Hitman (Andrew). "And pitching for the Angels, Gonzo!" Drake took the mound while Wheels (Aaron), Shark (Hunter), and Silk (Joshua) cheered from the dugout.

In the stands, Euan perused the field and asked any other parent who cared to answer, "Am I mistaken, or is every single kid playing a new position?"

Indeed they were. Ben had let the kids choose where they wanted to play, and it looked to be an experiment gone horribly wrong when the White Sox put up four runs in the top of the first inning. As the Angels prepared to take their first cuts, they found added incentive in the form of a big pink box.

"Here's the deal," Ben said, lifting the lid to reveal four dozen donut holes. "If you get a hit, you get a donut hole. If you put the ball in play, you get a donut hole. If you draw a walk, you get a donut hole, and even if you strike out, you get a donut hole—so long as you strike out swinging. No donut holes for you if you call a teammate by their real name, watch a called third strike, get picked off a base, or get caught picking your nose while on base." That drew a big laugh.

Boom-Boom led off. As he walked to the plate, he looked up in the stands at his father. Del was back. He did not appear amused, especially when Dante drew a walk and skipped to first base. The Angels played loose, battled back, and beat the White Sox. Maybe it was a relief after four straight losses. Maybe it was seeing the kids enjoy themselves. Maybe it was the way they forgave Logan and the way he acted like a model teammate. Maybe it was the way they'd won, coming from behind. Maybe it was the donut holes. Maybe it was all those things plus feelings he couldn't quite put a finger on, but Ben did not expect to feel so elated over watching his team win a game.

They had a chance to make it two in a row but came up short in the bottom of the sixth inning against the Mariners. Down one run with two outs and T-Roy at second base and Drake at third, Ben encouraged Dante to swing away. "Be a hitter. Let's end this here." The first pitch came right down the pike, a juicy strike. Dante started to swing, then hesitated and tried to square around to bunt and popped up a meek foul ball to the catcher to end the game. After the two teams shook hands, Ben pulled Dante aside. "You can't hit a home run if you're not up there swinging, right?" A dejected Dante nodded. After Dante shuffled off, Rubén pulled Ben aside.

"Del told him to bunt."

"What?"

"I saw him signal Dante from the stands. As he came up to bat, he looked up in the stands and Del gave him the bunt sign."

Ben chased after Dante, catching up to him as he and Del were leaving the ballpark.

"What's up, Boom-Boom, no snack shack, no chili cheese fries?"

"Call me a purist, Holden, but we don't reward failure," said Del.

"What are you talking about? Baseball is all about failure. Homer King makes an out two-thirds of the time he comes up to bat, and he is the highest-paid player in baseball."

"He's got a point," said Dante.

"He doesn't have a point," snapped Del.

"I just wanted to let you know, Boom-Boom, that you are going to be our starting pitcher on Saturday, so rest up and remember—no curve balls."

"What kind of crap is that?" asked Del.

"The snapping motion places unnecessary strain on developing arms."

"Not if the pitcher is taught proper mechanics."

"There is that school of thought, but then I did not come from that school," said Ben. Del caught his drift, as Coach had a strict no-curve-ball rule in high school. "I believe the risk is greater than the reward, so we preach throwing fastballs, mixing in the occasional changeup, and trusting our defense."

Del's expression screamed *Bullshit!* though he kept his mouth shut because the terms of his suspension stipulated that one more incident and he'd be banned from the ballpark for the remainder of the season.

As Del stalked off, Dante braved a smile. Ben should not have taken pleasure in it. But he did.

• • •

Later that evening, Ben attended a meeting of the Majors managers. The summit took place in the back room at McShane's for the purpose of nominating players for All-Stars. As Ben understood it, each manager was to put forward worthy players from his team for consideration. Who actually did the considering, Ben did not have the foggiest. All he knew is he felt woefully unprepared when other managers arrived with legal pads, index cards, and file folders. Roger Pollock arrived toting a three-inch three-ring binder. Ben brought a pen. And a dry one at that.

Ben took a seat to the right of Tom Doyle and to the left of the last empty chair in the room.

"Congrats on getting your first win, Coach," said Tom.

Keith Campbell sauntered in. Ben had always envied his saunter. In high school Keith would glide through the halls, feeling the vibe and swaying to its beat. Ben was tone-deaf when it came to the high school vibe. He tried to saunter but herked and jerked like a horse missing a shoe. Jili's high school beau eyed the open seat next to Ben, then scanned the room again just in case a chair had magically appeared in the two seconds he'd been standing there.

"Keith."

"Ben."

"What's up?"

"Nothing. You?"

"Nothing."

Ben felt fairly confident that this was the exact conversation he and Keith had had the last time they spoke, at Debbie Shoemaker's graduation party. They had seen each other out at the ballpark, but Ben had not engaged Keith so as to avoid a scenario he'd spun wherein he and Keith might actually hit it off and become friends and their families might start doing things together, maybe a barbecue and a swim, and Jili might glance furtively at Keith as he did flips off the diving board or sauntered hither and yon, causing Jili to question her choice in Ben and wonder why she ever broke it off with Keith. So, in a preemptive effort to save his marriage, Ben had opted not to engage Keith. Ben knew it was silly, and a couple of times he had thought about extending a proverbial olive branch, but now, given the events of the past week and the rift with Jili, there was no flipping way.

Roger Pollock spoke first. "I'd like to nominate my son, Channing Pollock." He opened the thick binder, which had color-coded paper and tab dividers. Ben figured Roger had organized dossiers on each of the players he planned to nominate. "Starting in Single-A, Channing has been an All-Star every year in the league. He is our team's number one starter and plays shortstop when he is not pitching. He throws right and bats both right and left. The numbers are pretty equal from both sides of the plate. No significant delta facing righties or lefties or playing day or night games. The only anomaly seems to be Tuesdays against right-handed pitchers who have had three or more calendar days' rest, but other than that he hits for average and power equally. He's got good plate discipline and excellent pitch recognition. He is generating significantly more power through the hips since we got him switched to a rotational hitter from a weight transfer hitter. He's been working hard on the tee and with soft toss, two hundred cuts every day. He's tightened his coil, shortened his stride, and optimized his launch position, and while I may be biased because he is my kid, the numbers don't lie: he is top three in batting average, hits, RBI, triples, and home runs and, by my calculation, leads the league in OPS."

"I don't have any stats like that on any of my players," Ben whispered to Tom.

"No one does."

"I can't wait to hear what he has to say about his next player," Ben cracked as Roger flipped a tab in the binder.

"As for pitching, Channing is now throwing from a three-quarter arm slot, which has improved the movement on his fastball, and his repertoire includes a dependable curve that he's not afraid to throw at any time in the count, a wicked circle change, and a split-finger we are looking to debut for All-Stars."

When it was Ben's turn he said, simply, "Our most deserving players are Logan Winters, Troy Watson, and Dante Mann. Each plays hard, plays smart, and plays to win and would be a solid addition to the team both on the field and in the dugout." Ben stood, collected his dry pen, and added, "That's everything you need to know. After all, we are talking about twelve-year-old children here. Thank you for your consideration, and if you will please excuse me, I need a beer."

The college kid manning the taps lit up when he saw Ben, as he provided a welcome excuse for the bartender to excuse himself from an older woman who appeared to be hassling him. Having not eaten after the game, Ben ordered Euan's deepest, darkest stout: dinner in a pint glass.

"Hey, I know you," the woman called to Ben.

In that moment Ben dearly wished Fritz had hung just one TV so that Ben could pretend to be engrossed in a game, any game. Alas, he was a sitting duck as the woman stool-hopped toward him. He hadn't gotten a good look at her when he walked up to the bar, and he wasn't about to look now, but his first impression said former teacher.

"Ben?"

He quaffed a big sip of courage and faced the woman. She wasn't older, just weathered. Apparently she either did not get or heed the memo about prolonged exposure to the sun.

"Don't tell me you don't remember me?"

Her face looked a bit like a child's drawing, disproportioned and colored outside the lines, as if the Botox took in spots but not in others.

"Of course I do," said Ben. "How are you, Liza?"

"I'm shitty," said Liza Heston. "That asshole bartender won't take my check." Liza helped herself to a long pull on Ben's beer. She moved to lick away the foam, but it had already seeped deep into the crevices of her upper lip. "That's good. Buy me one?"

Ben motioned to the bartender, who poured and delivered a pint of stout. Liza flashed the kid a sarcastic grin as if to say thanks for nothing. He smiled at Ben appreciatively for taking her off his hands and beat a hasty retreat. Liza downed a big gulp and burped irately at the bartender.

"Fucker."

Ben caught a whiff of her hair. The indelible scent of Liza Heston's flowing blond ringlets—strawberry cream with a hint of honeysuckle—had never left him, though it had long since left her. She smelled of menthol cigarettes and shrimp.

"So, Ben," she said, giving him the once-over. "You used to like me."

"Um, well, I suppose there was a time when I had what I guess you could call something of a crush."

"You liked me *a lot.* I know you did. And you know what? I liked you."

"You did? Really? When? I mean, at what point precisely? Or roughly?"

"Why not?" she proposed, downing a swig between words.

"Why not . . . what?"

"Why not . . . who?" Liza drained her pint with one disturbingly impressive chug. "Did we ever . . . ?"

"Did we ever what?"

Liza pounded her index finger into her fist.

"Uh, no," said Ben. "We did not."

"Do you want to?"

"I beg your pardon?"

"Yes, we did!"

"No, I'd remember."

"I could never forget. After graduation we all tossed our hats in the air and you jammed your tongue down my throat and then I gave you a hummer on the way to Debbie Shoemaker's party and then we did it in her garage in the back seat of her mom's station wagon and then I puked. I could never forget that."

"That wasn't me."

"I could never forget," she insisted with a wink.

"That was Gary Haverford."

"Who?"

"Gary Haverford."

Liza's expression went blank. "Never heard of him."

14.

An anxious telephone message and an e-mail bearing the urgent red exclamation point awaited Ben at work Friday morning, both from the Chicken Hawk. Ben did not answer either. By his estimation, he would have to work thirty-one hours a day, nine days a week to complete Tóuche's order on time. He prided himself on having never missed a deadline, and he'd have made hers if not for that blasted baseball software program. It was the computer equivalent of crack. He told himself he'd only do it for twenty minutes, and the next thing he knew five hours had passed. Ben drafted a list of options that included (a) calling Brad Pitt to see if he had any of Ben's bedroom pieces that he could buy back, and (b) cutting off the tip of one finger with a jigsaw and playing the injury card. But Ben had neither a high threshold for pain nor Brad Pitt's number, so he decided to come clean. On Monday.

Logan did not question or complain about his being skipped in the pitching rotation in favor of Dante. With only four teams advancing to the playoffs, three games left to play in the regular season, and the Angels fourth in the standings with a won-lost record of 8–7, conventional wisdom would have Logan pitch both this and the last game. A handful of players asked Ben why he made the switch, as did Mike and Rubén, as did a couple of parents via text messages from the bleachers, but Ben played the move close to his vest, ignoring the parents and telling the team only that he had his reasons.

Dante led off the top of the first inning. "Start us off, Boom-Boom. Be a hitter now." As Dante jogged to the plate, Ben saw him peek at the bleachers. From the first base coach's box Rubén nodded across the diamond at Ben before Dante laid down a picture-perfect bunt for a base hit. The Angels staked him to a 2–0 lead, and as they took the field in the bottom of the first, Ben let Dante get halfway to the mound before calling him back. Ben met him at the baseline and took a knee so as to talk to the boy at eye level. "I want you to relax and have fun out there, OK?" Dante nodded. "And remember, no curve balls, OK?" Dante's eyes darted away before returning to Ben. "Throw fastballs and trust your defense." As Dante trotted to the mound, Ben turned and spied Del standing in the back corner of the top row of the bleachers.

Dante fired a fastball over the plate for a strike. He came right back with another fastball and worked ahead of the batter, no balls and two strikes. Then suddenly, like Frosty the Snowman come springtime, Dante started to melt. His eyes drooped, his smile flipped, his shoulders sagged. Ben had seen him peer up into the stands. The boy stood there for a long moment, head bowed, staring at his shoe tops.

Ben pulled Logan close and whispered, "Grab your glove."

Dante lifted apologetic eyes to Ben. Then he rocked back and threw a curve ball that froze the batter and fell in for strike three.

"Time, Blue!" shouted Ben. He strode to the mound and put out his hand. Dante handed him the ball. The Angels fans voiced their displeasure, none louder than Del.

"What the hell are you doing?" he yelled, bounding down the stands and smacking the cyclone fence like it was a glass door he did not see. "He just struck the kid out on three pitches!"

With Ben's back to the stands, they could not see him smile at Dante and say, "It's all right, I understand. I'll fix this."

Dante scuffled to the dugout as Logan took the mound. Ben huddled with the home plate ump. "There is something I need to tend to. My first base coach is taking over." Ben then walked purposefully to Del, their noses all but touching through the fence. "I need to speak to you." Ben addressed the fans in the stands. "Excuse us, folks. Enjoy the game."

Del was waiting for Ben outside the dugout. Ben walked right past him to a more appropriate, more private spot along the left field line near his old patch of solitude and tranquillity. Del held his ground.

"Your son has played his last game," said Ben.

That got Del on his horse. In the time it took him to march from the dugout to Ben's face, Del conjugated the verb *screw* in the present, preterite, infinitive, imperative, present participle, past participle, present progressive, present perfect, future, future perfect, past progressive, past perfect, future progressive, present perfect progressive, past perfect progressive, and the future perfect progressive.

Ben let him spout, then said, calmly, "You quit signaling Dante from the stands, or he has played his last game."

"We were in first place, and now we are probably going to miss the playoffs."

"*We?* Who is *we?* I've got news for you, Del: you don't play Little League anymore."

"You've managed six games, and you've managed to lose five of them!"

"Is that what's bothering you? Or is it the fact that it does not bother me whether we win or lose?"

"What bothers me," Del growled, "is that my son is being taught to be a loser by a loser."

"Back off, Marion." Del did step back, surprised. "What, did you forget that I know your real name is Marion? Or that I remember your being so scared on the first day of school that you wet your pants on the playground? That's all this is," Ben said, motioning to the entirety of the baseball complex. "This is the grade school playground all over again—the posturing, the intimidation, the bravado. Guys like you are only out here to beat other guys like you. But it's not about you. It's about them," Ben said, pointing to the kids wearing uniforms on the field. "Make no mistake: if you so much as wink at Dante one more time, you can kiss the rest of his season and his shot at All-Stars goodbye."

The All-Stars arrow pierced deep. "You may be the manager. But you are no coach." Whether Del meant it as lowercase coach or uppercase Coach, the barb stung. Del grinned, figuring he'd had the last word.

"It was you," said Ben.

"Excuse me?"

"It was you."

"What was me?"

"Promgate."

Del scoffed and turned his back to Ben, whose voice took a solemn tone.

"I know it was you."

"You don't know shit," Del said, oozing smugness.

Ben placed his hands on his hips and stood slightly taller. He tilted his head just a hair to the right and pursed his lips and narrowed his eyes.

"What the hell are you doing?"

Ben told himself he could do this. He stood taller still, tilted his head a hair more to the right, pursed his lips a little tighter, narrowed his eyes and . . . nothing.

"What is wrong with you, Holden?"

Gazing at Del, Ben was struck by the bounty of his nose hair. It was quite something, almost as if he had small heads of broccoli protruding from each nostril. *The nostrils!*

Resetting, Ben placed his hands on his hips and stood slightly taller. He again tilted his head just a hair to the right and pursed his lips. He narrowed his eyes and flared his nostrils and . . . wait for it . . . patience . . . wait for it . . . *bam!*

The Gaze of Truth.

Del gasped, hit by a wave of emotional nudity, like a knight whose suit of armor has been ripped clean from his body by an invisible magnet. Clouds filled his mind, and in the haze Del struggled to separate answers from questions. *He does not know. Does he? How does he know?* Del connected a circle of dots: Coach was close to Principal Middleton . . . Principal Middleton went to his grave maintaining he not only knew who had defecated on his desk but also that he had proof . . . That proof may have been bequeathed to Coach . . . Coach may have bequeathed that proof to Ben.

"It was a prank," blurted Del.

"It worked!" gasped Ben.

"It was just a prank. I thought for sure they would think it was East Side High. I didn't know. It all just snowballed. I never imagined they would cancel prom. I never dreamed Principal Middleton would quit. I didn't mean for any of that to happen. You have to believe me. Please, you have to believe me."

"I believe you," said Ben as he tried to process not only solving *Promgate* but also, and more so, harnessing the Gaze of Truth. "Wait till I tell Jili!"

"You can't!" Del whimpered. "You can't tell anyone, ever. And you have to destroy the proof. Please, I'll do anything."

The voice of Yoda spoke to Ben. *"The dark side I sense in you. Once you start down the dark path, forever will it dominate your destiny, and consume you it will."*

Ben nodded, and Del heaved a sob of relief. Twenty-three years of bottled-up emotions all came gushing out. Logan got called for an illegal pitch when he started his motion but suddenly came to a screeching halt. Logan gaped toward left field. So did the infielders, then the outfielders, and the Angels bench, the Royals dugout, both bleachers, the ump, and the PA announcer, who offered, "Now there's something you don't see every day," as Ben hugged and consoled Del.

Ben flashed the OK sign and the game resumed. The Angels wound up losing on a play at home plate when Ben fell for one of the oldest tricks in the book. With two outs and down by one run, the Angels had Drake at first base and Ailsa at third. On the first pitch, Drake broke for second base. Conventional Little League wisdom would have the defense concede the stolen base and consider walking the batter to set up a force at any base. But the Royals catcher popped up and threw down toward second, and Ben sent Ailsa sprinting for home. The catcher's throw was, by design, not to second base but back to the pitcher, who underhanded the ball back to the catcher for an easy tag on Ailsa at the plate to end the game.

The loss dropped the Angels into fifth place with a record of 8–8. A loss to Keith Campbell and the Rangers in the next-to-last game would mathematically eliminate the Angels from the playoffs. This time, the cleat wound up on the other foot, as the Rangers loaded the bases with two outs in the last frame of a tie ball game. Andrew pitched solidly in relief of Dante, whose father offered nothing but encouragement as he sat and mingled with the other parents in the stands. Ben could see that Andrew was gassed, so he called time and gathered his squad on the mound.

When they broke the huddle, Andrew moved to third base and T-Roy came on to pitch. It appeared to be an inauspicious move, as eight straight warm-up throws hit everything but the catcher's mitt. "I know you're nervous," Ben shouted from the dugout. "Just calm down, take a deep breath, and try to get the ball over the plate."

In the third base coach's box, Keith told his runner, "Be ready. If the ball gets past the catcher, you go home."

T-Roy's first pitch sailed behind the back of the batter. As the runner charged home, so did T-Roy, catching the ball on a clean bounce off the wooden backstop and applying the tag as the runner slid.

"The runner is . . ." The ump double-checked whether T-Roy had possession of the ball, then cried, "Out!"

After the game, as the players and coaches shook hands, Ben stopped Keith. "I apologize if I have been less than friendly. We've had a lot going on, moving home and my dad's passing and then all this, but that's no excuse."

"I appreciate that," said Keith. "Don't sweat it. It's good to have you out here, and I'm really happy to see Jili so happy."

Ben stopped short of suggesting they get the families together for a barbecue.

As he lugged the gear out of the dugout, Ben spotted Fred leaning against the bleachers.

"You know, Coach always made the players carry the gear."

"Add that to the list of ways I do not measure up."

"I would, but there is a waiting list to add to that list." Fred slapped Ben lightly on the back. "I'm just kidding." It was not like Fred to backpedal from a gibe or to slap Ben's back without leaving a welt. "That was some kind of crazy way to win."

"We got a lucky bounce," said Ben.

Fred stepped in front of him. "Did you come up with that play, with the wild warm-up throws and the pitcher bouncing the ball to himself off the backstop?"

Ben would not admit it, but his wry grin did.

"Pretty ballsy," said Fred. His expression, one not often seen by Ben, conveyed genuine respect and admiration. "The old man would be proud."

Is fhearr fheuchainn na bhith san duil.

"Really, Mom, a tattoo?"

"It's totally hip, Grandma," said Kate.

"What the heck does it say?" asked Tommy.

"It's a Gaelic proverb," explained Patty. "It means, *'It's better to try than to hope.'*"

"How very apropos," said Jili.

Patty, Fred, Nancy and Paul, and their kids all came out for the big game between the Angels and the Orioles. With matching 9–8 records going into the last regular season game, the winners went to the playoffs and the losers started their summer vacation. Ben and his team waited restlessly on the patch of solitude and tranquillity as the game before theirs ran long. He spotted Cyn approaching and felt a rush of elation when his cell phone vibrated in his pocket.

"Ben Holden," he answered, motioning to Cyn that he had to take this. It was the Chicken Hawk.

"Mr. Holden, I have been trying to reach you for days."

"Right, sorry, I have been swamped."

"Busy making Tóuche's furniture, I suppose."

"I suppose."

"I am sorry to call on the weekend, Mr. Holden, but I need to know the status of the order."

"The status?"

"Yes."

"Of the order."

"Correct."

"Well, you know how statuses are, flexible and ever-changing and all."

"How many of the pieces are finished?"

"I guess that would depend on your definition of 'finished.'"

"Completed and ready for delivery."

"Completed *and* ready for delivery?"

"Yes."

"You know, I'd have to check to be sure. I am not at my shop right now; how about I give you a call on Monday or Thursday of next week."

"Monday is too late," insisted the Chicken Hawk. "By then the story will have broken."

"What story?"

The Chicken Hawk replied with a conflicted sigh. "Mr. Holden, Tóuche will pay for any pieces that are finished, and per the terms of the work order the initial deposit of $50,000 is nonrefundable."

"Do I sense a 'but' coming?"

"But the wedding is off."

"You don't say."

"You did not hear it from me. Their publicists are preparing statements to release to the press, and the story will break at noon tomorrow."

"I am sorry to hear that," said Ben. "For Tóuche's sake, I mean."

"Don't be, her ex-fiancé is a butthole."

Ben could not help but chuckle; when was the last time anyone called anybody a butthole? His infectious giggle drew a smile from Jili as she came to tell him it was game time.

"Please tell Tóuche not to worry about it, just give her my best. And let me know ahead of time next time she plays in these parts because my wife was jealous that I got to go to the concert and she didn't."

"What's up?" asked Jili.

Ben pocketed his phone. "Today could be my lucky day."

It was a good thing Ben didn't go to Vegas. Logan walked the Orioles leadoff batter, who ran down to first and immediately sprinted for second, catching the Angels unawares. Drake flung aside his catcher's mask and threw down to second, but no one was covering the bag. As the runner chugged toward third base, T-Roy raced in from center field and came up throwing but missed the mark and the runner waltzed home to score the game's first run. Roger Pollock seemed very pleased with himself.

The Angels got on the board in the third inning when T-Roy hit a solo home run. Down 5–1 in the fifth inning, they looked to rally as Ailsa raked a two-out single and Aaron drew a walk. With Hunter up to bat and riding a seven-year hitless streak, it was a fair bet that the Orioles would get out of the inning unscathed; still, Pollock brought his first baseman and his third baseman all the way in, past the pitcher and just feet in front of home plate. Pollock's plan to spook the poor kid worked, and Hunter struck out.

Logan worked a quick one-two-three top of the sixth inning, then Ben gathered the troops before their last ups.

"I had our resident brainiac Joshua here surf the Web on my cell phone for the greatest comeback in baseball history, and it turns out that the Cleveland Indians had two outs and nobody on base in the ninth inning of a game they were losing 13–5 then scored nine runs to win 14–13 over the Washington Senators."

"You mean the Washington Nationals," Duncan corrected him.

"No, I mean the Washington Senators. It happened back in 1901, but the point is it can be done, and we are just the team to do it, so let's go out there and make some history of our own!"

The good news was the Angels had the top of the order up. The bad news was Dante and Conor both made outs that could just as easily have been hits. Dante crushed a ball to the left fielder, who made a lucky "Hey, Ma, look what I found!" catch. Then Conor striped a line drive that ricocheted off the second baseman right to the shortstop, who made the throw to first. Drake drew a walk, then T-Roy blooped a single. Logan dribbled a routine grounder to the shortstop, who could not dig it out of his glove in time to get the force on T-Roy at second, and suddenly the Angels had the bases loaded and the tying run at the plate in Andrew Holden.

The great ones live for moments like this. Their parents, not so much. Ben's bowels churned, while Jili sat in the stands with her face buried in her hands. Kate posted real-time Facebook updates, while Tommy had last been seen three innings ago holding a snake by its tail and running around the picnic area scaring little girls. Fred foamed at the mouth. He would give his left nut to be in Andrew's shoes. Ben had never imagined a way in which he hoped his son might actually take after his uncle, until now. Everyone in both bleachers was on their feet. Players in both dugouts stood pressed against the fences. Spectators from adjacent fields bailed on their own kids' games to witness the spectacle at hand. Ben stood with his arms crossed in the third base batter's box trying to keep his emotions in check and his pulse under two hundred. The pitcher wound and delivered a rainbow that was way outside.

"Ball one!" shouted the ump.

There is no possible way.

Ben thought it, but he could not believe it. Then Pollock signaled his catcher by flashing four fingers. A sickening sensation turned Ben's stomach. He called time and paced across the diamond. Rubén thought Ben was coming to talk to him, but he bypassed his coach and approached the Orioles dugout.

"May I please have a word with you?" Ben said to Pollock.

"I have a word for you: playoffs, as in I am going and you are not!" Pollock laughed alone.

"Please don't do it."

"Get back in your dugout. We've got a ball game to win here."

"What's going on?" asked Rubén. The Orioles coaches and players appeared equally curious.

"You want to tell them?" Ben asked.

"What's to tell? I am playing the odds."

Like a *Price Is Right* model displaying a brand-new car, Ben presented the scene before them: children playing ball, families watching, the sun shining. "This is not about you playing the odds."

"What's he talking about, Dad?" Channing Pollock walked over from the pitcher's mound. "Why would you intentionally walk in a run?"

"Three runs," said Ben. "He's going to have you intentionally walk in three runs to get to our weakest batter."

"You're kidding." Channing turned to his father. "He's kidding, right?"

Pollock bolted out of the dugout, shouting, "Do not talk to my players, do not tell me how to manage, and do not come over here looking for sympathy just because your player sucks."

The ump told the managers to resume play. As Ben walked back to his dugout, Channing pleaded with his father. "We can get these guys out. We don't need to do this."

Pollock pointed a menacing finger in his son's face. "You intentionally walk the next three batters or I will find someone who will."

You kinda half expected a *Bad News Bears* moment reminiscent of when the dirtbag manager's kid held the ball and let Engelberg round the bases for an inside the park home run. But that was Hollywood and this was real life and the boy did as his father ordered, intentionally walking Andrew, Ailsa, and Aaron, making the score 5–4 and bringing Hunter to the plate.

Ben called the team together and got down on one knee. "OK, here's what we are going to do."

As before, Pollock brought his first baseman and his third baseman all the way in, past the pitcher and just feet in front of home plate. Hunter ambled toward the batter's box lugging T-Roy's big, long, heavy bat. It looked like a caveman's club in Hunter's little hands. Before stepping in, he took a practice swing, and the bat slipped out of his hands, clanging against the cyclone fence. Hunter cringed apologetically. He took another practice swing and the bat sailed out of his hands again, this time slamming into the dugout.

"You won't use a lighter bat?" Ben asked from the coach's box.

"I'm good. It's just kind of slippery." As Hunter dug in the batter's box, he looked at the first and third basemen and said, "Heads up, fellas."

The two Orioles backpedaled off the grass like it was on fire. Pollock barked for them to stay up, but there was no way they were going to risk getting decapitated. T-Roy's bat wasn't really that heavy or that slippery; Hunter was just that good an actor. Drama was his true calling. Still, he liked playing baseball, loved hanging around the ballpark with his friends, and while he dearly wanted and always tried to get a base hit, he did not mope when he didn't or let it get him down. He was a coach's dream: the twelfth kid who knew he was the twelfth kid and accepted being the twelfth kid, who never skipped or dogged a practice, who showed up ready to play and played hard with a smile on his face when he did get in, and who cheered on his teammates when he was on the bench. If only he'd open his eyes.

Hunter had an involuntary and seemingly incurable reflex that saw him shut his eyes when he swung the bat. If and when he ever did hit the ball, he would be the embodiment of the blind squirrel finding a nut. Channing fired two quick strikes past Hunter. The outcome was a fait accompli, but Channing stepped off the pitching rubber with the countenance of a reluctant executioner. Pollock signaled fastball; however, instead of bringing the heat, Channing lollipopped a pitch over the plate. Hunter's eyes grew wide as he watched the big, fat, juicy lob, the kind coaches throw the little guys in Single-A. Hunter shut his eyes, swung his bat, and missed the ball completely. Ball game.

Had the Orioles made the third out without intentionally walking in three runs to get to the weak kid, their fans would have rejoiced and the players would have poured out of the dugout onto the field. But as it was, Pollock celebrated solo, acting like the big brother who just pinned his little sister, pointing across the diamond and shouting at the Angels, "In your face, suckas!"

He was not the only one shouting and pointing. The umpire pointed at Channing and shouted, "Illegal pitch! Illegal pitch! The pitcher's foot was not touching the rubber!"

It took the better part of ten minutes for the Orioles coaches to corral Pollock and get him back in the dugout and calm enough for the game to resume. The penalty for a wild pitch is a called ball, putting Hunter back up to bat with a count of one ball and two strikes. Once again, Ben called the team together and got down on one knee.

"Do you all remember at the last practice when I was pitching and Hunter smacked that line drive that almost hit me in the nuts?" The kids all cracked up—until Ben lifted the leg of his cargo shorts to reveal a nasty greenish, purplish, black-and-blue bruise above his knee. "You can do this, Hunter. You know it, I know it, your teammates know it; the only people who don't know it are the Orioles. You just have to keep your eyes open, which is why I brought these invisible toothpicks."

Ben dug around his pocket and presented the team with a seemingly empty palm. He plucked one invisible toothpick and pinched it between his index finger and thumb then asked Rubén to hold the other. Ben held open Hunter's left eye and set the invisible toothpick in place. He took the other invisible toothpick back from Rubén, propped it between Hunter's right eyelids and said, "Voilà!"

Across the diamond, Pollock lit into Channing like a puppy that had just crapped on new white carpet, then turned his ire on the rest of the team with a stern warning about not blowing this for him.

"Quick!" whispered Ben. "Everybody start laughing really loud like you just heard the funniest thing ever!" The Angels all cracked up, doubling over laughing and drawing the attention of the Orioles away from Pollock.

"Don't look at them, listen to me!" screamed Pollock.

But he had lost them. Logan fell out of the dugout and rolled in the dirt grabbing his belly and begging, "Stop! Stop!" Dante squealed, "I think I just peed my pants!" The laughter caught on like The Wave, rippling from the Angels' dugout to the Angels' bleachers to the ump and the PA announcer to the Orioles' stands to the onlookers ringing the outfield fence. Pretty soon everyone was laughing except the Orioles.

Hunter hammed it up, sniggering in the batter's box. Channing missed with the next two pitches, running the count full.

"Toothpicks!" Hunter's father shouted from the first base coach's box. "Remember your toothpicks!" Pollock and Channing both eyed Rubén and wondered what the heck he was talking about.

"Time, Blue!" called Ben, and he ran down to talk to Hunter. "Watch this," he said. "I'll bet you an extra-large slushie from the snack shack that if we just hang here for a sec and pretend we are talking, their coach will get all antsy and come out and get up in his pitcher's head. He can't help himself." Sure enough, Pollock bounded out of the dugout and gave Channing an earful.

"Here we go," said Ben. He and Hunter shared a warm smile. "My dad used to say, 'You can't hit a home run—'"

"If you're not up there swinging. I got this, Coach." Hunter stepped in and started cracking up. He asked for time, stepped out and collected himself, then stood back in.

"End this," Pollock ordered. "Now!"

The toothpicks worked. Hunter smoked the ball right back where it came from.

"I did it!" yelled Hunter.

"You did it!" yelled Rubén.

"Run!" yelled his teammates.

The ball drilled Channing's protective cup with a disconcerting *thud!* then dropped at his feet as Channing dropped to his knees. Andrew broke for home. Ailsa rounded third base, hot on his heels. Hunter sprinted toward first base but veered out of the baseline and ran straight into his father's arms. From the ground Channing flipped the ball to the first baseman, standing on the bag.

"Out!" cried the ump.

Ball game.

	1	2	3	4	5	6	FINAL
Orioles	1	2	0	0	2	0	**5**
Angels	0	1	0	0	0	3	**4**

Players from both teams raced onto the field. The Orioles reached Hunter first, patting him on the head and the back and showering him with *attaboys*. The Angels hit like a tsunami, burying Hunter and the Orioles players in a massive dogpile. One after another, kids squirmed out from the bottom, backpedaled, took a running start, and launched themselves back on the pile. The Orioles and Angels coaches got together to keep the dogpile going while making sure none of the kids got hurt. Parents from both teams convened on the field, hugging their kids and congratulating Ben.

Pollock stood alone.

"It couldn't have happened to a nicer guy," remarked Del, walking past Pollock and over to Ben. "You proved me wrong, Holden."

"How's that?"

"Losing," said Del, taking in the jubilant scene, "officially does not suck."

15.

You'd never know they missed the playoffs," Del said, gawking at all twelve Angels crammed in the Jacuzzi like lobsters in a pot. The Yamagatas again graciously opened their home for the Angels' end-of-season team party. As Del poured margaritas for parents standing poolside, he admitted, "A few weeks ago I'd have thought it would be the end of the world."

"And now?" asked Rubén.

"It's just the start of summer."

Ben found Jili hoarding the ceviche. "Wanna slink away somewhere and get jiggy?" Jili crinkled her brow as though she would not rule it out entirely.

Del handed Jili a margarita as she popped another ceviche-laden tortilla chip in her mouth. Ben was already nursing a McShane's Limited Edition Angels Amber that Euan concocted specially for the occasion. Ben and Jili looked at one another and both called, "Dibs on drinking!" It appeared to be a photo finish.

"Don't look at me to settle that," said Euan, wisely.

"It's fine, I'll drive," she said. "You deserve it, Coach."

Del took Ben aside and thanked him for keeping mum about *Promgate* and for getting rid of the proof. He phrased it as a statement, though Ben detected the hint of uncertainty in his voice. Ben motioned as if to say his lips were locked, but he had already told Jili, in part because he'd learned his lesson about keeping secrets, but also because it's no fun knowing a secret unless you tell someone, which is the inherent flaw in any secret. As for the evidence, there was none. Principal Middleton had been bluffing, a fact that Ben had cajoled out of Coach years earlier.

Ben spied Kate spying Daniel Yamagata, Drake's studly sophomore older brother. Sidling up to Kate, Ben put his arm around his daughter and offered, "If this party is lame, I'll drive you home, honey."

"No, I'm fine," she said, busted.

Ben kissed her forehead, then a familiar song piped through the outdoor speakers: *"Shake your tush, shake your tush, shake your tushie good, girl!"*

Ben's face lit up.

"Dad!" Kate begged preemptively.

"But I know the moves!"

"I know, but . . ."

Seeing Daniel walking their way, Ben sighed, "Whatev."

"Thanks, Daddy," she said, kissing his cheek, then nudging him to move along.

"I've got to tell you, Ben," said Euan. "I didn't understand baseball before, and since you took over, I think I actually understand it even less. But you made it more enjoyable for Ailsa and for me and for everyone. Cheers." They toasted, and Ben polished off his beer. He fished around the beer tub for another but could not find what he was looking for. "Any more of those Angels Ambers?"

"In the fridge in the pool house laundry room," said Mike as he carried a tray of burgers to the barbecue.

She came to him in the laundry room. She followed him. As he grabbed a beer from the fridge, he heard the door shut, then lock, and he said, "All right, you horny little minx, let's make this fantasy come true." He closed the refrigerator door fully expecting to see Jili, not Cyn.

I can't . . .

He thought it, but before he could say it, Cyn's full, red lips were pressed firmly against his.

• • •

Ted Watson had been taking photos all season long, and he'd put together a slide show, set it to music, and burned it onto DVDs for each
family. The plan was to gather everyone to watch it after lunch, but
Ted could not wait to show Ben and Jili one of his favorite photos, a
priceless shot of Ben and Andrew that captured a son's pure elation
and a father's unbounded pride. Ted gave Jili a five-by-seven print
he'd made for them. Her heart melted. She showed Andrew, who was
dripping wet and shivering and drinking his third root beer. Andrew
smiled brightly and said, "Cool," high praise coming from him.

"Where is your father?" Jili asked.

"Getting beers from the fridge in the pool house laundry room,"
said Mike as he carried the empty tray from the barbecue back into the
house.

Ben could taste the warm blood in his mouth as Jili stood over him,
panting. She had walked into the pool house as Ben emerged from the
laundry room, his hair tousled and his expression disturbed. Without
a word, he took her by the arm, led her across the patio, inside the
house, up the stairs, and into a quiet room. He sat her down, though
she did not stay seated for long.

Ben recounted going to the fridge to get a beer. Cyn followed him,
and he made a suggestive comment thinking it was Jili, and before he
could say anything, her lips and her body were on his, and one of her
hands was grabbing his hair and the other was down around there, and
he pushed her off and ducked out past her.

"And that's when I bolted out of there and bumped into you coming into the pool house."

Jili said nothing for what seemed like forever.

"Your lip is bleeding," said Kate as the Angels and their families all
gathered on the patio.

"Yeah, I, um, bumped it."

"On what?"

"A door," Ben lied. He couldn't very well tell his daughter the truth: that he'd bumped his lip on her mother's head as they were having sweaty teenager sex in the guest room upstairs. Jili had plainly seen that Ben was telling the truth, and she was relieved to know that when opportunity knocked, he'd bolted out the door. His tousled hair was kinda cute, and she was ovulating and horny, and there they were, alone in the guest room she'd scouted during the team mixer, so she stripped naked and they fulfilled her fantasy, accidentally conking coconuts in the throes of passion.

He could taste the warm blood from his split lip as Jili stood over him, buttoning her blouse and panting. "As for your fantasy . . ."

"You," said Ben, "are my fantasy."

Mike Yamagata tinked his plastic fork against his bottle of Angels Amber. "Christine and I want to welcome everyone. It has been an eventful year, and even though we did not make the playoffs, I think I speak for everyone, players and parents, when I say that it has been a truly unforgettable season."

Tuckered out from swimming, Tommy sprawled across the couch he'd fashioned from his parents' laps. He looked up to his father and, with the pleading sincerity before which parents are helplessly defenseless, asked, "Daddy, will you coach my team next year?"

"Can we talk about that next year, little buddy?"

"I just want you and me to have fun like the way you and Andrew did."

Jili beamed. Ben felt his lips forming the *O* in *OK* when Tiffany Watson interjected, "How about a few words from the coach?"

Everybody applauded as Ben stood and faced the Angels.

"I came across an interesting statistic the other day. Interesting, surprising, and rather disturbing: seventy percent of children quit organized youth sports by the age of thirteen. And the number one reason they cite is pressure from their parents. My father, as most of you know, was a coach. I also recently came across his 'Three Single Most Important Keys to a Coach's Success.'" Ben produced Coach's spiral notebook and read from the last page.

Strive to make players better when they finish than when they start.
Work hard, but have fun.
Never be a kid's last coach.

"My father never wanted to be the reason a kid quit playing. He coached baseball for fifty years, and I only know of one kid who ever quit baseball because he didn't want him as his coach. A big part of me wishes I hadn't, but things happen for a reason—my father truly believed that—and I truly believe that this experience was destined to be the way that I learned to better understand who my father was and why he so loved coaching kids that he made it his life's work.

"I think we can all agree that when we gathered here a few months ago, not one of us could have predicted the way this season played out. We finished 9-9 and missed the playoffs, but the truth is we would've never even sniffed the playoffs if it weren't for Coach Del. Each and every one of these kids benefited greatly from his knowledge and passion for the game, and I'd like Coach Del to join me up here to say a few words about our team."

Del was surprised and touched by the gesture. He had nothing prepared, but then neither did Ben. They winged it, calling each player up one at a time, with Del speaking to his or her baseball skills and Ben talking about each child's personality and what each brought to the team.

Jili sidled up next to Cyn under the umbrella table with all the food. "You seriously need to give me your ceviche recipe."

"I'll e-mail it to you, I promise."

"That'd be great, thanks." Jili leaned a little closer. "And if you ever make a move on my husband again, I swear to God I will sew your lips shut with piano wire."

"I don't—"

Jili pinched Cyn's lips shut. "And I'm not talking about these that you had pumped full of ass fat."

Cyn nodded.

Jili let go.

They turned their attention back to the coaches paying tribute to the kids.

"I am not kidding," Jili whispered. "You seriously need to give me your ceviche recipe."

Tiffany Watson rose and presented Ben, Mike, Rubén, and Del each with a gift card to Pirate Pete's. "We also have something special for Ben," she said, presenting him with a large gift bag. Ben was just about to open it when Andrew stood. "May I please say something?" Jili shrodded at Ben, and he nodugged at her as Andrew stepped over and between his teammates, taking a place at his father's side.

"It's not very easy for me to get up here and speak in front of a bunch of adults, but I don't think it was very easy for my dad to step up and coach a bunch of kids. I think between Del and my dad we all learned a lot about baseball and also about other things like finishing what you start and coming together as a team and having fun. And even though we didn't make the playoffs, this is the best team I've ever been on and I'm really happy I got to share it with all of you guys but especially with my dad."

Ben pulled Andrew into a long hug. Tommy hollered, "Open your present already!"

The team had pitched in to buy Ben an authentic Angels dugout jacket. Embroidered over the left breast was the word *Coach*. It fit.

Acknowledgments

My sincere thanks to Pierre and Maria Breber, Matt and Lisa Middlebrook, Tim and Mary Boyle, Bill and René Rubach, Herb and Wendy Steiner, Ben and Lorraine Alexander, Kevin and Mary Imm, Chris Silva, and Victor Trione; to Lindsey Kennedy, Farley Chase, Holly Root, and Byrd Leavell; to Stacy Creamer, Trish Todd, David Falk, Meredith Kernan, Alessandra Preziosi, Jessica Roth, Renata DiBiase, Cherlynne Li, and Peg Haller; to Darrell Peart, Russ Peterich, Ari Hauptman, Bill Carroll, Bob Bone, Zac Ward, Jody Nash, Jennifer Lauck, and Shelley Twarowski; to Steve Smith and Dick Michaux; to David Kidd and Homer Kelley; to Willis L. Winter and Joshua R. Simon; to Swen and Hulda and Mickey and Edna; to Craig, Kristin, Todd, Marcia, Peter, Bob, Susie, Maia, Bill, Jim, and Dave; to Jasper; and to my blessed circle of phenomenal friends. My profound thanks to Scott Waxman, Justin Manask, Zach Schisgal, Armen Keteyian, and Allen and Dale Gummer. And my most heartfelt and humble thanks to Lars, Calvin, Swen, Ella, and my exquisite Lisa.

**Parents Behaving Badly:
Truth Is Stranger Than Fiction**

Have you got mind-boggling true stories
about overzealous moms, hyper-intense dads,
and lunatic coaches?

Share your stories on ParentsBehavingBadly.com.

Log on to share and to read real-life experiences about youth
sports gone wild. From the humorous to the mortifying,
peewees to varsity, boys and girls, any sport at every age—
you can't make this stuff up!

www.ParentsBehavingBadly.com